ARCHETYPE

M. D. WATERS lives with her family in Maryland. She is the author of *Archetype* and its sequel, *Prototype*.

Praise for *Archetype*

"*Archetype* finishes with a cliffhanger made even more tantalizing by Dutton's promise to publish the sequel, *Prototype*, in six months. The prospect has me more excited than the next *Hunger Games* movie."
—Associated Press

"This book . . . blew me away."
—*USA Today*

"Every now and then a book comes along that is truly unique, unforgettable, and genre-bending. Debut author Waters bursts onto the scene with a stunning first book of a duology. . . . Do not miss out!"
—*Romantic Times*

"M. D. Waters's *Archetype* is the equivalent of the big-budget summer movie—light on the bits that make you think but heavy on the stuff that drills right into the pleasure center of your brain. . . . What it does, it does magnificently."
—*Locus* magazine

"The story is carefully paced, slowly doling out clues about Emma's situation, until, like Emma, the reader is smacked with a bombshell of a twist (or two!). . . . Combining elements of science fiction, romance, and mystery, *Archetype* is a novel that will appeal to everyone."

"Stellar . . . Comparisons to Margaret Atwood's *The Handmaid's Tale* and S. J. Watson's *Before I Go to Sleep* abound. Readers looking for a great thriller with a strong female protagonist mixed with a hint of science fiction should pick this up immediately."
—*Library Journal* (starred)

"With its badass heroine, complicated love triangle, and dystopian setting, this novel most closely resembles an R-rated young-adult novel that has cut out most of the moping currently permeating that genre and replaced it with hot sex." —*A.V. Club*

"Waters has created a fascinating world in this well-plotted tale. A sequel, *Prototype*, is set to follow in less than a year. Definitely a writer to watch." —*Booklist*

"Emotional involvement powers this absorbing gothic thriller in science fiction trappings." —*Publishers Weekly*

"Best Bet for Speculative Fiction . . . Why you should read it: The setting of this story, a future where women are a rare commodity, lays the groundwork for a thought-provoking story with a strong female protagonist." —*Kirkus Reviews*

"*Archetype* heralds the arrival of a truly memorable character!"
—Tor.com

"Waters's breakout science-fiction debut." —LibraryJournal.com

"Get your hands on a copy, clear your calendar, turn off your phone, and inform your loved ones that you'll be taking a few hours to yourself. Once you get started, you will *not* want to put this book down." —Heroes and Heartbreakers

"M. D. Waters has given us that rare and wonderful action heroine who possesses both nerve and emotional depth. That rich characterization combined with an intricately crafted sci-fi mystery made *Archetype* an enthralling debut that I couldn't put down."
—Richelle Mead, #1 international bestselling author of
the Vampire Academy series

ARCHETYPE

A NOVEL

M.D. WATERS

A PLUME BOOK

PLUME
Published by the Penguin Group
Penguin Group (USA) LLC
375 Hudson Street
New York, New York 10014

USA | Canada | UK | Ireland | Australia | New Zealand | India | South Africa | China
penguin.com
A Penguin Random House Company

First published in the United States of America by Dutton, a member of Penguin
Group (USA) LLC, 2014
First Plume Printing 2014

 REGISTERED TRADEMARK—MARCA REGISTRADA

THE LIBRARY OF CONGRESS HAS CATALOGED THE DUTTON EDITION AS FOLLOWS:
Waters, M. D. 1976–
    Archetype : a novel / M. D. Waters.
        pages   cm
    ISBN 978-0-525-95423-1 (hc.)
    ISBN 978-0-14-218114-0 (pbk.)
    1. Women—Fiction. 2. Commodification—Fiction. I. Title.
    PS3623.A86889A73   2013
    813'.6—dc23   2013005468

Printed in the United States of America
10 9 8 7 6 5 4 3 2

Designed by Nancy Resnick

For Tad.

You're the one I'd search for in the darkest of places.

Seduce my mind and you can have my body, find my soul and I'm yours forever.

—Anonymous

ARCHETYPE

CHAPTER 1

My mind wakes, but the words essential to describe the stirring of my consciousness escape me.

I blink.

White light fills my vision, blindingly bright, darkening my peripheral to pitch. I have no words for variations, either, because while I understand shifts of color and luminescence in my surroundings, I cannot hold knowledge in my mind.

Voices articulate words—*No, we don't need her anymore; put her with the others*—and I struggle to make sense of them to no avail. I know what they say is important. So important. Vital. Yet all meaning flashes through the vast darkness of my mind, fleeting streaks of lightning. Alluring, coaxing, but gone before I can decipher patterns in the chaos.

I blink.

Dust particles float in the air, a fluid, graceful contrast to the vibrating hum of the light hanging above me. The motes dance around my slim, pale fingers, escaping my grasp, frustratingly transitory, like everything else I experience.

A hand pushes aside the sterile aluminum lamp seconds before a face appears. Cold fingers pry up the lid of one of my eyes. Gray eyes stare, unblinking, between a green cap and surgical mask. A pinprick of light forces tears. I squint and jerk my head, but the strong hand catches me around the forehead, fingers snagging on attached wires, and repeats the process on my other eye. I feebly bat his hand away.

The man leans straight-armed onto the table and stares at me. "Hm."

"*Hm*, what?" This voice comes from a man out of my line of vision but sounds very close.

The gray-eyed man lifts his head and pulls down the mask, revealing a bulbous nose and pockmarked skin. Matching gray whiskers shade his upper lip. He glances between me and the man who has yet to show himself. "It's too early to tell."

"But?"

"But . . ." The gray-haired man trails off and sighs. He scans me from head to toe, eyes narrowing. "But I think we have finally done it."

A soft chuckle sounds behind me. "You, my old friend. You have finally done it."

This gray-haired man reaches for my face. I instinctively jerk my head away, but he only pulls colored wires off my forehead, gathering a group of them in his palm. "Only time will tell," he says.

The moment drifts away as the words are absorbed into the vast space of my mind. By the time I think to be frustrated, it is too late. Nothing has meaning. Not time. Not words. Not the reason I am here.

I am simply tissue, blood, and bone.

New.

In the beginning of life.

The vibrant green leaves turn into shades of orange, red, and yellow. Sweltering heat becomes cool breezes through narrow slits in large, square windows.

With the passing of time comes a lasting comprehension of language, color, texture, and scents. He says I knew them all along, and what I have yet to learn, he will teach me. I think he will reward me one day if I can only get my lessons right. Except today he tells me something new, and one word I do not understand.

"You are my wife," he tells me.

I study his lips while they frame the words. He has a lovely mouth and I reach out to touch it often, but he never lets me. He says I must focus on one thing at a time.

"I am your wife," I say carefully, and the words sound right, so I smile.

His head falls forward and broad shoulders lift with a heavy sigh. Dark hair spills forward, hiding his expression. He is upset with me but I do not understand why. I tell him what he asks of me and only that. Is this not what he wanted?

"No, Emma."

He lifts his head, and eyes the color of seawater stare back at me. I know this color because it is in a large photograph in my room. They tell me the photograph is of the sea before, but they do not tell me before *what*.

"I do not understand," I say.

He leans back in his chair and combs hair away from his face with long, slender fingers. The dark strands slick back and hold in their usual style. "You're repeating my words only to please me."

He turns his head and squints into the sun shining through the windows. With an elbow propped on the chair's arm, he raises a hand to his chin and massages his jaw.

Leaning forward, I attempt to catch his gaze with my own. "This is what you wanted," I whisper.

Those beautiful eyes turn my way and he stops rubbing his chin, still saying nothing. He only watches me in agonizing silence. Then, abruptly, he stands and buttons the front of his suit jacket. It is dark blue today. I like this color on him.

Bending over me, he presses a whisper-soft kiss to my temple. "One day you will say it and believe it."

He leaves the room and now I understand. I must learn about this word "wife."

We spend day after endless day in this lounge, and I think I finally understand. "You are my husband, Declan Burke. I am your wife, Emma. We were married in a small ceremony with only our closest friends atop our mountain."

His smile, after so many weeks of frowns, warms my heart and brings a flutter to my stomach. He has an amazing smile. When he smiles, his cheeks crease deeply around the corners of full lips.

This particular smile brings a gleam to the sea in his eyes. "Yes, Emma, that's right. You were absolutely beautiful."

He reaches forward, carefully, and slides loose strands of my hair behind my ear. A tingle follows the trail of his fingers across my skin. I want more. *Have* wanted more than these fleeting touches.

"Do I frighten you?" I ask.

He chuckles and leans away, draping both arms over the top of the beige couch with red accent pillows. His fingertips dip into the beam of sun from the large windows. "No. Should you?"

I match him gaze for unblinking gaze. A smile twitches the corners of his lips and I cannot imagine why he finds this amusing. Is not a husband supposed to touch his wife? Am I not allowed to touch him in return?

I pull my feet up into my chair and twist to prop my elbow over the cushioned back. With my free hand, I pick at an imperfection of thread in the knee of my white scrub pants. "Is touching forbidden?" I ask him, casually raising my gaze to peer at him through my eyelashes.

I am learning about these rules, which they say are for my safety. Some I do not understand. Why should I not leave my room after seven each night? I want to see the stars. Need to see the stars. They pull at the core of me for reasons I cannot explain.

"I don't want to rush you," he says. While the amusement still tugs on his lips, he averts his eyes.

Rush me, I want to tell him, but do not. He knows what is best for me, but I believe I am ready for this step. No, I know I am.

Unfolding myself, I stand and hold out a hand. "I would like to see the gardens. And I wish for you to hold my hand while we walk."

He watches our hands meet, his twice the size of mine and barely a shade darker. Olive toned he calls it. He says when I am in the sun more, my skin becomes golden and rich in color, but for now, my skin is dull by comparison.

We leave the lounge where we meet every day, entering a sterile white hallway. The only color comes from a wall of paintings with random splashes of color. Declan calls it art, but the canvases look as if a child was set loose with a paintbrush. On more than one occasion, the idea that I could have done far better flits through my mind.

Opposite the wall of paintings, sunlight glares at us through large, square windows, but no worse than in the lounge, where the rays reflect off car windows in the parking lot. A rectangular lot cluttered with the same cars, day in and day out. Parked in the same exact places. Nothing changes in the surrounding manicured lawns sprouting trees and perfectly square hedges. Only the changing colors of the season. From my vantage point fifteen stories up, in this U-shaped building, these colors are my only proof that time passes at all.

We enter the enclosed garden area with exotic flora and a great domed roof with only a tease of sunlight through opaque windows. The space is heaven in shades of every color imaginable. The men in blue lab coats leave us to our walk without interruption. No one looks us in the eye, and I wonder why, but do not ask.

I wonder if I am scarred from the accident. Declan assures me I worry needlessly, but I have yet to see my reflection for myself. I only catch the short, angled tips of straight dark brown hair when it falls forward. I cannot recall my appearance at all, actually, so it pleases me to know this much.

"You're in a better mood today," Declan says mildly, which is saying something for a man with such a deep voice. "No nightmares last night?"

I shake my head. "Only good dreams last night. I think." I chuckle and pull close to him, hugging his arm. My hands wrap around a tight biceps. The top of my head just reaches his shoulder. Touching him like this, being this close, brings a warm sensation to my chest. "They must have been if I do not remember, yes?"

"Yes, I should think so."

"Maybe I have seen the last of them."

He kisses the top of my head. "We can only hope."

I float upright in a tank full of water. The occasional bubble sneaks past me and pops just above my head, but I cannot move my head to follow it.

I cannot blink.

I can only float and watch the world around me go on as if I do not exist. People come and go in silence, never staying long. They speak in whispered tones, leaving me to guess at their conversations. Any attentions they pay me are with furtive glances.

The room is pale gray with cracks snaking up walls into the ceiling. Unevenly stacked boxes rest in the middle of a tiled floor heavily decorated with black scuff marks. Tables topped with laptop computers line the outer walls of the large space. A monitor nearby beep ... beep ... beeps. *Another, separate monitor* beepbeepbeeps *a quicker rhythm.*

A woman, thin and tall, wearing a dark green jumpsuit under a white lab coat, checks the monitors regularly. Everyone calls her Sonya or Dr. Toro. She is dark skinned with hair cut nearly to her scalp. Like the others, she rarely looks at me. She watches the monitors and occasionally she watches ...

Him.

He sits in a folding chair at an angle to my tube of water, head bent forward, elbows resting on his knees. I cannot see his face. Layers of dark blond waves curl to his chin.

"Noah," the woman says. "You should get some rest."

The man does not turn around, but lifts his gaze to where I float helplessly in a tank of water I cannot escape. And I want to escape. I need to escape. But he will not let me out.

He never lets me out.

CHAPTER 2

I wake up panting and clawing at my sweat-soaked tank top. For a long moment, I believe I cannot breathe, that I float in water. But as my ragged breaths grow harsh against my raw throat, I remember where I am and tell myself for the millionth time that the nightmare was not real.

"Lights," I say, and the word is a croak.

Square panels on the lower halves of the walls flicker on with a soft hum and glow, illuminating my small room. Even the low setting makes my eyes water. I squint until they adjust.

I stand on shaky legs and clumsily run into the table with my pitcher of water and empty glass. The room-temperature water soothes my dry throat.

"Everything okay?" a male voice asks.

The abrupt sound startles me and I turn narrowed eyes up to the speaker protruding at an angle from the tan wall. The speaker is the only thing in my room that stands out and forces me to remember how I am never truly alone. The camera from which they watch me, I cannot find.

"Fine," I say.

Perched on the edge of my bed, I lean into the bouquet of indigo flowers delivered earlier in the evening. I had admitted my love for them to Declan on our walk and he had them arranged. The petals add color to my otherwise lifeless room, where even the green leafy plant in the corner is fake.

I spend the next few minutes searching the one large photograph in my room for something new. A dip in the sand I may have never noticed before or a new color in the sunset I may have just learned about. Are there more seagulls today? There never are, of course, but I still look. It calms me to look.

"Will you need a sedative?" the voice asks.

The time I take to consider this offer is short. I am too frightened to sleep on my own and need to sleep so I can be rested for Declan's visit tomorrow.

"Yes, please," I tell the speaker.

A *whoosh* of air precedes the arrival of a tube in the narrow air lock by the door. A tiny door opens and I reach inside for the slim aluminum cylinder. The top rolls aside and I tilt the end over my palm. One tiny, round white pill falls into it, wrapped in a clear plastic square.

A knock on the door startles me, a sign my nerves are still raw. I press a button by the door and Dr. Travista's face appears on the screen: spectacled gray eyes and pale skin scarred from some pocked ailment in his youth. He is much older than Declan, though Declan acts as if they were childhood friends.

"Yes?" I say into the tiny microphone under the screen.

"May I come in?"

His voice grates and I am too unnerved to listen to him and answer his many questions, but I cannot tell him no. I press another button and the door slides open with a barely audible *shiff*.

"Are you working late?" I ask amiably.

He nods, rocking slightly on the balls of his feet, and tucks his hands into the white lab coat he wears over a teal button-down shirt. I do not like this color teal. "You had another nightmare."

This is not a question, so I do not respond.

He motions for me to sit in a nearby chair. He kneels before me and begins taking my pulse with cool fingers. "Can you tell me about it?"

No! a voice yells inside my head. *Don't you dare!*

I listen to the voice because the voice belongs to me and why would I not listen to myself? I must have a reason to hide the truth, but I cannot think it is anything more than my uneasiness with this doctor, who is my husband's closest friend.

"I cannot recall," I say, if for no other reason than to calm the voice. She is always nervous I will tell Dr. Travista too much.

Gray eyes glance up at me over the rim of wire-framed glasses. "Hm." This is always his response. I dislike this, too. "Odd."

I tilt my head. "What is odd?"

"After all these months, you never recall the details of this nightmare you experience nearly every night. It's odd."

I shrug a single shoulder. "I suppose it is."

Dr. Travista continues checking my vitals without another word but watches me carefully. I cannot begin to guess what he looks for in my expression, which I keep carefully neutral. Experience has taught me that the calmer I act, the quicker he leaves.

Finally, he slaps his knees and stands. "You have your sedative and water. Is there anything else you need?"

I affect a pleasant expression. "No. I do not believe so. I will take it right now and go back to sleep."

"Good. Call if you need anything more."

I walk him to the door I am not allowed to pass through and lean into it when it slides closed behind him. The metal is cool against my warm skin and I roll my forehead over the flat surface.

"Stars," I whisper a moment later. "I should have asked to see the stars."

The stars shone bright tonight, but they always did this far from the city. These trips were always about taking the good with the bad. I hated them, but they were necessary.

"Time?" I asked.

"One hour."

"Good."

I lay down on the grassy knoll, ignoring the uncomfortable attachments to my black uniform. Or I tried to. I didn't dare remove anything.

Foster laughed. "What are you doing, Wade?"

Tucking my hands under my head, I settled in with a sigh. "I'm looking at the stars. Don't you miss the stars? They tell stories, you know."

He dropped to a knee beside me, a grin spreading over his face. His black curls peeked out from under a black cap and night-vision goggles, and his warm chocolate complexion looked darker under the night sky. Only the pale gray-blue hue of his eyes remained true in the dark of night, reflecting the moonlight.

"You can be such a girl sometimes," he said.

I reached up and smacked his uniformed shoulder. "I am a girl."

"No, you aren't," he said and shrugged. "Well, not always."

"My husband would tell you I am all the time."

"Your husband gets to go places no man has gone before." With a grunt, he dropped to his butt next to me. His heavy gear rustled and shifted while he settled.

I rolled my eyes. *"Jealous?"*

"Absolutely." Foster leaned back on his elbows and dropped his head back to look up at the sky. He released a deep sigh. *"Wow. That is nice."*

The tiny pinpricks of clustered light must have reached past a billion, more than I would ever count. In the city, I never saw this many.

"It's hard to believe men used to guide themselves using them," I said. *"I would get lost."*

Foster swiveled his head toward me and shot me a lopsided grin. *"Not you. You'll always know your true north."*

I wake with a start but remain perfectly calm. This was no nightmare. I liked this dream. It had been so real I could almost feel the items on my belt pressing into my hip and back. But it is the stars I want to remember, so I close my eyes and attempt to bring the image back. It is not the same but is good enough for now. It is more than I could have asked for.

A knock on the door brings me out of my dreamy half sleep. "Yes?"

"Breakfast."

I slide out of bed and am surprised to find the floor cooler than normal. I hiss and pick up the pace on tiptoes to press the UNLOCK and OPEN buttons. Randall, expression as impassive as ever, strolls right past me and sets my tray down. Like all of Dr. Travista's nurses, he wears gray scrubs over his skeletal frame. Thankfully,

the orderlies wear yellow scrubs, or I would never know the difference between the two groups of his all-male staff.

I eye the plate of fruit and whole wheat toast and stifle a groan.
Randall hates when I complain, and it does me no good anyway.
He is simply doing what he is told despite the fact that he considers
it below his job description to serve me breakfast in bed, as he so
curtly muttered under his breath a time or two.

Randall lifts the tiny cup of pills and holds them out with a
glass of water. The routine never changes. Swallow the pills in silence, open mouth and lift tongue to prove they are really washed
down. Then he takes my blood pressure and shines a light in my
eyes. He asks me questions about my hearing: better or worse?
Does my sense of touch feel any different? More sensitive? Less?
Any aches or pains? He checks my reflexes.

I do not understand the expectations. Nothing ever changes
and I say so every morning.

I follow through these steps without question, ignoring his
bored expression, trying not to take it personally. He simply hates
his job and it has nothing to do with me.

Randall leaves me within heartbeats of finishing his notations
on a computer tablet, and I cross the hall to the mirrorless bathroom. The space has many stalls and a shower area around a corner. It is meant to be shared, but I am the only patient on this floor.

I wash up and return to my cold, bland breakfast. The fruit is
tasteless, probably not in season, and I long for something sweet.

I remind myself that it will not always be like this. My life is in
a house in the mountains away from all this. I am much better now
and they will let me go home soon.

Until then, things will continue as they always have. One new
day at a time.

CHAPTER 3

Noah sits and stares at me in my tube, his face a mask of impassivity. My arms float lazily around me, my legs weightless. Like always, my eyes are unblinking. I cannot stand it.

He stands abruptly and spins around the room, his hands pushing the waves of hair back so tight, the force pulls his skin taut. A flush rises into his face and veins erupt on his forehead and around his eyes. He does not speak or yell but instead sweeps his arms over the tabletops. He knocks over boxes, scattering their contents, which I believe are medical supplies.

Computers and monitors clatter to the tiled floor. Sparks fly and disappear with a sizzle of electricity. The steady beeps of what I have come to believe are heartbeats go eerily silent. There are only the sounds of crashing.

Lastly, Noah turns to a large panel on the wall and throws open the door. The metal clangs against the wall and bounces. It hits his arm and he forces the door away with a touch more control. He then begins flipping switches.

I do not know what they are for until my air is gone. The icy sensation flowing into my veins ceases, though I had not realized this chill until it disappears. A pump hisses and slows to a standstill. A dark haze clouds my mind and fills my vision. My lungs burn. My heart drums like timpani in my ears.

The door swings open and Sonya runs into the room, glancing around in surprise. She finally sets her sights on Noah and gasps.

"What are you doing?" she yells.

"What does it look like?" His tone is harsh and dangerous.

She grips his broad shoulders and forces him aside. He stumbles away and something flashes in his eyes. His lips purse.

"You're killing her," she says through gritted teeth.

Sonya studies the switches, flipping them with quick snaps as she undoes his work. Nothing about his heaving stance frightens her. She moves as if he does not exceed her in height and weight. As if those clenched fists consist of stuffing rather than bone.

Noah glances around and his focus lands on the folding chair. In two large strides, he takes it into his hands and swings at my tube. The metal bounces off the surface, sloshing the water around me.

Sonya darts forward with outstretched arms, showing no concern for his weapon of choice. "Noah! Stop!"

He lifts the chair over his shoulder, preparing for another strike. "Why? She's already dead. This charade ends now."

"The nightmares are getting worse?" Declan asks.

I avoid his eyes and focus on the skeleton of a leafless tree through the lounge window. Bright yellow lights illuminate the otherwise dark parking lot and hide the night sky. My breath fogs the glass in circles, each of which race to disappear before the next one swallows it whole.

I wrap my indigo sweater tight around me for warmth. Declan's visit is later than usual—past my curfew time—and the room is cooler than I am accustomed to. He has explained that his late visit is authorized because he owns the hospital, and all the employees I believed were Dr. Travista's are in fact his. My husband is more powerful than I believed.

"Emma?"

He is getting braver because he touches me with ease now. His hands rest on my shoulders, then slide down my arms to fold me into his embrace. I sink into him. Cocooned the way I am, I allow myself to relax and attempt to forget.

"They are not that bad," I say, but I can still see Noah's enraged eyes in the last moments of my most recent nightmare. I do not know how it ended, whether he succeeded. It feels so real, which is the worst part. The not knowing is agony.

Am I dead?

I shiver. Of course not. I am here, am I not?

Declan's arms tighten. "You're cold."

"Yes. I miss the fall already." I hate the winter. With winter comes snow. I hate the snow even more. One day I will remember why.

"I don't understand your dislike for cold weather."

"I can think of no reason to love it the way you do," I say with a smile tugging the corners of my lips.

"Oh no? Lying by the fire, wrapped in nothing but each other?"

This statement is bold for him. He usually speaks of skiing and the love of extra blanket layers in bed. He does not venture to images of us making love. Now I can only imagine how wonderful it must be after he speaks of holding each other with such reverence.

"Something to look forward to, then," I say and twist around.

Long fingers gently trail over my cheek and along my jaw. His sea-colored gaze follows the languid movement, then rests on my lips. We have not kissed since my accident, and I have dreamed of this closeness. The way he looks at me tells me he wishes for nothing more.

"Will you ever kiss me?" I ask.

A light pink tongue darts out to wet full lips that quirk into a wavering smile. "Would you like me to?"

A nervous flutter warms in my belly and I bite down on my lip. We are married, but it is almost as if we are about to kiss for the first time. I do not know why I am nervous and wish I could remember every kiss we have ever shared.

"Yes," I say and am as breathless as if I had run down a long hall to get to him.

The time it takes his lips to meet mine is agonizingly long. And when they do, his kiss is gentle and hesitant. He is giving me time to pull away, I realize. But I do not want to pull away, so I part my lips to allow for his warm tongue to caress mine.

His arms wrap around tight and hold me as if I would run away and he could not bear it. But I will not. Not ever. I want to be with him always.

"I hate that he's not here," I said, my gaze glued to the cluster of stars.

Foster rolled his head toward me. "I take back the girl comment. You're definitely going chick on me."

"He's better at these situations than I am."

He sat up and wrapped his arms around upturned knees. "Yeah, he's probably super-pissed he can't be here. We've been planning this one for ages. But you're wrong. He isn't any better than you. You talk a good game, but when it comes down to it, you're doing what you were meant to do. You were born for this."

I wanted to deny his words with everything I had. I wasn't born for this. I was born for him.

Only him.

Dr. Travista pastes the last electrodes to my forehead. "Lie still, Emma. This will take a while. It is imperative you don't move."

We are in a bare white exam room with bright lights blinding me to most of the background. I usually come here only when I am not feeling well and Dr. Travista wants to run what he calls "extensive tests." I am also usually asleep for those. Today he asked me to come with no reason given.

I swallow and nod. "Of course. Can I ask what you are doing?"

He leans straight-armed on the stainless table, gripping the rounded steel side, and considers me a moment. "I'm concerned about your nightmares. They're causing stress to your body."

I finger and pinch my loose white scrub pants. "They are not that bad."

He shakes his head and pats my hand in a fatherly way. His skin is cool from the steel and sends a shiver over me. "Last I checked, I was the doctor. Do you want to get better?"

"I thought I *was* better."

"Almost. Not yet."

"I wish to go home, Dr. Travista." Despite owning the hospital and wishing me home, Declan defers to Dr. Travista when it comes to my recovery.

He runs a hand over my hair. "I know, I know, and believe me, I look forward to the day when I can say you are finally perfect. Unfortunately, that day has not arrived. Now"—he looks down and adjusts his head to peer through the lenses perched at the end of his nose—"I'm going to lower the incline of your bed." He must have found the button, because the upper part of my bed lowers me until I lie flat. "Remember, don't move."

He walks away, and for the first time I feel nervous. My limbs are jittery and I try in vain to hold perfectly still, but I think I only make it worse. I do not want Dr. Travista to scold me, so I try to relax by taking deep breaths and concentrating on the web-thin cracks in the white paint overhead. I like to imagine they form an elaborate message I have yet to discern.

A speaker clicks on and his voice sounds above my head. "I'm going to ask you a series of questions, Emma, all right?"

"Yes," I say so quietly I am sure he cannot hear me, so I clear my throat and repeat myself. "Yes."

"You may find some discomfort, but I need you to try very hard to be brave," he says in a soothing tone. "Can you do that?"

"Yes."

But I am not brave. I am frightened. What does he mean to do? Can he force me back into the nightmare? Would he? I cannot go back there. Noah will kill me. I know he will.

It is not real, I tell myself, and I do not realize I have spoken aloud until Dr. Travista says, "Did you say something?"

"I will be brave," I tell him.

Silence fills the room before the speaker clicks once and he says, "Let's start with your favorite memory. Do you have one?"

This will be easier than I thought. "Yes."

"I want you to focus on remembering it for a moment. You don't have to tell me anything."

I do as he asks and recall the first kiss with Declan, which happened several days ago but is still fresh in my mind. I want to feel his arms around me like that always. Feel his lips on mine and so much more. I want to go home if for no other reason than to do more.

Dr. Travista chuckles. "You must be thinking of your husband."

My cheeks warm. "Yes," I whisper.

He chuckles again. "I won't ask you to elaborate. I only need it for a baseline reading. Let's compare it to something else, though. I understand you like walking through my gardens."

"Oh yes," I say. "Very much."

"All right, let's picture a nice stroll, shall we? Let's see how this looks."

I imagine the garden, my fingertips brushing over indigo buds. I recall the cloying scent as I walk into the area for the first time and how the sweet smell overwhelms me.

Too late, I realize my fingers are making small circling motions over my thighs and pull them into tight fists at my sides.

"Very nice," he says. "Let's do one more. How about something you dislike."

This is easy. I imagine his teal shirt. His pockmarked skin. My daily breakfast of dry toast and tasteless fruit. No way to see the stars after months of isolation.

"Well, it seems you have a few things to complain about." He says this in good humor, so I have clearly not insulted him.

"Let's begin," he says after some time. "Tell me something about your nightmare."

I swallow nervously, wondering if these wires attached will catch my lie. "There is nothing to tell," I say and am happy there is no obvious tell to my tone. I sound perfectly at ease.

"Come now, Emma. We both know that's not true. You must remember something. No matter how small. How about the setting? Where are you? Outside? Inside?"

Surely there is no harm in telling him this much. I open my mouth to answer but it is difficult to find my voice. It is a simple answer and I should have no trouble with it.

"Picture it in your mind," he says. "Remember, you're safe, Emma."

But I cannot picture it. There is a wall around my nightmare I cannot penetrate. And my voice feels locked behind a lump in my throat. After some struggle, I strain to say, "Inside."

"Inside? Okay, excellent, Emma. What else? What do you see inside?"

Don't you tell him, that voice sounding very much like mine tells me. *Lie. Lie your goddamn ass off.*

I startle and suck in a deep breath. "I—I do not know."

"Emma, I asked you not to move."

"I have not moved, just as you asked." My voice pitches surprisingly high, and my heart, already pounding, stutters. Each breath hitches in my chest.

"Hm."

Holding my head as still as I can, I allow only my gaze to dart around the room. "Is something the matter?"

"What were you just thinking about? After you told me where the dream takes place?"

I bite into my lip and taste the metal of blood.

Lie, She tells me again, but I do not want to lie anymore and I do not understand why I should. Telling the truth will only make me better, and I want to go home.

My tongue rests behind my top front teeth, preparing to say something—anything—but the muscle locks and the air in my lungs refuses to support the sound. I strain to a point that my face feels hot.

"Emma?"

I shake my head, trying to force any word free. I cannot breathe now, and the harder I try to speak, the worse the pressure becomes.

Men in white lab coats and gray scrubs drive into the room the second I start to convulse. And yet, I continue to try. I have to overcome this. I want to go home.

I told you to lie, She says coolly. *You don't understand yet, but you will.*

I only understand that I am at war with myself, and I do not know why. One way or another, I will win.

CHAPTER 4

Dr. Travista crosses one leg over the other and settles a touch-screen tablet in his lap. He taps a few notations, with an audible *tickticktick* accompanying his fingers. He sighs before looking up at me. "How do you feel today?"

"Fine," I say.

"Any nightmares?"

"None." I am back to lying, only now I have my own reasons. The tests after the episode had been horrible. I do not want to relive them. "I am really great."

He tilts his head and removes his glasses. His expression is mocking and pitying all at once. I do not like this look. "We both know that's not true."

I bite the inside of my cheek. "They are not as bad anymore." This is the truth. Noah has been mysteriously—or not so mysteriously, considering Sonya's reaction—missing from them. Some nights I am utterly alone, and it is almost peaceful because there is no one to fear. "I swear this is the truth."

He points his glasses at me with emphasis. "Now, *that* I believe. Can you try describing them again? We aren't in the examination room. Just two friends talking in a comfortable setting."

The room *is* nice. Real plants and dark woods. Bookshelves with books I will never read because they have to do with chemistry and physics and physiology and other such complicated subjects. Dr. Travista is very smart. Declan calls him a genius.

The furniture is all burnt-red leather. I like this color. It makes me warm despite the colder days.

I caress the soft leather arm of my chair and consider the setting of my nightmare again. Nothing feels safe to talk about. I think words like "monitors" and "doctors." "Noah." This word especially gives me pain and threatens to withhold more oxygen. I wish I could tell Dr. Travista about the cylinder of water if for no other reason than to end his relentless questions. To prove to Her that She cannot control me.

I focus on the gray day outside a paned window. Autumn moves quickly into winter. Declan says we might see snow early this year.

"Emma?"

I return my attention to him. "Sorry. What was the question?"

"The dream. Is there anything you can tell me?"

The dream. Not the nightmare. He does not know there is a difference for me. I feel safe in the dream. Despite this, I still do not feel comfortable telling Dr. Travista anything other than, "Stars." I sense She waits close at hand for the moment when I would reveal too much, preparing to stop me.

"I thought you said it took place inside."

"Through a window," I lie. It bothers me how lying is becoming so easy. "It is the only time I get to see them. It is the only part of the dream I wish to relive."

"Stars, you say? Would you like to see them? I think we can arrange that."

I feel a noticeable shift in my expression to one of excitement, and it is unfamiliar to my muscles. I like this emotion and wish I had cause to feel it every day. "Could you? Tonight?"

Dr. Travista chuckles. "Yes, of course. Why didn't you just ask before?"

I want to say something really mean, but I bite my tongue. I should not have to ask, should I? "I would like a mirror," I say, though I understand I am pressing my luck. "Since we are discussing things I should ask for. I want to see my reflection."

The watered-down version I see in windows does nothing to appease my curiosity.

Dr. Travista shifts in his chair. "I'm not sure you're ready."

I do not understand this. Why would I not be ready? "Declan says I am not scarred and that I am still beautiful. Is there a reason why I should not look at myself?"

Dr. Travista's fingers tap over the rounded leather arm of his chair as he considers me thoughtfully. With a sigh, he then taps a few more commands into his tablet and hands it over.

I reach for it hesitantly. Is it this easy? I watch him for some sign that he will change his mind, but he seems decided.

I expect to see a photograph, but it appears he has activated a camera lens. I flinch in surprise when I find myself blinking at a woman's heart-shaped face over a slim neck. It takes several seconds to realize those hazel eyes surrounded by thick black lashes are mine. My fingers shake when I touch my cheekbone, rounded, high, and pink. My lips are full, the lower just a bit more than the upper. My nose is small and round on the tip. I do not like this part of me, but I cannot complain. It is me.

I move my hand over my dark hair. Lights overhead reflect over the silky texture, which angles perfectly against my chin line.

"There is nothing wrong with me," I say and note how my mouth quirks in a tilted smile and I speak mostly from that one side.

"Of course not," Dr. Travista says. "You're perfect."

He says this with some considerable amount of pride. Maybe because the accident had scarred me and he fixed me.

Dr. Travista allows me to hold on to the tablet for a while longer, asking his questions, and I answer as best I can while watching how my expressions shift with my thoughts. I see where I can hide things better. I am easy to read. I must work on this, but I do not know if this is because She wants this or I do.

It cannot hurt to learn such a skill, I tell myself, so with that, I practice schooling my expressions and watching them in the tablet's screen.

I learn fast.

"What do you think you're doing?"

The guard rushed toward the line and yanked my arm. His fingers bit into my skin and I yelped in pain.

"Nothing!" I yelled.

"Get back in line and keep your eyes forward," he commanded. "I'm watching you, girl."

For several minutes, I stared at the mousy brown braid of the girl in front of me wearing a thinning gray jumper identical to mine. Every half minute, the line edged forward one step toward the showers.

I clutched the thin black towel to my chest. I'd never had to shower with a group before. I didn't want any of them seeing me without my clothes. I was embarrassed by the small mounds of breasts beginning to show on my chest, and . . . other things. Embarrassing things. I hated my body and feared I'd never look as nice as some of these other girls who were filled out and almost ready for their assignments. No one would take me if I stayed like this.

The girl behind me tapped my shoulder. "What is the matter with you? Can't you do anything right?"

I started to turn my head to respond, but she stabbed me with a finger. "Don't turn around." She swore under her breath. "You have so much to learn."

"What do you mean?" I whispered.

Mousy-haired girl shot a glare over her shoulder but didn't say anything. I stuck my tongue out at her and she faced the front.

The girl behind me was a few years older—four maybe. New to this facility, I didn't know anyone's name yet. I'd noticed her when we'd first lined up, instantly jealous of her auburn hair and woman's figure.

"It's Wade, isn't it?" Before I could respond, she said, "I'm Toni Reece and I'm about to make your life here a lot easier. I don't know what WTC you came from, but here the guards are strict and won't hesitate to punish you in ways your twelve-year-old mind can't possibly imagine."

"I'm thirteen."

"Doesn't change the facts."

"Well, I can imagine a lot of things," I said indignantly. "Like death."

She laughed mockingly. "They won't kill you, twerp. We're too valuable to them. But that doesn't mean they won't bring you close to it. Sometimes I think death would be a better end."

"I just wanted to look outside," I said.

"Look outside on the wrong day, at the wrong time, and you'll wish you could turn back time. Trust me."

"So I shouldn't look outside?"

The line moved forward one step, slippered feet scuffling down the row.

"Or hide it better," she said. "You'll learn, and you'll have to learn fast. And who knows, maybe one day you'll put it to good use."

CHAPTER 5

The back wall in the gray room is no longer bare. It is no longer gray and cracked, either. Someone has painted it a calming shade of light blue and the boxes are unpacked. Traces of the organized chaos from before are gone.

On the wall, a large screen reaches from one side to the other. Sonya stands in the middle of the room, monitoring the men attaching the equipment to the wall. She directs them when one corner falls below level.

She smiles and shakes her head. "That bastard. This is quite the apology. And I deserve every square inch of it."

"Good, Dr. Toro?" one of the men asks. He kneels on top of the desk, breathing hard.

Sonya nods. "I think so. Let's see if this bad boy works."

She picks up a tablet computer from the desktop, and it clicks audibly with each tap of her finger. The screen in front blinks on to a monochrome blue. With pinched eyebrows, Sonya taps a few more instructions. Images appear on the right side of the screen. Boxes of

*information are too far away for me to read through my water-filled
tank, but I make out the humanoid figure with evenly splayed limbs
turning in a slow circle.* PATIENT 1 *is superimposed over the image,
an outline with a red dot blinking in time with the* beep ... beep ...
beep *sound filling the space.*

*The left side blinks on and off as if the information is having trou-
ble pulling to the large monitor.*

*"Patient 2 isn't reading," Sonya says, tapping her tablet again.
"Check those connections, will you?"*

I cannot hide this nightmare. I lurch up in bed and bite back a
scream. They are keeping two of us. Are we their lab rats?

I swipe absently at my forehead, and my fingertips come away
coated in sweat. A moment later, the air lock sounds with a *whoosh*
of air and the aluminum cylinder slides home with a soft *thunk*.
They do not ask me if I want a sedative anymore. It is automatic,
which means they know and will tell Dr. Travista about my nightmare.

I silently curse myself. I have hidden them for weeks now. I was
doing so well.

Standing, I spin in a slow circle. "I want out," I say to the walls.
"I need some air."

I do not care if I have to share a moment alone with an orderly.
I do not care if it is cold. I want to see the stars. *Need* to see the
stars.

My door slides open a few minutes later and Declan walks in.
He looks different, casually dressed in dark jeans and a nice green
sweater. He also looks tired.

"Declan?" I halt my pacing and blink several times in surprise. "What are you doing here?"

"Working late," he whispers. He reaches for my sweater, which hangs from a hook next to him, and holds out a hand. "Come. I will take you up."

"Up" is the roof. Since mentioning it to Dr. Travista, I have been allowed up to the roof whenever I request it but never allowed privacy there.

I shake my head. "If you are working, I am more than willing to wait for—"

A tilted smile breaks the tired mold of his expression. It takes years off his relatively young age. "Don't be silly. I need some air, too."

I slide into the sweater he offers without another word and follow him out.

On the roof, the air bites at my skin and I wrap my sweater tight around me. When I stop and look up at the sky, Declan beckons with open arms and I nestle in. I close my eyes to the hazy night with only a hint of starlight and focus on the warmth of his cheek against mine. His lips find my neck and warm breath sends a shiver down my spine.

"See?" he murmurs against my skin. "The cold isn't so bad."

I sink deeper into him. "You are right. I could get used to this."

The cool tip of his nose brushes my ear. His lips kiss my lobe. "Better?"

I understand without asking that he is referring to my nightmare. "I was fine before."

"No, you weren't," he says in that patient way of his.

I turn and wrap my arms around his waist. He is slim but broad.

I can barely grip my wrists around his back. His heart beats solid and steady in his chest; I pace mine to match. It soothes me.

"I thought the nightmares were over." His breath is warm against the crown of my head.

"This was different." The lie comes of its own volition, as does the follow-up. "I dreamed of never breathing fresh air or seeing the sun. I believe I am getting cabin fever."

My automatic response comes with a new phrase I did not realize existed, but I am careful not to react. I find I already understand its meaning, too. It bothers me how I know without knowing, but still chance upon most discoveries as if I am a child. I am anxious for the day when this is no longer the case.

He laughs and there is a rumbling sound inside his chest. "I can understand that. I'll talk to Arthur."

He uses Dr. Travista's first name so easily. I will never feel this close to the doctor because our situations are very different. Dr. Travista has an established, friendly association with Declan and never looks on my husband with anything more than respect and fondness. But me, he watches with careful calculation and study. Even in moments when he seems friendly, he scrutinizes every nuance.

"You've been inactive for a long time," Declan continues. "I think you just need something to do."

"I wish to go home," I say, burying my face in his chest, inhaling the scent of heavy spice and musk. It erases the smell of crisp wintery air and hint of ozone.

His hand grips the back of my head and holds me tight to him. His cheek presses into my crown. "I know. Me, too. Soon. Very soon. Arthur is pleased with how you're progressing."

I lift my chin to look into his eyes, hardly able to believe I am about to say what I mean to say. "In time to lie by the heat of a fire, I hope."

Declan's eyes widen only a fraction, and he smiles. "That would be a dream come true."

"For me as well."

I wear the spandex top and pants Randall leaves with my breakfast. I am intrigued, and he says I am to wear them once I clean up. Having spent most of my time in loose scrubs and gowns—the tightest item being my nightly tank top—I am curious about how my body looks in these form-fitting clothes. I wonder if I am meant to be so thin. I have no muscle like Declan or Randall.

An orderly arrives to escort me later, and I follow him to a floor I have never been to. There is one big room where men bounce an orange ball around the floor and throw it into two nets. Their shoes screech and squeal against a shiny floor.

In another room, men lift large black objects. Veins protrude from reddened faces. They do not seem to be having fun like the men playing ball, yet they continue to do it. It seems a large waste of time, in my opinion.

Finally, we reach another room with Dr. Travista standing beside a table of instruments. Behind him is a big circle in the floor. The word for it comes to me after only seconds: track.

The orderly pushes open the glass door and leaves me alone with the doctor.

"There you are," Dr. Travista says, waving me closer. He begins fiddling with the things sitting on the table. "When I spoke to Declan last night, I knew just the thing to help you with your— How did he put it? Cabin fever. This will allow you some activity and I can monitor your vitals. The exercise will test your endurance, and over time you will see your staying power build."

Five minutes later, he has me covered in electrodes and I have a moment of self-consciousness. No one else in the area is being tested. Only me. Their exercise is unobserved and I am jealous. I would almost prefer the non-fun-looking exercise in the other room to this.

Almost.

I eye the track almost hungrily. Running. I know running.

"Well, go on," he says, waving toward the track. "You can walk or run. Whatever you're comfortable with."

My first lap is slow, and I am especially warm when I come back around. The second lap makes me forget the electrodes and witnesses. The run is freeing. My breathing increases and I break a sweat. My lungs burn.

I am sad when I cannot run any longer. The time is too short, but my legs feel soft and it is hard to breathe. Dr. Travista assures me this is normal, and I am glad. I want to do this again.

"How long until I will feel okay?" I ask in starts and stops. "Can I try again in a few minutes?"

He laughs. "No, Emma. That was good for today. Your body will take some time to adjust to this new experience. We can try again tomorrow if you wish."

I smile and nod. "Yes. Please."

"Run," Toni told me. She pushed her spade into the soft earth and used her shoulder to push away some of the stray auburn hairs that had come loose from her braid. "Whenever you get a chance. Tell them it's recreational. Tell them you have cabin fever and need to

burn off some energy. That works for me every time. They fear cabin fever. It makes people crazy."

She sat back on her heels and brushed aside more hair with the back of her hand. "One day you'll need to run for real and you'll have to outlast them."

CHAPTER 6

I run every day. I run with sore muscles and aches in my knees I fear will never go away. I will live with this pain because during this time I can focus on something that is not a nightmare or Her voice in my head. She must like to run, too, because She never talks to me during these sessions.

Declan sees how much I love this exercise and brings me special shoes and more clothes to wear. He says they are made specifically for runners. I like this new label.

I am a runner.

Patient.

Wife.

Runner.

Foster stood and reached out for my hand. "Time to go, Major."

. . .

I pace down the row of books in Dr. Travista's office, my fingertips skimming over the soft black covers with gold embossed letters. The titles are in English but may as well be in Swahili for all the sense they make to me. Arthur Travista really is a genius if he can read all these books.

The books lining his shelves are sandwiched with bookends: large chess pieces, gargoyles, or mini replications of *The Thinker* to start. Almost hidden between one-half of a pewter globe set and bronze scrolls sits a digital frame. Scrolling through are images of a young brunette woman. She is not exceptionally beautiful but is undeniably pretty enough to turn more than a few heads. Her only imperfection, if you could call it one, is the dark mole on her right cheek. I pause to study her visage during my visits but have yet to gather the nerve to ask about her.

Until now. "Is this girl your daughter?" I ask, but I do not see a resemblance. The age difference fits, though.

When I face Dr. Travista, he is looking at his clasped hands in his lap. "No."

There is a finality to his answer, but I have contained my curiosity long enough to not hold back now. "Wife, then?"

He looks up and a brief smile glances across his face but does not touch his eyes. "Once upon a time, she might have been."

"What is her name?" He clearly still cares for her despite his somber mood.

"Her name was Jodi."

"Was?"

"She's gone now. Has been for more than twenty years."

"Oh, I am sorry. I should not have pried."

He waves me off. "It's been a long time, Emma. Let's get back to you, shall we? How do you feel?"

"I am well."

He leans into one side of his chair, a hand tapping a quick rhythm over his knee. "Exercise seems to agree with you. You're very relaxed these days."

I shrug and return to the books with names that I can only guess refer to researching the body and all its parts. He has a particular interest in the brain and memory and, according to the bindings, has authored a few himself. "I like running."

Dr. Travista is silent a long time, but I can almost feel him watching me. Always observing me. Always waiting to see what I will do next. I believe he is waiting for me to elaborate. He will be waiting a long time.

Finally, he says, "Do you like to read, Emma?"

I turn to catch him making notes in his computer tablet. This question has surprised me because I do not know the answer and I should. "I do not know."

He barely glances my way, still typing in his notes. "Is there anything you would like to read?"

"I do not know," I say again and then turn fully to face him. "Why do I not know this? Should I not know what I like to read? If I read at all?"

Dr. Travista removes his glasses and nibbles on the end. "In time, maybe. You had a serious accident. All of this will take time."

"What kind of accident?" I ask.

"That answer, too, will come in time."

I clench my teeth and breathe slowly in, then out of my nose. "Will it never be the time of my choosing?"

"In time," he repeats and taps something else into the tablet.

I turn away to hide my annoyance. When I trust my voice not to quiver, I say, "You choose."

"Choose what?"

I stare blindly at gold letters and soft black covers. "The book. We will find out what I like."

No classics, She says.

"A classic," I say.

Because you'd rather sleep than read? She says in a dry tone. *Don't be so difficult.*

"Never mind," I say grudgingly. "No classics."

"No classics," Dr. Travista repeats. "Any other instructions?"

I wait for Her to tell me, but She is silent. "No."

"Then I shall have a few options sent to your room."

I walk to the window now, and cold seeps through the panes. A light layer of snow coats the parking lot. No footprints mar the perfection, so the fall must be recent. "It snowed," I say.

"Yes. A couple of hours ago. Do you remember snow?"

I press my fingertips to the cold glass. My breath fogs the surface, obscuring my vision. My answer sits behind a sudden lump in my throat. *Oh yes.* I remember.

I shivered in the courtyard, my feet buried in snow. My slippers did nothing to protect them from the icy feel, and my toes had long ago gone numb.

Victor Porch, the captain of the guard, paced in front of us, his dark eyes narrowed and his hands clasped behind his back. Unlike the large group of girls he looked at, he wore a fur-lined coat and boots.

"One of you," he started, his voice startling me with its thunderous nature, "has decided that our rules are not to her liking."

My body went rigid. They knew what I did. How did they know?

"What is our number one rule?"

The group around me answered in unison. "Do not leave the compound."

I sighed in relief. Not me. Definitely not me. I fingered the indigo petals in my smock pocket and decided I would bury the flower tonight before they did catch me. What number was the rule for stealing? Four? Five? Regardless, a bloody whipping and a week of solitary confinement.

"That's right," Captain Porch said. "And we haven't had any violators of this rule in years. So many, in fact, you probably don't understand the severity of punishment that goes along with this crime."

Crime? Was he serious? He spoke as if this was the ultimate in crimes against humanity. My gut clenched for the hapless girl; her punishment would no doubt be painful. But I understood wanting to escape. The fact that I stood in snow to my ankles was only one reason.

Toni spoke of escape almost daily and planned to make it out before her time came. Before she was chosen. I admired her courage to speak openly about things the others were too frightened to consider. One day I would find the same courage in myself.

"You're about to witness this punishment firsthand." Gray teeth flashed from behind a vicious smile. "Your only assignment is to tell the tale, girls."

He motioned to another guard, who opened the side door to one of the windowless detention rooms. In seconds, he dragged Toni out by her auburn waves, clutching so tightly to the crown of her head that she walked on her tiptoes. To her credit, she didn't so much as whimper through her clenched teeth as she tripped along the path he dragged her on.

I gasped behind both hands. She hadn't been at breakfast, and I had assumed she was only skipping the meal she skipped frequently because she preferred sleeping in to the bland food.

Toni's entire body shivered in the cold. Her skin had turned a sick shade of blue. They'd been freezing her to death in there, I realized.

The guard threw her to her knees in front of Captain Porch. The soft snow flew away from her in a cloud. Slowly, she rose on shaking legs. She gritted her jaw and lifted her chin in a show of defiance. It must have taken all the strength she had to fight the urge to curl up into a warm ball, begging for his mercy.

"You understand what you have done wrong?" he asked loudly.

"Yes." She didn't hesitate.

"Then you understand what is in store for you?"

Toni met my eyes then, and I wish I could have read her mind. What must she be feeling? Did that determined gaze camouflage fear?

"I understand and accept it gladly," she said and returned her fierce gaze to the captain. "Go on. Get it over with. I'm freezing."

My legs weaken under me and I brace myself on the windowsill. Tears flood my eyes but they do not fall. Not yet. Behind me, Dr. Travista is standing. He is saying something I cannot hear.

I hear only Her.

Don't you dare speak of it, She says. *You are strong because of her. She wants you to fight.*

But I do not want to fight, and I do not want to look at the snow,

so I close my eyes. But this is worse because now I see Captain
Porch reach for his handgun and press it to Toni's head.

I open my eyes.

Now all I see is her blood in the snow.

And I am angry.

CHAPTER 7

*C*alm down.

No, I think. *What are you doing to me? You manipulate my dreams, and now you use them in my waking hours to taunt me.*

Not dreams.

I clutch the sides of my head and clench my teeth. *Shut up! They are dreams. Toni and Wade and Foster and Noah and Sonya . . . they are not real.* You *are not real.*

"Emma?" Dr. Travista grips my wrists and pulls them away from my head. "What's the matter? Talk to me."

"Nothing," I say, but we both know this is a lie. I scramble for another response but can hardly think clearly through the pounding of my own heartbeat in my ears. "Headache."

Dr. Travista feels my head, takes my pulse. "Let's go run some tests."

I yank my trembling hands free. "It is only a headache."

The doctor edges around his massive decorative desk and presses a button. "I won't hurt you, Emma. You know that."

The tears I have been fighting fall freely now. I know what is coming and would rather tell the truth than deal with what he intends to do. "I do not want tests. Please. No more tests. I am lying. I do not have a headache."

It is the truth he believes is a lie. I know this by the way he tilts his head in a mocking gesture.

They only believe what they want to believe, She says.

Get out of my head!

You have to calm down. You're making this worse on yourself.

My fingers grip tight to my hair and I drop to my knees. *Leave me alone!*

I wish I could, She says, and I almost believe She is as sad as She sounds. *But that would mean giving up. Unfortunately for you, I don't give up.*

Well, neither do I.

That's all I want to hear.

I wake up under a large white bulb. Several, actually. They form concentric circles under a single aluminum lamp hood. Dust particles float in the air. Dr. Travista's gray eyes watch me from behind a blank expression.

"How do you feel?" he asks.

I hate this question. "Where am I? How did I get here?"

"I had to sedate you," he says. "How do you feel?"

The lights make my eyes water and I squint. I try to use one of my arms for cover but they do not lift. When I look down, I find I am bound to the table by Velcro straps. Instinctively, I jerk and the bindings burn and pinch my wrists.

"What are you doing?" I ask, panicked.

"I'll remove them when I think you're no longer a danger to yourself."

I gape at him. "I am no danger to myself."

Dr. Travista lifts a tablet from the table and enters a few commands. When he turns it on me, my reflection blinks back. My skin is pale and my eyes are wide and darting. On either side of my face, long red gouges mar my skin.

I gasp. "I did that?"

"Yes," he says simply.

"But why?"

"You tell me." He leans on the table and narrows his eyes. "It's time to come clean, Emma; otherwise, I can't help you."

I do not need his help.

The thought is automatic, and I do not understand it. But I know from experience that it does not matter. I cannot tell him what is wrong. Even if I wanted to, I cannot. I will never forget the suppression of air in my lungs. How my throat locked. I do not want to feel that again.

Dr. Travista sighs and nods once to someone nearby. I am suddenly surrounded by his nurses. Randall twists my arm and forces a needle into the crook of my elbow.

I jerk in surprise. "What are you doing?"

"What I must," Dr. Travista says evenly.

Another nurse pastes electrodes to my chest and head. He does not look me in the eyes. None of them do.

"Put the stirrups up," Dr. Travista orders someone. He snaps a rubber glove over one hand. "May as well run a few extra tests while I'm at it."

No, I think, but my tongue is too heavy to voice the word aloud. I do not want this to happen.

Cool hands lift my heavy legs as the *clink* of metal locks into place. I am asleep before the cold metal stirrups fully rest against my bare calves.

"Just relax," the strange doctor said.

I squeezed my eyes shut and tried pretending I lay somewhere else. That I didn't lay propped open by stirrups, my legs spread for a strange, gangly man. I'd feared turning sixteen for this very reason.

The gynecologist appointment.

The regular bimonthly visits that would continue until we turned eighteen. From what I'd heard, they didn't stop even then.

The doctor worked and talked as if poking around in my womb was normal. My answers and responses were as simple as I could make them.

Toni would tell me, don't give anything away. Keep your answers short so you don't tell them something you don't mean to. Keep as close to the truth as you can. They can spot a flat-out lie a mile away. Evade, evade, evade.

I didn't need her instructional reminders today, though. My jittery nerves kept me from elaborating anything. But it helped to remember her voice. I've tried to remember it every day for the last two years. I can't forget what she taught me.

I wake in my room. I notice right away the bruised and achy feeling in my lower belly. My throat is dry and I cough.

"There you are."

Declan rises from a chair in the corner and lays a book down on the table. He does not look at me as he fills a cup with water. His beautiful lips are set in a frown.

I sit up and accept the glass he offers me. "What happened?"

He sits on the edge of my bed and appears to focus on his clasped hands. "You've had a setback. Arthur says we've been allowing you to do too much and it's causing stress to your body."

My spine snaps to attention and heat floods my chest. It takes everything I have not to react irrationally by lashing out with accusations and arguments to the contrary. And in the end, I still cannot halt the strained words that finally slip past my throat. "I do not do too much. I am not allowed."

If my reaction surprises him, he does not show it when he meets my gaze unflinchingly. "We're restricting your activities for a while."

"What? No!"

He nods once. "I'm sorry, but your health means more than anything else."

Scorching hot tears threaten, and a roll of heat moves up my chest and into my face. Declan's eyes widen when I throw my sheet off my lower body and stand opposite him. I barely notice the coolness of the floor under my bare feet.

Declan rises slowly and his eyes, usually soft and kind, narrow and harden. His thinned lips say what he does not: *Be careful where you go next.*

But I do not care. "You cannot do this to me," I say and do not recognize my own voice. It is low and wells up from the deep recesses of my chest.

"I can and I will," he says, his tone even and deep.

I am unaccustomed to him speaking to me this way and should

be scared, but I am too furious about the loss of what little freedom I have been able to gain.

Hide your anger, She says. *Play on his sympathies.*

I straighten and close my eyes. Drop my shoulders. Take a calming breath. "I had a headache," I say softly, then look at him, letting tears glaze over my vision. "And Dr. Travista overreacted. He scared me. How else was I supposed to respond? I was afraid he was going to hurt me. And I was right, because he did." I rest a hand over my throbbing abdomen. "He hurt me and you trust him?"

"Some of his tests are necessary," he says, and his expression softens. His gaze drops to my stomach and he swallows deeply.

I have made my way through his defenses.

I round the end of the bed. "I did not drink enough water after my run and I got a small headache. I told him and he started acting strangely. I was scared and only wanted to get away from him. Did his tests show anything was actually wrong with me?"

He looks hesitant to answer. "We are still waiting on some test results."

I take his hand. "Declan, please. You have to believe me."

He sits on the bed and pulls me down beside him. His hand caresses my cheek and he sighs. "I want to believe you."

Kiss him.

I do not hesitate and kiss him. In his surprise, he is slow to return it but quick to make up for it. His soft lips taste of the fresh water he must have drunk while waiting for me to awaken. While his kiss is malleable, the stubble of his day-old beard burns my skin.

His lips guide mine open and my tongue darts out to meet his, igniting a fluid heat between my legs. This explorative kiss must release something new in him, too, because his hands graze my cheekbones on their way to the sides of my head, where he grips me tighter, deepening the kiss.

The heat of anger swiftly turns into something different, and I know instinctively that this is the heat of lust. Warmth swirls in my belly and snakes up my core, flaming out into my limbs to give them new life, new courage. While part of me is nervous about what I am doing, another part of me is willing to do whatever it takes and does not mind this course of action.

I maneuver up and straddle his lap, never allowing my lips to leave his. His fingers gouge deep, penetrating grooves into the small of my back, and I arch closer to him, feeling the swift beating of his heart against mine. His heat is my heat. His air is my air.

I grind my hips down over his obvious erection. This new sensation jolts me, and my breath hitches on a sharp inhalation. Our widened gazes meet in surprise and lust. It nearly shocks me into retreat. We are swiftly reaching the point of no return, and I wonder how far I am willing to take this.

Whatever it takes, She whispers.

With trembling fingers, I find the knot in his tie. His gaze holds mine as I yank it free with surprising ease and slip it over his head. My fingers have found their nerve again by the time I undo the first button of his shirt.

His slender fingers run a hot trail over the throbbing pulse in my neck and up to my swollen lips, his gaze following hungrily after. His hands tighten like a vise around my head again, and he slants his mouth over mine. All gentle pretenses are gone. He is lost in his lust and I am not far behind.

My fingers grip the bottom of his shirt and pull. He yanks the rest of it free of his pants, shifting awkwardly under me to do so. I push the fabric over his shoulders, allowing my hands to slide over his skin. His shoulders are round and creased in muscle that he has hidden well until this moment. Each indentation shifts under my hands as he wrestles to pull himself free of the shirt.

I am disappointed to find another layer of clothing in the form of a tank top, but this does not stop me. I guide him to lie on his back and oscillate my hips against him. He groans, and this pleases me. I want to elicit more of these sounds from him.

His hands maneuver under my top and are hot against my skin. I have no memory of his touch on me like this, and it makes my breath catch. He smiles against my mouth and strokes his hands farther up. They stop and his thumbs trace over the bottom of my rib cage, so close to my breasts, and it is agony to my body.

I bite his lower lip in retaliation.

Smiling, his eyes glisten as he holds back his kiss in return.

I reach for something he cannot keep from me. My hand closes over his erection and his eyes widen. His jaw falls open and holds. His chest lays unmoving under me and he forgets to deny me his mouth.

"I am not as fragile as he would have you believe," I whisper over his lips, and I do not know where the words come from. I had not meant to say anything. I only meant to see this through to completion because I am bottled heat with no release.

In an instant, I am on my back and he shoves off the bed, his chest heaving. He reaches for his shirt and I prop up on my elbows, dazed. He cannot look me in the eyes and his lips draw down in a frown.

"What is the matter?" I ask, though I can guess.

He buttons his shirt and says, "I will speak to Arthur."

He turns and I scramble off the bed. "Where are you going? I thought—I thought we . . ." I trail off, more willing to perform the act than speak it aloud.

His gaze meets mine for the first time, and there is no gleam of happiness. Only a hard edge. "You made your point. I won't force you to do something you have no desire to actually perform."

Declan is out of the room before I can respond.

The door slides closed and She says, *Well done, Emma. Very well done.*

CHAPTER 8

Whatever Declan said to Dr. Travista worked, because they allow me to run today. I welcome this run. I need this run. I run hard and fast, using each step to release the anger raging inside. I am angry with myself for what I did to my own husband. I am angry with Dr. Travista for the violating tests he performed. And most of all, I am angry with *Her*. This is all Her fault.

Are you complaining? She asks. *You got what you wanted in the end, didn't you?*

I widen my strides and pump my arms. My breathing increases.

You're ignoring me? She laughs, and it is low and deep. *You can't ignore me. It's literally impossible. There's nowhere you can run.*

I do not respond and She falls silent. Before I know it, it is only me and the whisper of my feet over the rubber track.

My quick, even breaths.

The slide of my arms against the silky material of my top.

. . .

I ducked behind the wide trunk of a tree and searched for Foster. He peered around the trunk of another tree nearby, fingers playing over the barrel of his plasma rifle. He caught my gaze a moment later and nodded. His expression mirrored the intense, focused feelings coursing through my veins.

We're ready.

He motioned the all clear and the team moved as one silent, deadly entity. Pride washed over me for my well-oiled team as they ducked and rolled out of the shadow. The night was silent except for the whisper of our boots through the grass.

She remains silent, but I know this is Her doing. The waking dream stops my breath and I stumble. My knees knock against the rubber floor and my palms slap hard and sting.

In seconds, two orderlies are on either side of me. One prepares to fill me full of a sedative, while the other reaches out to restrain me.

I raise my hands defensively. "I am okay. I . . . I twisted my ankle."

A lie, but I am desperate to stop what they plan to do. I cannot afford another "setback," especially over something as ridiculous as a dream.

Rather than pump me full of drugs, the orderlies help me to my feet and I affect a limp of my right ankle. I even wince at the appropriate moments.

We are nearing the glass door when Dr. Travista and Declan rush through. Declan lifts me off my feet and carries me to a bench. The orderlies must have explained the situation to Dr. Travista because I am barely seated before he eases my shoe off and presses his thumbs and fingers into my foot and ankle.

"I don't feel anything out of place," he says. His eyes narrow when he looks at me, and I fear he might question my noninjury. "How bad does it hurt?" His gaze does not leave my face as he waits for my answer.

I clear my throat. "Not very. Just a twist. It surprised me. I did not mean to scare anyone."

Declan exchanges a quick glance with the doctor, and his attention is back to me before I can blink. "Can you stand?"

I do, and when they request that I press down on my foot, I do that, too. I wince but assure them it is already better and that I do not require assistance to my room. Declan is beginning to insist, when a young man in a suit enters the room.

"Mr. Burke," he says, "sorry to interrupt, but you asked me to let you know if any of the board members showed up unannounced."

"Which one?" Declan asks, his voice tight.

"Mr. Thomas and Mr. Barbosa, sir. They insist on seeing the—"

"Mr. Tulley," Dr. Travista interrupts and gives Declan a passing glance, "why don't you and I go upstairs where I can greet these men myself?" He looks at Declan. "If that's all right with you, of course."

Declan takes him by the elbow and they move several steps away. He lowers his voice, but his words carry easily to me due to the room's acoustics. "I want to know *exactly* what they know and how they found out. I want to know who talked."

Dr. Travista lays a hand on his shoulder. "Don't worry. I'll handle everything."

Declan squares his shoulders and glances at me. "Thank you. I'll be along shortly."

The room clears, with Declan never taking his gaze off the glass separating the room from the hallway. He stands rubbing his chin, a million miles away.

"Is everything all right?" I ask. I cannot make any sense of what has happened, but he is clearly upset about it.

"Fine," he says and faces me with a guarded expression.

It is the first we have been alone since last night, and I have been going crazy over what we would say to each other. By the look he gives me, his usual kind words will not come easy. And they shouldn't. The fault lies with me, and only I can clear the air.

"I want to apologize," I say. "But also, I think you misunderstood my intentions last night."

Declan sighs as if a weight has lifted and averts his eyes. "I forget you aren't who you used to be. I should be apologizing to you."

This takes me aback. He never talks of how I used to be, but if he had, I never would have expected this. "I do not understand. What was I like?"

His eyelids fall shut and he shakes his head. "Never mind." He takes my hands and draws me close. There is an abrupt softening in his expression, and I wonder how he can swiftly change—or hide—his emotions like that. The sea in his eyes now shines as they look into mine. "I love you more and more with each passing day. I never believed that was possible."

I am on the verge of tears because of this declaration, and my insides twist knowing how I have truly deceived him.

Put on your big-girl panties and get the fuck over it, She says.

I ignore Her and draw close to Declan. "Come to my room with me?"

He smiles, biting his lower lip. "I can't. Not with"—he waves a hand absently toward the ceiling—"the sudden business I need to attend to. Besides, it isn't private. I completely lost my head last night when I let it go that far."

I pout and he kisses me, then murmurs against my lips. "Soon,

my love. Just keep getting better and we'll go home where we'll
have all the privacy we need."

My cylinder now faces the opposite direction. I know I am closer to
the new monitors because the heartbeats are louder and Sonya now
faces the wall to my right to read the screens. I still do not know who
Patient 2 is, and this bothers me.

Instead of computers, I now face a row of hospital beds dressed in
white sheets with inclined backs. White cabinets cover the walls. Cur-
tains hang between beds for privacy, but as of now, there are no pa-
tients.

Noah scans the room when he enters. Maybe this is his first time
visiting since the rearrangement. "Looks good in here."

Sonya, who sits in a wheeled stool with a heavy book in her lap,
looks up and slaps the tome closed. "You should throw a few more
tantrums."

His face does not shift in emotion one way or the other. "It's what
she wanted. Tantrum or no, you know you would have gotten all of
this anyway."

Silence is her response, and she presses the book to her chest as
makeshift armor. The title, Infertility in the New Era, *is all I can*
read, as her arms cover the author's name.

Noah shifts his weight on his feet. He brings his hands up to his
waist, and one is coated in dried blood. Sonya must see it, too, be-
cause she curses under her breath.

"You went with them, didn't you?" she says in a reprimanding
tone.

She walks to a cabinet across the room with a purposeful stride,
shaking her head in a disapproving manner that makes even me

want to look away in shame. She drops the book on the shelf under the cabinet.

"I haven't cleared you for duty," she tells him and yanks open a cabinet door.

"I don't need your approval," he says without pause.

He meets her eyes and they stare each other down in a battle of wills that she eventually wins, because he looks away first.

I think I like her.

She nods her head toward a bed, and he hesitates but eventually strolls over. He sits and passes over his hand. As she wipes it down with an antiseptic, she glances up at his face every now and then, waiting for him to shift his attention back to her. Or maybe she waits for him to look my way. I know I am waiting. He has not looked at me once since arriving. He fixes his gaze on the floor.

"They're fine," *she says quietly,* "in case you're curious."

Not a single flinch of muscle breaks his stony expression. "I assumed as much. I hadn't heard otherwise, so I figured she's still kicking."

Her hand freezes over his for a moment before finishing. She throws the swab in a trash can and unwraps a bandage.

"What's her name?" *she asks casually.* "Referring to her by a patient number is getting ridiculous."

Noah's jaw sets firmly and he nods toward the bandage. "I have somewhere else to be."

Sonya slaps the bandage on his hand, making him wince. "Get a fucking haircut and shave that shit off your face. You may not be human on the inside, but you could at least look the part."

Anger flushes his cheeks, but at least now she has his full attention. "What the hell's that supposed to mean?"

"It means grow a fucking set and man up." *Her eyes scan him from scruff to scuffed boot.* "If she could see you—"

He jumps off the bed. "Well, it's a good goddamn thing she can't,"
he says and storms out of the room.

The door slams behind him and Sonya flinches. "—she'd kick your
ass," she finishes quietly, and the words seem to echo in the empty
room.

Yes. I definitely like her.

Declan clips an Electric Indigo lotus flower from their dedicated
section in the garden and passes it to me. He knows these hybrid
lotus flowers are my favorite.

"Tell me again how we met," I say and bury my nose in the cloying scent of the flower.

He smiles as if he loves reliving this memory as much as I love
hearing it. They are only stories to me, and I hope to remember
them for myself one day.

"You were eating lunch by yourself in a park. I happened to be
in Richmond for a business meeting. Before it even began I decided
the perfect spring day was too beautiful to waste and found myself
drawn to the park."

I do not ask him about Richmond anymore. I have no memory
of glass skyscrapers and paved roads and walkways and hundreds
of people, but I can imagine now what it must look like from the
books I have been reading. It must be amazing to see buildings
made of steel and glass, domed or pointed or slanted or square
roofs. The men who design them do amazing things. Impossible
things.

"You drew me in like a magnet," he continues. "And in the days
that followed, we met there for lunch and conversation. Same time,
same place."

"Was I madly in love with you?" I ask for the first time.

His sea-green gaze darts to me and back to the gray paving stones under our feet that are wet around the edges from the recent spray. He tucks his hands into his pockets, bunching the sides of his suit jacket back.

"I like to imagine you were," he answers carefully.

"I was not?"

"It took you some time; that's all. You were difficult to"—he pauses for the space of two heartbeats—"acquire."

I laugh, but there is something about this word "acquire" that rings of another meaning. "You make it sound like I was a difficult purchase."

He sighs and slows to a stop. "There are a lot of things about the world we live in that you don't understand. Things you'll find out in time."

My heart begins pounding and my previously happy feelings melt away. "The time is not now?"

"You aren't ready. Your mind is still fragile from the accident and I'm wary to rush you." He edges closer and cups my face. "I don't want to lose you. Taking it slow is our best chance."

I don't know what he sees in my face, but he pulls me out of the view of curious glances from the employees working in the garden. He pushes us through a doorway I have never noticed before and into a small, empty hallway. More nondescript doors lead off to places I am unaware of.

My curiosity is piqued and I want to inquire about this place but am suddenly against the wall and his mouth is on mine. He is not careful and my body heat rises in response. His fingers thread into my hair, and when he pulls away, it is only to leave us heaving for air and filled with longing.

"I love you so much," he says. "More than you'll ever imagine."

I reach up and cover his hands with mine. I do not understand this outburst of emotion, but I know what my response should be. "I love you, too."

Liar, liar, pants on fire, She says and chuckles. *You're much better at this than I ever gave you credit for.*

She is right. It is a lie. I care for him, but I cannot say it is love. Not yet.

Declan's smile is wide and amazing and I cannot help but smile in response. "When this is all over with, I want to renew our vows. Will you do that for me?"

I nod, but my stomach twists uneasily. Still, I affect a smile of utter happiness. I do not need to see a reflection of myself to know it is perfect. "Of course. Anything."

Anything to go home.

CHAPTER 9

Dr. Travista does not ask me how I am. He has not asked since that day. Instead, he watches me read the bindings of his books again and again. I will read them until they are in tatters and still have no idea what they are for. It makes no difference, because I only wish to stay far away from the window and the thick layer of snow on the ground.

"Have you read any of the books I sent you?" he asks.

I shrug one shoulder. "It seems I am not much of a reader." She likes them, so I stopped reading to spite Her. If She wants to screw with me, I can screw with Her. "I think I will stick with the gardens and running for now. I like to do those things."

"What about the stars? You like the stars. Maybe you have an interest in astronomy. We could manage a telescope—"

"I only think they are pretty," I say. I have no interest in studying them. "The mystery of them is what holds my interest." The mystery of some niggling memory drawing me to them, actually. I feel it is just there, at the back of my memory, trying to dig its way to the surface.

"That makes sense." He taps something into his tablet, adjusts his eyeglasses, and then clears his throat. "Declan says you two are becoming close again."

Hiding my face to answer would only help the lie, so I give him a glassy-eyed look and smile broadly at him. "Oh yes. I love him very much."

"I'm curious. What do you foresee for your marriage?"

My breath catches, but I do not think he notices. "I do not understand the question."

"What are your plans when you get home? When people are married, they have hopes and dreams for a particular future. What are yours?"

I do not have an answer for this. I have not thought beyond returning home.

The answer is family, She says. *Living happily ever after.*

I want to ignore Her, but I need an answer for the doctor and have no other response than the one She has given me. "I would like to have children," I say.

This answer intrigues him, and his thick wiry eyebrows rise as he pulls the glasses from his face. "Oh? And how many do you think you'd like to have?"

Be vague, She warns. *Specifics will only lead to trouble.*

"I do not know," I say and fold into the leather chair across from him. The cold leather seeps through my thin pants but only slightly penetrates my sweater. "I have not thought too much about it."

Audible clicks time perfectly with the taps of his fingers over the tablet. "Well, I'm happy to report to you that children are very possible. Your tests came back with positive results."

This makes my mouth and throat run dry. "There was a question?"

He sets the tablet aside and crosses his legs. His arms spread over the overstuffed sides of his leather chair. "Well, yes. Fertility is questionable with a majority of the female population, and because of your accident, we feared you would lose the ability to bear children."

I sit up, curiosity piqued by only one thing he has said. The other I could come back to later. "Fertility is questionable? How so?"

He shrugs very slightly. "That seems to be the big enigma for us all. Nobody can seem to pinpoint the exact reason, so they blame it on Mother Nature. Her way of compensating for the overpopulation of our species.

"Unfortunately, we'd already begun taking the steps to take care of this ourselves. Globally limiting families to one child, and at that time—oh, I'd say this started roughly two hundred years ago—couples could change the sex of their child to whatever they wanted. Men wanted their family lines to continue, you see, so they chose male children more often than not.

"The women who are fertile these days," he continues while he stands and moves to one of his bookcases, "are only fertile into their late twenties, early thirties at most. It isn't disease or genetics, just the unfortunate way things have progressed."

"But if you have the ability to change a child's sex, why not make more girls?" I say when I am sure his long explanation has ended.

He finds the book he was looking for and pulls it free, then heads back to his chair. "It has been outlawed after what happened last time. We do not want to risk a shortage of boys. Forcing nature to do our bidding is a risky business."

"I see."

He hands me the heavy book, then sits. "You are blessed with the ability to bear children, so you don't have to worry about it. At least not for a few years yet. You're still young."

I am unable to respond because I am staring at the very book Dr. Sonya Toro was reading in my last nightmare. And Dr. Travista wrote it. Under the title *Infertility in the New Era*, it reads, *Our Steps to a Cure.*

My head feels light, but I cannot allow Dr. Travista to realize anything is wrong. He will ask too many questions, so I shift my focus back to his last statement in order to continue the conversation. "Does Declan know?"

"That you can carry a child? Of course. I told him right away. This has been a concern of his since the accident."

I bite my lip and shift my weight in the chair. "I wish to know about this accident."

He stands and pats my shoulder. "You should focus on your future, on becoming better so you can go home."

He is good at diversion.

I want to be better.

I will be better.

We reached the outer walls and everyone wordlessly painted themselves into the dark stone structure and shadow. I glanced to either side of me, settling on Foster's cool expression. His gaze searched high and I followed it to the empty night sky. This close to the compound, the glow of lights drowned out the cluster of stars.

"Where are they?" he asked.

"They'll come." I was confident they would, but the timing was off. I didn't like it. "They'll come," I repeated.

Foster nodded.

"And if not, we'll just create our own diversion."

I grinned, and his tilted smile followed a moment later. "No doubt it'll be better, too."

"At the very least it'll be more fun."

His elbow knocked into my side. "You're the only person I know who can turn war into a good time."

"Somebody has to."

"Might as well be you."

Discovering the door and its subsequent hallway days before opens my eyes to what I have been missing with my focus so narrowed on nightmares I would rather forget, my husband, and returning home. With fewer visits from Declan these days, I have plenty of opportunities to enlighten myself.

I find a new exhilaration in my daily garden walk. Not because of the exercise it affords or because of the flowers and their amazing aroma, but because of what I learn in my covert search. I find ways to listen to conversations before anyone realizes I stand nearby, learning names and, in very few cases, about families.

This is how I learn the workers in blue lab coats are botanists studying the medicinal applications of the plants in the greenhouse garden. I suppose it makes sense to employ this type of study in a hospital.

Once I satisfy my garden walk, I take leisurely strolls through the corridors, keeping to the far wall, well away from the half windows lining the outside walls. The nearly white sky tells me there has been a heavy snowfall.

I pass men—I am the only woman here—in various colors of lab coats: white, pale blue, and bright red. Dr. Travista and the other doctors who assist him wear white. While there is a concentration of white lab coats in my set of hallways, the occasional red coat appears and pays me special attention. They think I have not noticed because I pretend to study any one of the multiple abstract paintings, fingering the dips of paint, the texture of the canvas. In reality, I watch everyone's destination, and in particular Dr. Travista's.

I have a good view near a cross section of the hallway that splits to three others. Each white hallway is identical to the next. I do not leave my hallway. Not yet, anyway.

Dr. Travista visits one room in particular across this epicenter every day. He never knocks or begs permission to enter this room as he does mine. Instead, he enters with a "Hello, dear. How are you feeling today?" Then the door slides behind him and I learn nothing else, but my instinct tells me I am not the only patient on this floor as I have long believed.

"Do you like the paintings, Emma?"

I sit with my back to the windows in Dr. Travista's office, my sweater wrapped tightly around me. This question, though simple enough, tells me the red-coated men are not only watching me but reporting my actions. I have suspected they are security and now know for certain. "Yes, I like them very much."

"Would you like one in your room?"

I cannot bear to have even one of these atrocious abstracts hang near my photograph of the sea. "No, thank you."

"If you change your mind . . ."

I smile at him. "I will let you know."

. . .

I find paint and canvas in my room. Below the easel is a tan drop cloth. I should be exasperated by this gesture because I have shown no interest in painting. Perched on the edge of my bed, I study the simple setup for a long time. My fingers scratch slowly up and down my thighs, itching to touch a brush, and I bite my lip. Can I do this?

Just try it, She tells me. *You might like it.*

Her nudging sends another image to my mind, one where I stand and knock it all to the ground, but I cannot bring myself to do this. It feels very wrong. Wasteful. That, and I realize I would like to try it.

Standing, I approach the table and rifle through a box of ten white tubes with colors on the ends indicating the hue inside. A rectangular board with a hole in one corner. A cup full of brushes. A jar of water. Folded blue rags.

It feels natural to slide my thumb through the hole in the board and squeeze on the colors: titanium white, cadmium yellow medium, cadmium orange, cadmium red medium, alizarin crimson, phthalo green, phthalo blue, dioxazine purple, burnt sienna, and ivory black.

Beginner colors, She says.

I am a beginner, I say.

She does not respond.

I study the blank canvas for a long moment and am resolved to mimic one of the paintings in the halls, but another idea forms. I do not know if I can do it, but I can only try. If I try something, I am one step closer to my goal.

Freedom, She says.

Diversion, I think, which is only a fancy word for appeasing my curiosity about the hallways and their occupants.

I choose a brush. Before I realize what I am doing, I am mixing colors and making long strokes over the surface of the canvas. I angle the tip of the brush in ways to smudge the lines, which changes the look and texture of the paint.

I am surprised when I am done, and I have no sense of how much time has passed. I have painted the sea. A beach with an archway wound in soft white fabric flowing in a breeze. Indigo flower petals litter the sand. The sun dips low in the background, casting the sky in burnt oranges and reds.

And carefully, very carefully, almost unseen to the naked eye, I have painted a symbol into the peaks and dips of the sand: intertwined hearts. My mind conjures the word "luckenbooth." It is near the bottom left corner and almost obscured in beach grass.

It's beautiful, She says. *You've captured it almost exactly.*

CHAPTER 10

Noah finds the metal chair and opens it. The legs vibrate audibly over the tile as he places it in front of my tube. He stands over the metal seat, hesitating, eyeing it as if he thinks it may swallow him whole. At last, he eases down and settles in.

His hair is short now and looks closer to brown than blond. The waves are hidden in this shorter cut, and the top is styled with messy lifts and spikes. It is the first time I have seen him so cleanly shaven, and this makes him look nice. Handsome.

When he looks up at me, it is in silence, and I really study him for the first time. He has a sharply angled chin and nice, full lips. His nose is narrow. His eyes, wide set, are a shocking shade of amber surrounded by thick, dark lashes. The almond shape angles down on either side, dipping into smile lines.

Yes, he is handsome. Very handsome.

He leans forward on his knees. His gaze finds the floor, and a minute later, he hoods his eyes with a hand. His back heaves and jerks *and I realize he is crying. My captor, the man who will not let me go, cries. I do not understand this change of events.*

Where is the angry man from before? Him, I understood.

When the door opens a minute later, Sonya strolls in with a small entourage of men. They all come to an abrupt stop and Sonya's arm flies up to hold the others back. A moment later, she ushers them back out of the room, asking for a few minutes alone.

Noah pinches his eyes and the bridge of his nose. He runs a hand over his face and sighs. "Sorry," he says. "I thought you'd be gone for a while."

"My schedule changed. I'm glad you came."

He looks up at me and his eyes are an amber flame.

"And you cleaned up," she adds.

"Yeah. Thought it would make me feel human again." One side of his mouth jerks, threatening a smile that never comes. His eyes cast down again. "I'm still numb."

Sonya rolls a round stool over and straddles it. She is close enough to touch him but does not. "We all are. It was a shock to everyone."

His face crumbles and he presses his forehead into his palms. "My wife is dead."

The words hold a heavy release in them, and there is shock enough on Sonya's face at hearing them said aloud that she turns away from him. From me. She does not look but reaches a hand out and lays it unmoving on his heaving shoulder.

"She was the best of all of us," he says after a while. "The strongest."

"A part of her lives on," Sonya whispers.

Noah nods and looks up at me. Tears stream unhindered over his cheeks. It seems to take everything he has to utter the following words. "Her name is Adrienne."

. . .

I run to forget the dream. It is no longer a nightmare. I do not know when this changed, but I am no longer frightened of Noah. He is sad. They all are. I feel their sadness as if it is my own, and I do not understand why. It is only a dream and, given a name, has nothing to do with me.

Adrienne.

It is a beautiful name, She says, and She is as sad as they are.

Declan enters the room and smiles broadly at me. My heart leaps at the sight of him, and I run into his open arms. He does not seem to mind my sweat-coated skin even though he wears a nice suit. He kisses me and swings me up into his strong arms.

"I have missed you. Where have you been?" I ask breathlessly, fingering back hair that has fallen over his forehead.

"Oh, don't ask," he growls and sets me on my feet. "Business, but it's over now. I called to check on you every day. Arthur said you're painting?"

I nod. "Yes. I like it."

"And good at it from what I understand. I can't wait to see."

A new weight sinks in my stomach. "I did not paint before now?" Even I have to admit my paintings are good. I assumed Dr. Travista left everything knowing I would pick the hobby back up.

"Not in the time I've known you," he says, then his hand strokes my cheek and pinches my chin to angle my head up more. His lips press to my forehead and the tip of my nose. Finally, my lips. "I missed you."

"Then you did not miss much," I say and laugh.

His expression turns serious. "I missed everything."

I cup his neck in my palms and bring his lips back to mine. They are warm and pliable and, when his tongue strokes mine a moment later, hungry.

I come to my senses—not an easy feat—and push away from him. "I should shower. I am going to ruin your nice suit." It is the dark blue today. My favorite.

"I don't care about my suit, but while you do that, I'll just check in with Arthur."

We stroll hand in hand to my floor, where we part outside my room. It takes only a moment to retrieve a clean set of scrubs and another ten minutes to shower.

I walk into my room, towel-drying my hair, and find Declan flipping through the canvases leaning against one wall. Dr. Travista says he will have someone come by to hang them for me.

"You like beaches," he says. It is not a question.

My chest tightens and I have an urge to explain, as if he has caught me doing something bad, but why should I? I have done nothing wrong. They are only beaches.

"It is the photograph." I point to the wall behind me, where the photograph of the ocean hangs. "I have spent many nights wondering what the rest of that beach must look like."

He nods, and when he smiles at me, it is tight. His eyelids narrow slightly. "You're very talented, Emma."

Questions are burning a trail through me, none of which he will have the answer to if my painting is new for him, too. Like where I learned to paint. Why I am drawn to the beach and why he seems disturbed by it.

Questions best left unsaid, She says, and I am inclined to agree for once. There is something about this that bothers my husband, and I do not want to fuel this fire.

I lay down my towel and force myself to smile. "Thank you. I will try painting something new. Is there anything you would like to see?"

His expression softens and he takes me into his arms. "The mountains. Do you have any memory of our home yet?"

I shake my head. "No. Not yet."

"I will bring you some pictures. Arthur says it is a good time to try and jog your memory."

My smile is genuine now. "Really? I cannot wait."

Today I decide to leave the safety of my hallway. Dr. Travista has already disappeared into the room with the woman he calls "dear." I spy a painting near the cross section and do not waste time.

Act like you belong, She says. *That's the key.*

I do. At least, I hope I do. I run my fingers over the paintings as I pass, stopping to analyze paint strokes. It is everything I do in my hallway.

I am nearing my goal and passing the door I suspect to be a room for travel, where all the colors enter or exit. I slow my pace only a little, hoping the door will slide open and give me a peek inside. In my peripheral, the silver doors slide apart and two white lab coats emerge. As casually as I can manage, I kneel and lift a pant leg to scratch my ankle. It is enough to allow me the view of several rows of clear plastic tubes that reach from floor to ceiling and are large enough to hold up to three people, if I had to guess.

Those take you out of the building, She tells me. *Probably to other floors, too. They're teleportation units. Teleport. Teleporting. Teleportation. You know, teleporters.*

Teleporters?

There is the sensation that She is now rolling Her eyes. *They split you into a million different pieces and send your bits to your destination. You tell it where you want to port and it sends you there. Get it? Tell—a—port.*

This gives me pause and I blink at the painting I finally come to without really looking at it. *That sounds dangerous.*

She sighs. *It used to be. Eons of years ago.*

I know She exaggerates about eons. She is using Her sarcastic, bored voice. She is never patient with my questions.

This is how I will get home, I say.

Yes, Padawan learner. This is how you will get home.

What is a Pa—

Never mind.

"Mrs. Burke."

I turn to face the red coat, whom I somehow had not noticed before. "Yes?"

"I'm afraid I'm going to have to escort you back to your section of the hospital."

"I am waiting on Dr. Travista." I cannot let this man take me back when I am so close.

"I'm only doing my job, ma'am. Please come with me."

Squaring my shoulders, I begin to refuse a second time, but behind me, the hospital room door slides aside. Dr. Travista begins to exit, his head bent to look at a tablet computer he holds. I look past him to the woman sitting in a wheelchair and bite back a gasp. She looks a lot older, her brown hair streaked with gray, but I have stared and stared at her picture for months.

Jodi. The woman Dr. Travista said died, or so I thought. His exact words were "has been gone," but how else was I supposed to interpret that? And maybe he had not lied, because she sits limp in a chair, jaw slack, her stare devoid of life.

I shift my focus to the red coat, who refuses to leave, the moment I see Dr. Travista raise his head in my peripheral.

"Emma?" He is quick to steer me away by the elbow. "What are you doing here?" He waves off the disgruntled red coat as if batting at a fly.

"I apologize for bothering you," I say. I am finding it difficult to focus on the lie I have devised, but I manage what I hope is an apologetic smile. "I saw you enter this room and tried to catch you. Was it okay that I waited?"

He glances between me and the now shut room. "Of course. What can I do for you?"

I lift my right hand. "My wrist has been aching a little. From painting, maybe. I was hoping for a pain reliever?"

We stop in the epicenter. The male staff flow around us like water around rock. I let Dr. Travista examine my wrist, which is perfectly fine, watching him carefully through my lashes. His expression gives nothing away, so I imagine he does not feel caught in his lie. This can only mean I have been successful in fooling him, which is surprising considering I am screaming on the inside. The woman he claims to love, Jodi, is *alive,* and I am dying to find out what has happened to her.

Dr. Travista releases my hand. "There doesn't seem to be anything wrong, but we could take some images—"

"It is only a little throbbing."

He studies me for a protracted moment, then nods. "All right. Pain reliever it is, then. But if the pain persists, I will have to insist on images."

I nod. "Yes, of course. Thank you."

Dr. Travista leads me down the hallway toward his office, and we pass the same lounge with the same beige furniture and red pillows, but one thing is not the same. A girl with a man I have never seen before. She stares out the window over the snow-white day with blank eyes. Her cropped blond hair is short like a man's and she is very, very thin. I think she is no more than skin over bones.

Whoa, She says. *Somebody needs to feed the waif.*

The man wears a nice suit like one Declan might wear. He is not as tall as my husband but is just as well groomed. His face is set into hard lines and every part of me wishes to run, but I am frozen by the sight of yet another woman. After all this time of seeing not a single woman outside my dreams, I see two in one day, and neither of them seems capable of interaction.

"My name is Chuck," the man says. "I'm your husband."

She does not respond, and his face flushes a deep purple. He slams a palm to the table between them and she does not blink. She only stares.

Orderlies rush by me, grazing my shoulder, followed soon by Dr. Travista. They move as if I do not exist.

"Patience," Dr. Travista tells this man. "You can't rush her progress, and you must take special care not to frighten her."

The orderlies lift the woman from her chair and lead her away.

A hand slips into mine and I jump. "Declan," I say breathily, holding a hand over my drumming heart. "When did you arrive?"

"A little while ago." He answers me but watches the scene inside the room. "I see you've stumbled across your new floor mate."

Which one? "Floor mate?"

He wraps an arm over my shoulder and maneuvers me toward my bedroom. "Her name is Ruby. She had an accident like you."

"Like me?" I stop and turn to watch the orderlies lead Ruby down the hall. She does not take a single step without the guidance of one of the orderlies. "Declan, was I like that, too?"

He is hesitant to answer but finally says, "Yes. It's the most difficult time." He lifts my chin to take back my attention, smiles in that soft, loving way of his, and brushes my hair back. "You're much better now. And if Chuck is patient, Ruby will be better, too."

Movement nearby grabs our attention and we turn to see Dr. Travista leaving the lounge with Chuck. The man does a double take when he sees me and leaves the doctor's side without a word. Dr. Travista's mouth freezes in the middle of a sentence but he follows a moment later.

My muscles lock and warning bells go off in my head. I do not know this man, but his reaction to his wife a moment ago tells me he is not a kind person. And he is heading right for *me*.

Declan angles to stand in front of me. "Charles," he says in a cool tone.

The man points a stubby finger around my husband at me. "I want to talk to her."

"No." Simple. Direct.

He lays fisted hands on his hips, making his suit jacket flare. "I need to know I'm not wasting my money."

Declan glances back at me very quickly. "You aren't."

Chuck or Charles narrows his eyes. "The video—"

"Watch what you say in front of my wife," Declan says, and this time his even tone sends icicles over my spine.

Chuck's gaze jumps between Declan and me. "I need more proof. I don't like wasting my time. You never said it would be like"—he waves absently toward the lounge—"*that*."

"Didn't I?" Warning laces Declan's tone.

Danger, danger, She says.

No kidding. I have no idea what this is about, but I do not want to be here anymore.

I touch Declan's arm with only my fingertips, afraid anything more would turn the anger on me. "I wish to go to my room."

His gaze never leaves Charles's. "Good idea. I will see you there shortly."

CHAPTER 11

Ruby sits in the lounge staring out the window for the third day in a row. Her husband has not been back and I am sad for her. Declan is gone more now, but he was around when I needed him most. I need no further proof to see the difference between what kind of man her husband is and what kind mine is.

I am hesitant but resolved to get to know her. "Hello," I say.

She blinks one time, but there is no sign that she knows I am even here.

"My name is Emma. Your name is Ruby."

She swallows and blinks again. Her eyes are lovely: light brown with flecks of gold and green. Her light pink lips part to say one word. "Ruby."

I smile. "Yes, that is right. Ruby is a pretty name."

"Pretty."

Dr. Travista appears in the doorway and comes to a stop. His eyes widen when he sees me, and I am about to stand because he must not want me talking to this woman. Instead, he nods to show me he approves.

"You are named for a gemstone," I say. "One of my favorites. The color is red. Would you like to see red?"

I do not wait for the answer she will not give me. I move to my painting supplies and drag what I need over. I have been painting winter landscapes to please Declan. I have painted enough beaches, though I am saddened by this decision for reasons I cannot explain.

Today, for Ruby, I paint a red desert. I bring it to life from memory. Not because I recall being in a desert, but because I have seen the landmark in a book. Ayers Rock in Australia. I find it easy to give this place life, but as with the winter landscapes, I do not feel as though I belong there.

I belong on the beach with sand between my toes and cool surf flooding my feet. I can almost feel the water receding and claiming the sand below me.

The packed sand slid away from either side of my feet and I stood as long as I dared, testing the strength of my dissolving foundation. I lasted a long time.

I closed my eyes and lost myself in the peaceful surroundings—the warm surf over my feet, a gentle breeze lifting my hair, the caw of seagulls. Crashing waves.

Arms surrounded my waist and a bristly chin nuzzled my neck.

I linked the fingers of my left hand with his right. On the webbing between my thumb and index finger, a tiny brand marred my skin—linked hearts. The luckenbooth on my left hand matched the one on his right hand.

His thumb played with mine, his skin a shade lighter, as he planted soft kisses on my neck.

I pressed my back into him as his arms tightened. He smelled of soap and a gentle musk. He smelled of home. He smelled of mine.

"How much longer do you plan to stand out here?" he asked in a near whisper.

He wanted me to come inside so we could make love. He wasn't fooling anyone.

I bit my lip as I smiled and continued watching the surf. "I was thinking a few more days at least."

He chuckled, and it came from somewhere deep, making me tingle in places only he could connect with. "You're cruel."

"You love me, Mr. Tucker."

"With every part of my soul, Ms. Wade," he agreed.

I begin to turn toward the man in this waking dream, my heart warm and pounding, and find myself sliding out of my chair. The shock of reality, the sterile recycled air and scent of acrylic paint, turns my blood cold. I am back in the lounge, and Ruby watches me paint, but I have not set brush to canvas in some time. The painting sits half-finished, and I no longer have the desire to give it life.

Life is on a beach.

As another woman.

With another man.

Who is not my husband.

I sit alone at a table in the lounge. Dr. Travista gave me a tablet and unlocked only one file out of what could be hundreds. I understand why now. I am frustrated and angry and no longer focused on each individual picture. I swipe my finger over each one, skipping to the next, waiting for one to offer some shred of recognition.

I do not remember my wedding.

Our wedding took place on a mountain, just as Declan said. My dress is not as lovely as he claimed: long, lacy sleeves and a heart-shaped front, full skirt made of silk. I do not think this is my taste. No, I do not *feel* this is my taste.

Our honeymoon pictures are just as infuriating. A villa in Tuscany. I have been to Italy?

Not unless you suddenly lost your fear of flying, She says.

Just the idea of flying in a plane sends cold shivers of fear over my spine, and beads of sweat break out across my hairline. Flying is not natural. My feet belong on the ground. No question.

But I look happy, I think.

That you do, She agrees.

Maybe I took a sedative to get to Italy. It is possible I was knocked out the entire trip.

Anything's possible, She says dryly. *Obviously.*

We could have taken a teleporter. Though the idea of this, too, does not sound much better. Splitting into millions of pieces cannot possibly be safe.

There's human advancement, and then there's science fiction. You're grasping.

She does not continue and I am glad. She is making my mood worse.

I cannot blame it all on Her, or even the pictures I do not recognize. Since the last waking memory of the man on the beach, I feel frustrated. Even if I had seen his face, because I called him Mr.

Tucker, I know for certain he was not Declan. He was not my husband.

To recall the love I felt for this man makes me heavy with guilt because what I feel for Declan is merely a glimmer of that.

And then there are the brands on our hands. A brand I do not even have, a name that is not mine, so this cannot be me, but . . .

It does not matter. They are only dreams of someone else's life. Vivid dreams, but dreams nonetheless.

I turn off the tablet and slide it away. Near me, in a chair facing the outside, Ruby slides fingers over the skin of her cheek, then looks at them, then returns them. She does this several times.

"Skin," I tell her and she looks at me with a thin line between her eyes. I touch my cheek. "See? I have the same thing. Would you like to feel?"

She does not answer, but I move close to her and she reaches out. Her fingers are very soft, far softer than mine. Soft like finely ground powder is soft.

I let her touch me like this for a long time. Soon she moves on to analyze our hands and fingers. I remember discovering these parts for myself. It was hard to grasp how they were meant to do so many other things. Now I paint and write and touch.

"Skin," she whispers.

"Yes," I say.

"Emma." The male voice startles me and I turn toward it. Dr. Travista waves me over, then jerks his head toward the hallway.

I follow him out and find Ruby's husband, Chuck, ambling our way. He narrows his eyes when he sees me in the angry way I am growing accustomed to. I do not understand the reason for this emotion, but he is beginning to scare me. I hope to never find myself alone with this man. So far, I have been very lucky to avoid this.

I avert my eyes and whisper, "Why does he hate me?"

Dr. Travista takes me gently by the elbow. "He doesn't understand why you are well and his wife isn't."

"But she will be, will she not?"

"Yes, of course, but it takes a lot of time and patience. And she doesn't respond to him the way she responds to you. He doesn't like that, either."

"He is not kind to her."

Dr. Travista's lips form thin lines. "No. He isn't."

I am not surprised he agrees with me after seeing how he enters Jodi's room on a daily basis calling her "dear." He must still love her if he continues to care for her after all this time.

"How is Ruby progressing?" I ask.

He smiles down at me. "Slowly, but I'm not concerned."

"Are her nightmares bad?"

He seems taken aback by this question. "I almost forgot about that. She doesn't have nightmares the way you did."

Now I am the one surprised and stop walking. "Really?"

He laughs at my response. "Really."

I drop my gaze, dejected. "That does not seem fair."

Dr. Travista wraps an arm around my shoulders and brings us back into a stroll. "You are well now; that's all that matters. Speaking of which, how would you like to go home?"

I stop again. "If you are teasing me, this is a cruel trick."

"Oh, I'm not teasing. Probationary, of course. You'll spend your nights at home and return during the day for observation. I'm sure Ruby will appreciate your company as well."

I am so excited that I hug Dr. Travista. It is uncomfortable for both of us, but I am unable to stop it from happening. I would hug anyone who happens to walk by.

"Starting tonight," he says when I release him. "Declan will be by to pick you up shortly."

Warm tears brim my eyes. "I feel this is a dream."

"Not a dream. This is very much reality, my dear Emma."

I hug him again. "Thank you. Thank you so much."

He pushes me away. "Don't thank me just yet. As I said, this is probationary. The second I think you're regressing, you'll be back."

"I will not regress," I say, and I hope this is true.

"Let's hope not. I'll see you in the morning first thing." He raises both bushy eyebrows to be sure I understand.

"Yes. Your office, first thing." I bite my lip and attempt to bury the overlarge smile longing to beam and take out the entire floor. "The very second I arrive."

The ground rumbled under my feet and I braced my back to the wall. I couldn't make them out, but the single-man aircraft sounded in the night sky, dropping missiles over the outskirts of the compound. The deadly projectiles carefully avoided the compound itself. And us. Fire lifted into the sky and licked at a dark cloud obscuring what remained of the stars.

"They made it," Foster said.

I nodded. "Better late than never."

Foster waved an arm in the air. "Let's go!"

I closed my eyes for a moment and prayed. Each time I did this, the risk of never making it home hit me too late to turn back. It was always harder when I left him behind. But I left him with memories of a warm bed and a soft touch. It was always like this when the other

had to go out. We made love as if it would be the last time. The unspo-
ken rule.

Foster tapped my arm and I opened my eyes.

"Ready?" he asked.

"Yeah, let's do this already. The sooner we're done, the sooner I can
get home."

CHAPTER 12

My nerves are on high alert while Declan walks me toward the transporter room I only recently discovered—this is what Declan has just recently called it. I grip his hand so tight he must suffer from a loss of feeling, but he does not seem to mind. In fact, I think his hand grips mine tighter than usual as well.

The doors to the transporter room slide open soundlessly and a man in white exiting the room steps out of our way. His head bows once to us. "Mr. Burke."

He does not greet me, but nobody ever does. I am used to this.

Declan leads us to the left and swings open a door in the tube.

"Is it safe?" I ask and swallow hard against a dry throat.

He laughs. "Yes. Very."

Declan nudges me inside and the floor gives slightly under me. With the addition of his weight, it bounces more, turning my stomach. A set of projected numbers appears on the surface of the clear tube in red and I now know why the floor moves. It measures our weight. Total mass, water, body fat, and even our clothes are calculated.

"You're going to smell something funny," Declan whispers. "It's only a numbing agent. Without it, this would hurt like hell."

I want to whimper and beg to get off. I think I would rather fly in a plane. "What if it doesn't work?"

He squeezes my hand. "It will."

A projected numeric pad appears beside our calculations and he says, "This is where you enter the port number."

Unclench, She says. *I promise you won't feel a thing.*

Says the imaginary person in my head.

She laughs.

Then I smell it. The spearmint is aromatic at first, but I quickly realize it covers something rancid that upsets my stomach. In a millisecond, I am completely numb. Like I am only a set of floating eyes.

I try to speak but cannot feel my mouth or tongue, or even my lungs to breathe. Panic sets in instantly, but the outside world shivers and appears to melt, then blends into different colors. Fluorescent lights become a natural, brilliant white light. The view slows and solidifies. The blinding white is sun reflecting off snow, and it is *everywhere.*

Startled, I step back so quickly I hit my head against the clear tube. My feeling is back and a tiny headache spreads from the back of my head toward my eyes. Declan holds me in the space of a heartbeat.

"Are you all right? I know it's strange, but—"

"The snow," I gasp out. "You didn't tell me about the snow."

"It's outside." He sounds confused.

I peer around him and relief fills me. We are indoors, but the outside walls are giant windows. The walls—what there are of them—are pale wood slats with black knots. A kitchen is equipped with only a single counter. A thin breakfast bar stands between that and a sunken living room. Toward the back, a bed is visible through an open door.

Declan slides the tube open and helps me out. My jaw aches from clenching my teeth, and I try to relax. It is only snow. It is only my home. Right? I wanted to be here more than anything.

"This is it," he says and walks down two steps into the living room. His heels make sharp raps against the wood floor, which has shades of brown that vary from pale to dark in random placements. He looks right at home in his cream-and-burgundy sweater and pressed jeans.

He spins and smiles up at me. "What do you think?"

I bite my lip and look around more closely. Now that I'm near the living area, I notice the grayish redbrick fireplace in the corner and the large fur rug lying in front. I hope it is a fake. There is so much wood in the place that it smells of the outdoors, like cedar maybe. Cedar and burning wood. The furniture is pale wood like the walls, with dark brown square cushions.

Declan lifts the lid of a chest and pulls out a throw blanket. He lays the folded fleece in a large chair near the fire and points toward the bedroom. "You can change out of those scrubs if you want and I'll start a fire."

What I want is to fold into a ball and lie on the floor with my eyes shut tight. There is so much snow and it is cold and I am really alone with my husband for the first time. I do not know who I am in this mountain home with this man who claims to love me.

My fear must show on my face because he jumps the stairs and pulls me into his arms. "We'll take it slow, Emma, I promise. Just breathe."

The burn of my oxygen-free lungs surprises me and I gulp air. "I am sorry," I whisper. "I think I need a minute."

He smiles gently down at me and brushes my hair back. "I know just what you need."

He leads me into the bedroom and through an archway into a bathroom. The room is huge, and like the rest of the house, one side of the room is a window to the outdoors. In a corner across from the window, Declan spins the tap over a large tub.

"A bath?" I ask.

He lifts a small blue box. "With lavender and chamomile to help you relax. You can turn on the jets and soak."

He arranges the bath as if he has done this for me a million times. He lights candles and pours the bath salt into the water. My fingers itch to do something other than watch, but I do not know what else I can do.

Once he has everything set up, he lays out a thick white towel and a red robe.

"I'll leave you to it," he says and kisses my forehead. "Take your time."

He kisses me again, this time on the lips, and I want to bask in the seawater of his eyes. I am lucky, I realize, and do not deserve him.

"I love you," I tell him.

This brings a smile to his face that lights his eyes. "And I love you." He glances over his shoulder at the running bath. "Go on. Get in. Call if you need anything."

Left to my own devices, I slide into the bath before it is ready, but it is enough to make me sigh. The water is soft against my skin and the smell is amazing. And the heat . . . I want to live in the heat of this bath. Once I shut the water off, I let my eyes slide closed and drift into semiconsciousness.

Every few seconds, a single drop of water pinged against the bathwater and small ripples traveled to the end where I lay against his hot chest. The hot water turned the room into a sauna, and beads of sweat tickled my brow.

The sun's reflection off the ocean shimmered on the slatted blinds above the tub. The color shifted from a soft yellow to burnt orange as the day turned late. With each passing day, I grew to regret the sunset no matter how progressively beautiful the atmospheric effects became. They signaled another day gone, and I didn't want to leave.

I shifted, lifting an elbow up out of the water to rest on the cool porcelain. "Let's stay," I said, my voice a bomb in the quiet space.

He nuzzled his abrasive chin into my neck. "Say the word. We never have to go back."

I reached back and ran a hand over the side of his head, fingering his sideburns. Across the tub, I watched the next drop of water build in the faucet. "In another lifetime, I wouldn't give it a second thought."

A kiss whispered over my ear. "I know. I promise we'll come back to stay. In our lifetime."

"And not when we're old and wrinkled."

His chuckle was nearly silent. "No, of course not. In a few years when we're ready to start a family."

"If I'm still fertile th—"

"You will be." His hands found mine under the water, and the dying suds lapped up against my breasts. He linked our fingers and wrapped our arms around my abdomen, holding me tighter. "We'll

be responsible for populating the world with so many Tuckers, the world won't know what to do with them."

I laughed. "Especially if they're anything like you."

"The men in this world won't stand a chance with one of our daughters in the room. Not if they look like you."

"Badass?"

He chuckled. "I was going to say beautiful, but that works, too."

CHAPTER 13

I jolt upright, gasping. I turn to find I am alone in the bath Declan prepared for me. The fading light outside is wrong, and cold winter air seeps through the windows. My mind floats in the remains of the dream and the shock of reality confuses me.

The room is warm, not hot, and the light is graying and yellow, not orange. There are no slatted shutters. There is no man relaxing behind me speaking of our future children. A man whose face remains hidden from me but is most definitely Tucker from the beach dream. And as impossible as it sounds, his absence shreds my heart and twists my stomach. His absence feels like death. If not for the missing brand, I might believe I have a right to this grief. But it belongs to Wade, whoever she is.

I grip the edge of the tub and press my forehead to the porcelain surface. I breathe deeply of the soothing scents and tell myself to calm down. I am on the verge of a possible breakdown and need to get my head on straight. I cannot show this weakness to

Declan or he will tell Dr. Travista. I cannot live in the hospital again. I will not.

I coat my cool face with the warm water and pull my knees into my chest. The only sound in the room now comes from the single heavy drops *ping*ing in my bathwater. It is too close to the dream, so I stand and let the water fall from my body in a shower. I flip the drain switch with my toe and climb out.

I leave the bathroom in the soft red robe and find a navy blue turtleneck and jeans lying on the bed with a set of nice undergarments. I flush thinking about how Declan picked out the flesh-toned silk underwear and bra.

A knock sounds on the door. "Emma?"

I jump and tighten my robe. "I am just getting dressed. I will be out in a moment."

"Okay."

My hands shake as I slide the silk over my thighs. Hooking my bra with trembling fingers is an even bigger feat. After pulling the rest on, I am calmer and ready to face what is to come. I hope.

I press the button near the door and it slides aside with a soft *shiff*. The temperature difference is significant. Declan has started a fire that lights the entire living area. The heat warms my face and wraps around my bones.

Then I smell dinner. I am tired of the bland food I eat every day. I need something rich in flavor.

"*Mmmm*," I moan and step toward the kitchen. "What did you make?"

Declan lifts a large pan and spoons food over two plates. "Asiago cheese tortellini."

I bend over the nearest plate. A creamy sauce, mushrooms, and spinach cover the cheese-filled pasta shells. Steam coats my nose and chin.

Declan takes me by the shoulders, turns me, and points to a candle-lit table in a nook of sorts surrounded by now dark windows.

"Go sit," he says and kisses the top of my head.

I go, ignoring all my negative thoughts about being so near the windows. I will make the most of my first night here and will report to Dr. Travista that I am still well enough to stay home.

The fire's warmth reaches into the dining area, dispelling my fear of feeling the winter chill through the windows. I sit and run a palm over the soft white cloth covering the table. It is as pristine as everything else. Not a single wrinkle.

There are two tapered candles, but there is also a small vase of indigo flowers. I want to pick them up and bury my face in them but do not wish to risk petals falling anywhere.

Declan sets my plate on the table and sits diagonally from me. He watches me carefully. Maybe my nerves are apparent in my expression. Can he see the inkling of guilt that remains after the dream I experienced only minutes ago?

I reach over and slide my hand into his. His fingers are warm and slightly damp from washing them. "Everything looks lovely," I say, smiling.

He lets out a breath and a smile breaks out over his face. "Thank you."

His fingers squeeze mine before releasing our hands to take up the heavy, ornate silverware. Its weight does not feel natural in my hand but I do not complain. For all I know, I picked this set out myself. The tablecloth could be pristine because I like it that way.

Maybe I always set flowers out on the table. Maybe I wanted this house and all its windows.

I'd rather live in a well, She says.

Not now, I tell Her.

Declan picks up our empty plates and stands. "Go sit by the fire and relax."

"Let me help you with the dishes."

His head nods toward the living area, a tiny smile playing over his mouth. "Go."

"You are doing so much," I say, taking the steps down.

"I don't mind taking care of you. You're worth it."

I pick up the fleece blanket automatically and sit angled on the couch so I can watch Declan. His focus is on his task, which sets a crease between his eyebrows and his lips into a fine line. He clearly does not like this menial task, but he does it without complaint.

He must sense me watching because he looks up from where he wipes the island countertop and the creases and hard edges vanish. He smiles and it is brilliant. I wonder how such a handsome man can manage these two contrasting faces in the space of an eye blink.

"What?" he says.

"Nothing. I like watching you."

He turns, still smiling, to finish. "I like you being here to watch me."

A log snaps in the fireplace and startles me. I turn to watch the embers fly toward the protective screen and die out. The logs shift and reassemble.

Declan appears in front of the fire and removes the screen. He kneels and uses a poker to stoke the glowing embers below the logs until the fire blazes to twice its height, then adds two more small logs.

Finished, he brushes his hands together. "That should do us for a while. Is there anything you need?"

"No."

I pat the seat beside me when he looks unsure of where to sit. He angles into the corner and props a knee up behind me so I can sit between his legs. I hesitate at first, recalling the dream in the tub, but decide to go with it. He is my husband. Why should I not sit this close to him?

I turn and lie down on his chest. His arms fold around me automatically, his hands seeking mine. He links the fingers of his manicured right hand with my left and I stare down at our skin. Mine a shade lighter. No branded hearts.

"Why do we not have marks?" I ask and feel Her annoyance. I have asked something before She was able to stop me.

"Marks?"

"The linked hearts."

His chest stills under me for so long I worry enough to turn. He stares at me through narrowed eyes but does not appear angry.

"You said 'we,'" he says carefully. "As in both of us?"

I twist slightly to look at him. "Yes."

Declan's eyes focus on the fire across the room, his thumb absently rubbing my skin. "Men don't mark their skin. As for you, I chose to leave you unbranded. You are not in the city long, if ever, and so there is no need to worry about another man claiming you."

"Claiming me?"

His dark eyebrows pinch together and his eyelids narrow. "You remember the brand, but not why?"

I twist my legs around farther to sit more comfortably. "It must be part of the process. Some things I know, while others are still in the dark place with my past. I wish I could explain it."

But the truth is you only know because of a dream you can't admit to, She says. *You have to nip this line of questioning in the bud. It will only lead to trouble. Trust me.*

"There is a very specific law," he begins slowly, "that says a man cannot take another man's property. His wife. The brand signifies that she is taken. A ring can be forgotten, while a brand can never be removed."

I do not like this word "property." It causes a rise of heat to flush my cheeks. "I am your property?"

He shakes his head, his nostrils flaring. "You are here by your own free will, but out there"—he points over the couch toward the obsidian night—"you are my property because it will save you from another man taking you as his own."

There are too many questions and too many pieces to put together. I cannot keep quiet as She asks. "What is the reason for this fear? Why would another man want me so badly?"

"There are not enough women to go around," he says. The threat of anger in his voice seems to be diffusing. "And even less to bear children."

I recall the things Dr. Travista told me, in addition to things I have learned from my dreams, and the pieces finally fall together. "You purchased me."

His gaze looks past me to the fire. The flames reflect in his eyes, obscuring the sea-green color. "I chose you and created a life for us that I swear will never reflect the outside world. I don't want that life for you or for us." He looks into my eyes and brushes my hair back. "I will not mark your skin because that means I am giving in to that world, which already rules my every waking decision as it is. You are my peace from that."

Guilt washes through me for doubting him. He has never treated me like a piece of property, and after seeing Charles and Ruby, I know the difference. She will not be as lucky as I am.

CHAPTER 14

Trinda tapped her heel beside me and cinched the skirt of her yellow dress into her fist. I watched her from the corner of my eye as she gnawed her lower lip to shreds and blood appeared.

"Stop it," I whispered harshly. "You'll have no lips left if you keep at it."

She pressed her lips together until all blood disappeared. The tapping didn't stop, and I waited for the guard to turn his back before I slammed my knuckles into her thigh.

"Cut it the fuck out."

On Trinda's other side, Melanie leaned forward to wordlessly thank me. From a row of chairs in front of us, Uganda bit back a laugh. This was all fun and games now, but when they dragged Trinda off and punished her for it, the laughter would end in a hurry.

"I'm nervous," Trinda whispered. "I'm sorry."

"You meet asshole men every day," I said. "We call them guards. This will be no different."

"They'll dress better," Melanie said.

"I bet they'll smell better, too," Polly said from directly in front of me.

Uganda added, *"Fuck better."*

Everyone gaped at her, but I schooled my face to impassivity. *"The rest of us wouldn't know anything about that."*

"Right?" Trinda said, pinching her face in disgust. *"So disgusting, Ugie."*

Uganda shrugged a single shoulder. I knew all about her and what she did with the guards. Had known. We had the same goal, she and I, only I didn't plan to spread my thighs for those murdering bastards. I'd get out of here with my self-respect intact, thank you very much.

Guard Taggert entered the room, and both rows of girls—nineteen in all—sat up straight and crossed ankles. Hands folded into laps. Eyes forward. Utter silence filled the room.

"Thirty seconds, girls," he said. *"You know the drill. If your number is called, stand and walk through that door."* He pointed to the door to the left of a large mirror. *"From then on, remember your manners and everything will work out just fine."*

In other words, there'd be no beatings, no starvation, and no solitary confinement. Too bad I couldn't add slave labor to the list.

Taggert left the room and it began. I'd been through this twice already. This time around was my final callback. Someone wanted me. According to the repeat faces, more than one someone. Only one was semi-good-looking, and I wasn't holding my breath he'd outbid the others.

When I turned eighteen in a couple of weeks, the winner would be revealed. With any luck, I wouldn't be around to find out.

Guard Mack lifted a hand to his ear and then nodded to the room. We stood and walked in single file past the mirror, then stopped in

the center to pose. One thing was for sure: We looked great. We wore
standard issue while in the camp, but for this—the big sale—they
gave us nice dresses. We saw a hair stylist and makeup artist, too.
They gave me a teal wrap dress made from a soft, flowing material.
In another life, I might have loved this dress. In another life, its sole
purpose wasn't to dress me up for sale on the open market. I couldn't
wait to throw it into an open flame.

I was just about to take my turn in front of the mirror when Guard
Taggert ran into the room. "Wade, you're with me."

I nearly tripped in my damn heels. Not that I cared, but had all of
my suitors just rejected me? I didn't ask and didn't miss a step on the
way into the hall.

"You've been taken out of the running," he said.

"My suitor changed his mind?" Curiosity was a huge weakness of
mine.

Guard Taggert hesitated. "Not exactly. They've been denied. Your
buyer . . . well, let's just say he doesn't need to wait in line."

My heart stuttered in my chest and my mouth went dry. "He has
to wait for my birthday, right? That hasn't changed." It couldn't
change. I wasn't ready.

He scowled down at me. "The law hasn't changed, and no man is
above the law."

I resisted a relieved sigh. "Too bad."

This made him laugh. "Is that right? You ready for what's in store,
are you? Think you're the shit?"

I shrugged and trained my gaze on the hallway perpendicular to
ours just ahead. "Of course not. I'm only a simple girl."

He scoffed. "Simple. Right. And I'm the queen of South America."

. . .

"How was your first night?" Dr. Travista asks.

I run a hand over the smooth leather arm. I am surprised I have not worn it thin after all this time. "It was fine."

"Not what you expected?"

He asks this as if he already expected this answer. "Not exactly."

"Would you like to elaborate?"

"I am a stranger there." I sigh and watch him nod absently, tapping something into his tablet. "I know who I am here. But not there."

Dr. Travista puts the tablet aside and removes his glasses. "Are you up to continuing this trial?"

Yes.

"Yes. I do not wish to give up."

Quitters never win.

The doctor watches me for a long moment, then says, "I spoke to Declan early this morning. He says you asked about the luckenbooth."

Play dumb, you idiot. I told you.

I raise my eyebrows. "The what?"

"The brands. The hearts."

I nod theatrically. "Oh yes."

Easy. Remember—

I know, I tell Her. *Short answers as near the truth as possible.*

Good girl.

He folds his hands over his lap. "Where did you hear about them? My staff is all male, so they won't have one, and you've never had one yourself."

"A memory, I think," I tell him.

"A memory? Of what?" He raises his bushy eyebrows and nibbles the earpiece of his glasses.

"A hand."

Good God.

"A hand?" he asks.

I nod.

"Anything else?"

I shake my head. "I am sorry, but there is nothing more I can tell you. I really do not understand it myself."

Not a single lie.

I take a long route to the lounge and "study" the paintings. It is early and the red coats are out and about. I will not get far, so I do not try to enter a new hallway. Not only that, but I am not in scrubs today and must stand out.

You're a girl in a sea of guys, She says. *You already stand out.*

Shut up.

I miss my old scrubs now that I do not have them. I am sure I will find some in my room, but I cannot backtrack. I must move forward, and if that means wearing real clothes, then I will wear real clothes.

I chose my outfit this morning, though Declan offered to help. Little does he know that I carry a fashion adviser in my head and She knows what She likes. The fitted white top has a wide neck that shows a lot of my collarbone and three-quarter sleeves. I liked the jeans, so I am wearing them again. And low-heeled boots. My feet will need some time to grow accustomed to the close fit.

I had been unsure of this outfit until I saw myself in the mirror. I look pretty. Sexy, even. I did not expect that.

I am nearing the lounge, thinking about taking the time to paint. I want to paint a bathroom with pale wood and the setting sun reflecting off slatted windows. But I will paint mountains and trees with so much snow that branches weigh down at impossible angles.

I peel to a stop outside the lounge, my boot heels sliding over the floor. I brace a hand on the frame to keep from falling.

Or you won't paint, She says.

The inside of the lounge is covered in what can only be described as caveman art. Handprints cover the windows. Circles and swirls decorate the thin beige carpet. I think one head-shaped thing on a wall might have horns.

Ruby.

Ruby, I agree.

You can't stand in a fucking hallway for five goddamn seconds before security is on you and she redecorates the entire lounge like she's some prehistoric troglodyte. What the hell was everyone doing? Taking a break? Eating donuts?

My paint tubes are misshapen and empty. Ruby actually twisted them into shapes and used them as centerpieces to some of the floor art. I might have thought this was clever but am too hurt to care.

You'll get more, She says, and to Her credit, She really is trying to make this better.

I step farther into the room and try not to look in the corner where I left a few paintings the other day. I already know what I will find.

It's like ripping off a Band-Aid.

I turn.

My beaches. My beaches are littered in Ruby graffiti.

My legs give way under me. I am so heartbroken by this I cannot breathe. It is not the paintings or the work I put into creating them but the intrusion on something so personal. Personal for reasons I cannot explain even to myself.

I crawl to the painting with globs of cadmium yellow winding out of the canvas like cake icing. I drop to my butt and hold the painting over my lap. It is much too large to hold like this, but I try. All I want to do is save it.

Tears splatter beside my hand as I try to scrape off the still-wet paint. It only smears and makes it worse.

Emma. Her voice is soft and sad. *It's only a painting. It will never be the real thing.*

There is no real thing.

It's here with me. You can have it anytime you want. Whenever you're ready.

Why should I believe you? You work against me whenever you get a chance.

I work on another glob, but my fingers are too full of the paint I have already scraped off. It is too late to save and I smear my hand over the canvas in disgust. Now there is an Emma-size caveman handprint on my painting.

One day, Emma, you'll understand.

"You are just like them," I say aloud. I stand and throw the painting into the others. More of the same. "Keep your fucking secrets. I do not want any of them."

CHAPTER 15

Declan takes one look at me and chuckles. "Don't painters wear smocks or something?"

I do not laugh. There is nothing funny about the yellow paint on my white shirt. It is a reminder of how betrayed I am by the simpleton. I never should have left my supplies in the lounge.

I stand from the bed. "Can we leave? I am ready to go."

A crease appears between his eyes and he steps farther into the room I have not left since Dr. Travista walked me out of the lounge with his pointless apologies. "Have you been crying?"

I fold my arms. "I got a little upset."

"I'm going to go talk to Arthur for a few minutes. Can you sit tight until I get back?"

It is not like he is giving me a choice, so I sit and turn away.

Only seconds pass before Dr. Travista's voice echoes in the hall. "Declan. I didn't expect you for a couple hours."

"What happened?" His tone is almost accusing. Protective.

The doctor stands in the doorway and frowns in my direction.

"Ruby happened. We had an incident while Emma and I were in session. Her paintings were . . . redecorated."

"She ruined them," I spit out without hesitation. Anger reignites a fire in my chest and I bite my lip to thwart any further words.

Declan nods and releases a sigh. "I see."

A wayward tear slips down my cheek. They do not understand and I cannot explain it to them. I will not even bother trying. "I want to go home," I say. "Can I go home?"

"Yes, of course," Dr. Travista says. "Whenever Declan is ready."

"Any reason I need to stay?" Declan asks.

The doctor takes a few moments to respond. "No, I don't think so. We can talk tomorrow."

Declan nods and reaches out a hand for me. "Let's go, love."

I let him walk me to the transportation bay and do not hesitate to enter the tube this time. I want out of this place where nothing is mine. Nothing is sacred. No one can be trusted.

Declan watches me carefully before entering the port number into the projected keypad. "You're upset."

"That is an understatement."

Spearmint wafts around us, deadening our vocal cords, and his response freezes in his throat.

Until we appear in the house. "Emma—"

I push out of the tube and head for the bedroom. I want to seal the door behind me, but I do not want to anger him. So I stand in front of the closet with my back to him, his gaze scorching me from the doorway.

"I cannot explain why I am so upset," I say, barely turning my head. "I just am."

"She destroyed your paintings. You should be upset. It's only natural. What can I do?"

If only it were the paintings I was so upset about. Paintings I can re-create but will not for the sake of his distaste for my beaches. The beaches were precious to me, and though a few remain untouched, each was a link to the next. Now my link is cracked. Ruby's foreign footprints mar the sand. She touched my world. My private world.

"I do not know what I need," I say with a resigned sigh. "Other than a shirt, I suppose. I have ruined this one." I finger the hem. "I am sorry about that. I will be more careful in the future."

"I don't care about the clothes." He comes to stand behind me, and his hands move over my shoulders and upper arms in a soothing way. "Did you run today?"

"No. I was too upset."

"Then you will run before dinner," he says simply. "You need an outlet for your frustration."

He is right. I should have done that first thing. "Where will I run?" I do not want to go back to the hospital tonight.

He opens a drawer and lays clothes on the bed for me. "Put these on."

He then opens another drawer and pulls out more clothes. Turning his back to me, he proceeds to undo his tie and remove his suit. He is placing it on a hanger before I strip out of my shirt. He has kept his back to me, but I am still nervous that he is in the room. He does not seem to hold the same reservations, because he strips down to his boxer briefs and I have to bite down on my tongue. His body is amazing.

I turn my back to him, my stomach aflutter, but the image of his back and taut butt have been branded in my mind. He is all lean muscle, his back creased down the middle, and long dimples over the curves of his backside. With each movement of his arms, the lines of muscle over his shoulder blades appear. His shoulders themselves are round and grooved in muscle and I remember how good they felt the night we almost had sex.

I am dressed when Declan brings forth a light jacket made of the same light material as my outfit. He holds it while I push my arms through.

"Ready?" he asks. He is dressed for exercise, too.

I nod, trying to ignore the shoulders peeking out of his sleeveless shirt.

We are back in the teleporter tube and he keys in a port number that takes us to someplace I have never been. It is a basketball court. To our left is another room encased in glass. Exercise equipment fills the space beyond.

"This is my private gym," he says, stepping out. He points up to a level above us. It looks like a narrow walkway that spans all four walls. "The track is there." He points to my right. "Stairs will take you up." He points to the glass-encased room. "I'll be there."

I am about to go to the stairs when he raises a finger for me to wait. "I almost forgot. I got you something. Arthur says you like music when you run."

This is such a recent development that I really had not given it much thought. "Yes."

He jogs over to a table and lifts a pair of wristbands and two other small devices from it. He pins one device over his ear on the way back, then pins the other to mine. It pinches slightly, but the earpiece slides into my ear and the fit will not jostle when I move. He then slides the thin band over my wrist. The controls are on the inside of my wrist, and a song title slides across the top of the screen, ready for me to press PLAY.

"At the top of the music menu is a CALL button," he says. "If you want to call me for a leisurely chat," he adds with a wry smirk. "Or if you just need to get my attention. I play my music pretty loud."

I am in awe over the trouble he goes to for me. "You think of everything."

He laughs. "I seriously doubt that."

I push up on my toes and grab him by the neck to pull his head down. I kiss him softly, letting the moment linger, and when I pull away, the space between us is practically nonexistent.

"Thank you," I whisper.

His smile quirks up on one end. "It's just music."

"It is more than music."

He kisses me on the space just between my eyebrows. "Go run." He leaves me, holding lightly to my fingers until the last possible second.

I take the stairs up and find the second floor is no more than a track. No doors and no windows. Overhead are steel girders and fluorescent lighting. The ventilation system pushes cool air along the track, which is too cold right now but will be perfect once I get going.

A *click* in my ear startles me and Declan's voice comes through the earpiece. "Emma?"

I flip my wrist and tap ANSWER on the wristband. I peer over the railing and find Declan standing inside the doorway of his exercise room. "Yes?"

"I love you." He sounds the most serious I have ever heard him. "There is nothing I wouldn't do for you."

Now, that, She says, *I believe.*

. . .

We are covered in sweat and smiling when we return to the house. Declan was right about a run relieving me of my frustrations. I am still very upset with Ruby, but I understand now how I must not blame her for what happened. She does not understand her own name, let alone the property of others.

As for my paintings, I am upset over a lost connection to something that is not real. That beach and the man there do not exist. Like Her, they are a figment of my imagination. How can it be real?

Declan said himself that men do not brand themselves. I have only to look at my own hand to know I am not the woman on the beach. It is not my life. Not my past. Not my future. Only a dream. Just like the woman Adrienne who floats in a tank. Just like Foster and Toni and all the other dreams She shows me about a girl named Wade. It is all a manipulation with a purpose I have yet to decipher.

Declan is real. This home he has given to me is real. I will focus on that.

Declan shoves me playfully toward the bedroom. "You can shower first. You smell the worst."

I gape at him. "I do not. And I really think that is physically impossible."

He raises an eyebrow. "Showering?"

I giggle. "Smelling worse than you. You can go first. I will wait."

He swallows hard, walking backward toward the room. "There is another solution, you know."

"And that would be?"

"We could shower together."

The idea of showering together turns my heart into a jackhammer.

No, you can't, She says. *He calls it a solution. I call it a mistake.*

That's what he's offering you. A really big mistake. You can't uncross this t or undot this i.

This does not concern you, I tell Her. *You did not mind the idea of sex when we were in the hospital.*

That incident ended precisely when it needed to. This is different.

You are right. It is. I want to do this.

She has no response, so I simply nod and let Declan lead me into the bedroom.

CHAPTER 16

Declan kicks off his shoes at the foot of the bed and so do I. His eyes barely meet mine, and I take some comfort in the fact that maybe he is nervous, too. He disappears into the bathroom, and a heartbeat later, the shower starts. The sound is like an electric shock to my heart. Declan appears in the doorway, shirtless. He leans a smooth shoulder into the arched frame and folds his arms. Forget the electric shock to my heart. The sight of him like this— covered in sweat and curved in more muscle than is *ever* necessary—jolts my entire core.

"Emma..." His voice trails off and he drops his gaze. "Take your time," he says and turns back into the bathroom.

The shower doors thump against each other a moment later, and the sound sets my feet in motion.

The shower's glass has a layer of steam coating it, turning Declan into an opaque version of himself. His back is to me, both hands running over his head under the shower spray. The clean, almost sweet scent of shampoo fills the room. Heavy smacks of water intermingle with softer sprays as he moves, his body slick with water.

I slide out of my clothes, taking deep breaths. He will make this okay. He will not hurt me.

I take both handles in my hands and slide the doors apart. They are silent, as if sliding on air instead of metal. The movement alerts him to my presence, but he does not turn around. His head turns only slightly and his shoulders lift with his next intake of breath.

Declan edges aside. "Come here."

He guides me around him and places me under the spray. I tilt my head back and wait for the kiss that will start it all, but instead, he puts all his attention into washing my hair. While his fingers massage my scalp, I memorize the way water drips from the end of his nose and beads on his face. I watch his chest expand with each measured inhalation, and the drumming of the pulse in his neck.

His gaze lowers to meet mine and his smile is soft. His dark hair looks heavy and black from its recent wash. A thick strand falls forward and the tip grazes his cheekbone. I reach up and brush it aside, then let my fingers linger and trail his cheekbone and chin.

He turns his mouth into my palm and kisses it gently before moving my hand back to my side. I am confused until I realize he is reaching for a body sponge and coats it with a vanilla-scented wash. Now when he washes me, he does not follow his movements. I wonder if he is afraid to look at me. Regardless, I do not know if I am ready for him to.

The sponge slows over my breasts, and my breath quickens. My body is on fire and my mouth a desert. My insides are molten and aching with the most pleasurable pain.

I reach forward with shaking fingers, finding his abdomen with their tips. His muscles draw in taut under my touch and his breath

ARCHETYPE 125

catches. The hitching sound is almost inaudible over the spray hitting my back. Water trails over his skin and I move my fingers up against its current, over ridges and smooth plains of muscle. It is not until my hands reach his collarbone that he draws in a shaky breath.

I lay my fingers over the quickened pulse in his neck. "Are you nervous?" I ask.

"Of course I am," he says, his tone husky in a way that leaves me breathless. "Being touched by you—being able to touch you—" He stops abruptly and slides a hand over my cheek. His thumb gently outlines my lower lip. Raw desire fills his eyes, which are turning a fiery shade of green. But not only desire—tenderness. Love. "I have no words to describe this," he says finally.

My heart spins wildly in my chest, and the heat in my belly rises in dangerous tides, threatening to roll me under, and I grow dizzy, but a good dizzy.

I slide my hands behind his neck and up, clutching his damp hair in my fingers. I have only to rise on my tiptoes to meet his mouth halfway. He tastes of warm, clean water, and his skin is akin to the flame of my own.

Our skin meets and a delicious shudder takes my breath. I press into him and mold with my pliable bones and raw nerve endings. His palms flatten across my back, and we are so close, I truly believe I might slip right into his skin. And yet we are not nearly close enough.

"Make love to me," I whisper over his mouth and can hardly believe I found the nerve.

The water shuts off and I am swiftly off my feet and carried through the bathroom. His mouth glances over my neck, his nose brushes my ear. Hot, humid breaths send waves of goose bumps over my wet skin. Yet the fire inside me rages on, and I expect steam to rise from my skin any second now.

There is no concern for the carpet or comforter as we drip water over everything. He lays me down with such care, as if I am delicate china, and hovers over me a moment later. My skin begs for him to touch me again.

His chest heaves and his eyes smolder through dark lashes as they look into mine. Dripping strands of his hair hang forward and I reach up to push them back. This time, when my fingers trail over his cheekbone and his lips press into my palm, he does not push my hand away. His eyes close and his mouth slides down to my wrist. His lips are smooth and his skin is a coarse contrast of beard shadow. My skin tingles and burns in the wake of his kiss.

When he opens his eyes a heartbeat later, the hunger in them is sharp but controlled. "I need to look at you," he says and he is not asking.

This whole time his gaze has never traveled low enough to see me, really see me, giving me some small amount of privacy. Just the idea of his gaze rolling over me is fuel to my fire. My teeth press into my lower lip until all feeling is gone and I nod.

His gaze drops to my lips. "Roll over," he whispers, and I do.

He does not touch me for so long, and if it were not for the acute awareness of him, I would almost forget he is there. It is as if my skin can sense him, which direction, how close or far. So when his hands slide up the sides of my hips to my waist, I am not surprised but am finally able to take a long-needed breath. His palms are hot on my skin, his mouth and tongue in the dip of my back smoldering. The trail he places over my spine calls up my flame, speaking its language. *Burn,* it says. *Need.* And, oh, how I need. Ache. *Melt.*

His fingers move up my back, tracing agonizingly slowly over every curve and angle. His lips brush over my ear. "Turn over."

My body is so alive at this point that I cannot imagine surviving his touch. I am a live wire. His gaze on my breasts alone is as good as a simple touch. I arch up slightly as if he has pulled some string, his eyes reeling me in.

His fingers hover, trembling, over my breastbone for several thumping heartbeats, before skimming over my skin. The trail between my breasts is hot on its way to where he widens and splays his palm over my stomach. The tips of his fingers press gently into my skin and his mouth falls desperately to my breast. My breath hitches at this new sensation. Where my skin was tender before, my nipples are a million times that. He suckles and grazes his teeth over them, drawing moans of pleasure from me.

I thread my fingers into his hair, holding him to me until I can no longer take it. I find the strength to pull him free and up. His mouth falls on mine, tasting of the tang of skin. His lips force mine apart with a new desperation in our kiss. Something deep and primal and nowhere enough to sate our needs.

His knees nudge my thighs apart. If I could breathe, I would whimper or sigh with relief. I no longer fear this; the need is too much for this trivial feeling. His gaze dances over my face, watching me carefully before sliding inside.

The shock of this sensation takes my breath. I knew nothing of heat until now. *Nothing.* With each gliding inch of him, shock wave after shock wave of heat envelops me. I cannot breathe, and only the weight of his gaze keeps me from floating into this sensation.

When he is as deep as he can possibly go, he holds very still, mouth parted, shoulders bunched and corded with muscle over me. Neither of us exchanges a single breath. Time is frozen, yet I am writhing in flames.

"Don't move," he whispers.

His palm eases over my hip and thigh. Fingers press behind my knee and pull my leg up and back. He rests my calf over his shoulder, opening me up further so he can sink deeper. And deeper is where he goes. I cry out and arch up. A shudder drives over him and he holds again, filling me, eyes closed.

"Declan," I whimper, desperate for him to feed this insatiable hunger building in me.

"Shhh . . . Not yet."

His kiss paints the underside of my chin. His tongue dips into the lines of my neck. And still he does not move out of me.

He tortures me with this pleasure, and when he slides away, there is no relief because then I am empty of him. I am in agony, burning. The need for him returns me to the mindless woman I was months ago who knew nothing of the world. I am no more than tissue, blood, and bone. And *need*. Oh God, the need. The hunger. The pain of needing him to fill me, the torture of pleasure when he finally does.

A smile shapes his lips and he watches me intently as if memorizing my face. Soaking in the details of each mask I wear, the creations he himself helps forge. I watch his as well, wondering if my expression is as open as his. If my desire is as clear.

I know one thing for certain; I will never again see Declan as honest as he is in this moment.

My fingers trace over this raw honesty, this desire, *his* need. I grasp his face and pull his mouth down over mine. His lips are oxygen to my fire, and suddenly I cannot take it anymore. I buck up against him and he is too surprised to stop me. He rolls to his back and I grind my hips down against him. His head tilts back into the pillow under him and a moan of pleasure passes his swollen lips, sounding very much like my name.

He is still swimming in this sensation when I pull up again. I tighten my muscles over the head of his erection and slide down slowly this time.

"Oh God," he says, his eyes rolling up, fingers kneading into my hips.

I do this again and his arms tighten around me impatiently. I am suddenly on my back again. He rocks into me with a new purpose, a new drive, a new goal.

"Come," he says breathily, his gaze boring into me. "Come for me."

He does not need to tell me to because I am already there. The eruption is too much to take in silence, yet I cannot catch my breath to scream as I need to. Declan rides into the shuddering waves of my body until I am raw and tender and then holds me to him until his own climax peaks. He does not scream out, either, but is red and breathless. His jaw clenches tight, as do his eyes, and when he is finally capable of breath, he collapses over me.

It is a full minute before he pushes away and kisses me. The hunger and longing and need are all gone. What remains is far sweeter.

"How are you?" he asks.

I bite my lip and smile. Now that it is over, my nerves are back on high alert and I am all too aware of how he lies spent and pulsing gently inside me. "Perfect."

He grins and the sea in his eyes is alight. "Are you blushing?"

I turn my face away and try to hide behind my hands. He removes them before they can rest.

"You're beautiful when you blush," he says and kisses the tip of my nose.

"Too bad I cannot blush on command. I would do it simply for the compliments."

"I've been working hard to give you all this and all you needed were compliments?" He laughs. "Why didn't you say so? Would have saved me a lot of trouble."

I cup his face and kiss him. "All I need is you." I stop and consider something else to add. "And dinner. I am starving."

CHAPTER 17

I woke to a deep, sinking warmth. It came from the sun peeking through the slatted windows but also from the heat of skin pressed against my back. Deep and even breaths told me he still slept, spooning behind me in the same way we'd fallen asleep.

Near my head, his hand lay over mine. It twitched once. I removed my hand and covered his, letting my thumb trace over the luckenbooth.

I begged him not to do it. It wasn't necessary for him to brand himself just to prove his love for me.

"No one will take you seriously," I'd warned.

"No one has to know. I'll wear Plasti-skin over it."

I'd laughed at him. What an absurd annoyance for him to go through. "Every day?"

He waved a hand. "It won't be every day. Just when I have to meet with clients."

"So every day."

"I'm doing it. The only way you're changing my mind is if you refuse to marry me."

"I won't do that."

"Then it's settled."

I hadn't been able to tell him the brand meant something dif-ferent for me. I'd grown up thinking of the linked hearts as a ball and chain to slavery. This wasn't what I wanted for us, but he seemed determined to turn this horrible memory into something special.

Now, looking at the sign of something I'd grown to despise on his hand, I realized he was right. He was mine, just as I was his. The two of us linked.

Forever.

I start awake and bolt upright in the dark room. No light comes through the windows, which do not have curtains, let alone blinds. Only the moon's glowing reflection off the snow gives me a sense of time. A sense of where I am.

My heart drives in my chest and my quickened breath is diffi-cult to tame. I am beginning to think of these dreams as night-mares because each one only adds to my confusion. Why do I dream of this woman's life?

I study my hand to be sure there is no brand, that I have not dreamed this, too. It is the only proof that these dreams are not memories. That I am Emma Burke. That I am where I belong.

The bed shifts and dips beside me. Declan runs a hand over my bare shoulder. "Bad dream?"

"Yes." The word comes out of my mouth before I have a chance to stop it. "I mean, no."

"You don't have to lie, Emma. I'm not going to think you're hav-ing a setback because you have an honest-to-God nightmare."

I peer over my shoulder. "It was not a nightmare. I promise. Just . . . uncomfortable."

"In what way?"

"It does not matter." I lie down and stare up at the shadowed ceiling. "It was only a dream."

He scoops an arm under me and curls me into him until I rest on his shoulder. My hand lies over his chest and his heart thumps steadily against my palm.

"You're shivering," he says and pulls up the comforter.

Goose bumps rise on my arm as if on command. "I am a little cold."

"House control, increase heat two degrees," he says into the room. A tiny *click* sounds before an almost imperceptible *whoosh* of air in the ventilation.

"Thank you, but will you be too hot?"

"I can sleep outside the covers if I have to." He slides my hair back and kisses my forehead. "Go back to sleep."

"Declan?"

"Hm?"

"Why do I have to go back to the hospital?"

The air in his chest stills and he does not speak for a long time. "Arthur wants to make sure you adjust okay. It won't be long now."

I push up on my elbow and watch my hand moving over his chest to avoid his eyes. "I am adjusting. The first day was difficult, but I did okay tonight. I am comfortable here. I am comfortable with you."

"Is this about Ruby?"

This surprises me and I give him my full attention, bringing my hand to a complete stop. He lifts a hand to tuck my hair back.

"No," I tell him. "Ruby does not understand things. I was not careful, so what happened was my fault. I should never have left my belongings in the lounge."

A small smile plays on his lips. "You're really good with her, you know?"

"She is like me. I understand her."

He nods. "I'll talk to Arthur. Maybe we can shorten your days."

This is enough and I smile. "Really?"

He kisses me. "Really."

"Declan is happy to have you home," Dr. Travista says. "The week has gone by rather quickly, with no problems."

I stand with folded arms near the window, looking out at the melting snow. Living in Declan's home makes this easier. "It gets easier every day, and Declan works hard to make it so. He is very kind and patient with me."

"He is much like his mother in that respect."

I turn, careful to hide my surprise. This is the first I am hearing of parents. "His mother? Did you know her?"

He smiles. "I've worked for the Burkes my entire career. His father, Andrew, hired me right out of college. Andrew and Eliza are gone now." He looks down at his lap and frowns. "Eight years now, I think."

He uses the word "gone" and I cannot help but wonder if I will find them in a hospital room just as I did Jodi. I do not want to wait and find out, so I probe deeper. "Both? At the same time?"

"Oh no, of course not. No, Eliza died during her second pregnancy and Andrew had a heart attack."

"How sad," I say. "What about me? Do I have parents?" I doubt

I do because I would have seen them. At least I think I would have. So much about this world confounds me.

"No." He does not elaborate.

"Are they dead, too?"

He taps his screen a few times and reads something. "There is nothing here in your WTC record about your parents."

I recognize the acronym from one of my earlier dreams with Toni. "WTC?"

"Women's Training Center. Where all our young women are prepared for marriage."

I bite the inside of my cheek and swallow the words "work camp." He makes the WTC sound warm and fuzzy. Instead, I move back to the previous topic. "If there is no record of my parents, what does that mean?"

Dr. Travista considers me for a long moment. I know this look. It is the can-she-handle-the-truth look. I am tired of being coddled.

Finally, he says, "There is no official record of your birth, which means you come from West America."

Land of the free, She says, and I nearly jump in surprise. She has not spoken since before Declan and I made love. She was not happy with my decision, but I did not expect Her to disappear the way She had.

I turn my back on the doctor. "But they could be alive?"

"Unknown."

What he means is that nobody crosses into the east without deadly consequences. This is a man's land. Corporations with their eye on the prize: survival by any means necessary, but only if it makes a lot of money. They took you from your parents.

I school my face to hide my annoyance at Her outlandish accusations. "I will never know."

"No," he agrees. "Not likely."

I turn to smile at the doctor even though my insides are empty of happiness. "It does not matter. I have Declan. We will have the family I never had."

"Maybe you are already well on your way."

I blink rapidly in surprise. "What?"

"You're a fertile woman and you've been home for a week. According to your cycle, you're ovulating."

Heat floods my chest and flares up my neck. "You know my cycle?"

He waves a hand as if my personal business is no big deal. "Of course. I'm your doctor. Why don't we run some tests and see? Imagine the look on Declan's face if you could tell him he's about to be a father."

He stands to leave but I cannot bring my feet to move. Pregnant? I could be pregnant. I want to be sick when I should be thrilled. Why had I not thought of this possibility?

I believe I mentioned the word "mistake" recently, She says.

Dr. Travista's eyebrows pinch together. "Are you all right? You look very pale."

I swallow. "I did not think . . ." I drop into the chair and turn away from him. "Is it really possible?"

He sits back down and leans forward. "What is it, Emma? I thought you wanted this. You told me you couldn't wait to start a family."

He is right. I did. But it had been a lie. "It is an easy enough thing to say. To feel. But faced with it . . . I do not think I am ready."

He leans back into his chair and sighs. "Emma." He says this with an air of condescension, and I ball my hand into a fist before I reach out and slap him.

"No." I turn to face him. "I am only just getting used to being home. I need time."

He slaps his hands to his knees and stands. "I'm afraid you don't have a choice. Birth control is illegal. Abortion is illegal, with a very severe punishment. Emma, pregnancy is not a choice. I'm sorry."

I follow him out but do not see anything but my future slipping out of my control.

CHAPTER 18

I manage to contain my joy until I am alone and show very little even then because of the cameras. I am not pregnant. I want to cry from relief. Dr. Travista will no doubt tell Declan, who will be sad, but for now, I cannot care. I can only be happy that I have been given a few more weeks if my cycle remains true to its course. I am told there is no further chance until next month.

Declan finds me painting in the lounge, and it is clear by the distant look in his eyes that he has already spoken to Dr. Travista.

"I am sorry," I say. I stand from my stool and embrace him.

He kisses the top of my head. "For what, my love?"

"He told you about the test. I am sorry for the result. You must be disappointed."

"No. There's plenty of time."

I step out of his arms and nod at the painting. "I am almost finished. Do you mind waiting?"

He sits and loosens his tie, squinting at my work. "This is very good, Emma."

I tilt my head and examine the mountain scene I have painted. It is the view from the living room, but what I imagine spring to look like. I am tired of snow. "Do you think so?"

"Hm. I think this is already my favorite. We'll have to hang this one at home."

"Oh no, I do not think it is that good." It is not that special.

"We can hang it over the fireplace."

I lay my paintbrush down and rise from the stool. "Never mind. I am finished."

He stands, still eyeing the painting. "You don't like it?"

I shake my head. "It is not right. I will start over tomorrow."

He takes my hand and we stroll toward the transporter room. "I have something to show you before we go home."

I eye him with curiosity. He speaks as if he is pleased with himself. "Where?"

"It's a surprise."

We step into the teleporter tube and he says, "The port number is 037-5138-1."

I commit this to memory with our home and the hospital port numbers. I cannot repeat it aloud because the spearmint fills the space and the outside room melts into an empty room with white walls. Not only the sidewalls but the ceiling and floor. Upon closer examination, I see the walls are not painted. The surface is a flat, screen-like material.

In the middle of the room is a lonely cluster of art supplies that includes an easel and a small table with paint, brushes, and jars for water. Am I supposed to paint here? In this bare room with nothing to look at?

I step out and spin slowly. "What is this place?"

He must see the confusion on my face, because he chuckles and gathers up a small computer tablet from the stool in front of the easel. He presses the screen a few times and the room comes to life.

"Holograms," he says.

I spin again, gaping. I stand in a desert complete with mountainous sand dunes and the brightest sun I can imagine. The scene changes a moment later and I stand in a jungle with dark roots twisting around my feet. Dark green vines hang from slender trees and water drips from the largest leaves I have ever seen. A snake slithers on a branch above me and I yelp.

Declan runs a hand through a nearby tree trunk. "It isn't real. You're perfectly safe in the case of a jungle cat or some other predator appearing. I have no idea how extensive this is, but it's the best money could buy."

He shows me a huge closet full of canvases in every size imaginable, every paint supply I will ever need, smocks, and drop cloths. In the room next to it, a bathroom complete with a small shower— in case I have a paint catastrophe.

"Where is this room located? The hospital?" I ask. I do not think our house is big enough for this room.

Declan looks around at the mountains I have keyed into the tablet. I am happy to see there is no snow. "We're in Richmond. I had this room put into the basement of my main office building. I have an office upstairs."

I look around again. Other than the closet and bathroom, there are no other doors. "There is no exit."

"I didn't put one in." He cannot meet my eyes. "It's for your protection. A door will allow others in, and while I trust a lot of people, I don't trust all of them. You and I are the only two with the port number. Arthur's only stipulation is that you alert him when you're leaving, just as you would if you decide to go home."

I nod. "Yes, of course."

He pulls out a phone that resembles my tablet computer but is far smaller. "And, obviously, I'll know where you are if you leave the hospital."

I do not need this reminder as if I did not hear the first twenty times he told me after he gave me the home port number, but I nod my understanding anyway. I will not complain when he has given me something so amazing.

"Declan, this is the most thoughtful gift." The sting of tears threatens my eyes and I turn from him. I try to focus on the range of mountains and the wildflowers blooming in the clearing around me. A wind blows through, rustling the grass, but I feel nothing but still, warm air.

His arms come around me and his fingers tap over the menu on the tablet in my hand. "I made sure they put in this one in particular," he whispers.

Now I stand on a beach. Seagulls dance over the water and waves crash audibly on the shore. It takes my breath away.

"One last thing," he says. "If you approve, of course."

I turn in his arms and he folds me in. "I approve."

He laughs. "I haven't told you anything yet."

"It does not matter. I will do anything."

"I was thinking," he begins hesitantly, "you would like to have a show. Burke Enterprises owns an art gallery a few blocks from here. If you would like to do a series, we can have a show and maybe find some buyers. What do you think?"

I am nearly speechless. "I am not that good."

He raises an eyebrow. "Actually, the gentleman running the studio was very impressed with your work and asked to see more." He places a finger over my lips when I begin to speak. "I sent in a man he wouldn't know, and he didn't tell him you were my wife, so there was no bias."

"I do not know what to say." My heart pounds and I cannot tell if it is from excitement or fear. Maybe both.

"Think about it," he says and shrugs. "There's no time limit on the offer and you aren't obligated. I just thought your work was too good to simply sit in the hospital, and by the speed with which you paint, I'm going to have to rent space just so the work has a home." He laughs. "Which I will absolutely do if the need arises."

I bite my lip because I am dangerously near tears. "What does Dr. Travista think?"

He tilts his head, narrowing his eyes. "Not that it matters, but I got the idea from Arthur. He said in passing that he would consider buying your work if he'd seen it somewhere, so I decided to look into it. When I told him what the gallery manager said, he agreed it would be a positive experience for you."

"Will I have to be at the show?"

"You would prefer not to be?"

"I do not know. This is a lot to consider."

He nods. "It is, so think about it. Enjoy your new studio and paint your heart out. If you decide to go through with it, say the word. I'll get my people on it right away."

I step away and look around the room. Behind Declan, the beach expands for what appears to be some distance and ends in a row of cliffs. It is really as if we stand on the shore.

With some hesitation, I shut it down and the room returns to nothing more than white walls. I blink several times to adjust, even though I knew what I would see. The difference is still shocking.

"You don't have to come home right away," Declan says. "I can always find something to do upstairs and we can order takeout later."

I lay the tablet down on the stool in front of the easel. "No, we can go home. It has been a long day."

Declan sweeps me off my feet and carries me into the tele-porter. "I was hoping you'd say that."

My entire body wakes in anticipation and I grin. "Something on your mind, Mr. Burke?"

"Always, Mrs. Burke. Always."

His mouth slants over mine and I press into him as much as I can. When I get a moment to speak, I say, "We are going to need that takeout. Neither of us is leaving the bedroom tonight."

His arm reached around and took the paintbrush from my hand. "This isn't quite right."

He mixed and added a new color to the brush and, in a few strokes, altered the color of my sunset.

I peered around the canvas and saw the change for myself. The sky beyond the ocean had turned a deeper shade of red and purple. "It didn't look like that a few minutes ago."

He chuckled and returned the brush to my hand. "A lot can change in a few minutes."

I sent an elbow back into his gut, laughing. "And in a few more, it will be dark. What are your plans for my masterpiece then, huh?"

His hand tapped my hip and he said, "I just thought of something to add. Get up."

I lifted and he slid under me, repositioning me on his lap so I faced the painting head-on. I held the board while he got a clean brush and then added the color I'd already mixed for the sand.

I watched him add shadow to one corner of the canvas, altering the shape of the sand. "What are you doing?"

"Signing it."

"But it's my painting."

"I helped."

I shook my head and watched his final strokes paint in linked hearts. They were so well hidden in the shadow of the sand dune that no one would ever see them unless they specifically looked for them.

He laid down the brush and kissed my shoulder. "There. What do you think? An original by Emma and—"

"Oh, no you don't," I said, laughing. "You aren't claiming my work. An original by Emma and Emma alone."

"You know," he said thoughtfully, "I would buy this original by Emma and Emma alone. I particularly like the colors you chose for the sunset."

I rise from the stool so fast it falls and knocks against the floor with its hologram of sand dunes and beach grass. Not only do I stare at an exact replica of the dream's painting with its hidden luckenbooth, but Wade has been given a first name.

Mine.

Now I understand the longing and grief I suffer over Tucker. Unless the name is a coincidence—*God, let it be a coincidence*—these dreams are not dreams at all, but memories. And because I have been married to Declan for eight years, the entirety of my adult life, this can mean only one thing.

I have been unfaithful to my husband.

CHAPTER 19

Declan stands to take our dinner plates and I finally find the nerve to speak.

"I decided to do it."

He laughs and returns to his seat. "You can't hit me with a conversation without a topic first."

It has been more than a week since he gave me the studio, and though I spend a lot of time trying to reach a decision, we never talk about it.

I give him a tilted smile. "Sorry. The show. For my paintings."

He sits up straighter and blinks at me in surprise.

"I have waited too long to decide," I say. "It is too late?"

"No. No, of course not. I told you to take your time." He smiles and takes my hand. "I assumed you didn't want to because you didn't answer right away, but I'm glad you decided to do it."

He stands again and turns away with our plates. "Did you decide on a theme?"

I meet him at the sink and take the rinsed plates from him. I am sliding them into the dishwasher when I say, "You will not like it."

"Why would you think that?"

I avoid his eyes. "I want to paint the beaches."

The paintings are all I can think about. Them and Tucker, which adds to my guilt daily. I think I must paint the beaches to get them out of my system once and for all. A way of giving myself completely to my marriage. I think I paint them because each stroke of the brush brings me closer to the truth behind the dreams. Are they memories of a past I am better off without? I know I paint them because in them all my blank spaces are gone. Filled. Complete.

Declan passes over the rinsed silverware in silence. After a few tense moments, he leans his hip into the counter and folds his arms. "It's not that I don't like them, Emma, but I wonder why you have such a fascination with them. And you put so much more time and care into them."

I force myself to meet his eyes. "It is nothing more than what I told you the first time. The photograph in my old room. Most of my earliest memories since waking from the accident are centered around it."

"Are you sure that's all?"

I do not understand his disbelief in my words, though his distrust is completely justified. I will never tell him how I dream of another man on a beach. A man whom I may or may not have had an affair with.

"What other reason would there be?" I ask.

He shakes his head and turns away. "None, I guess. I'm just being paranoid."

I want him to elaborate why he feels this way, but I sense a warning from Her, though She has not voiced anything. I need to let this subject drop. I have gotten what I wanted and should leave it at that.

I close the dishwasher and reach out to embrace him. "You know . . . in all this time, we have never made love in front of the fireplace."

His grin is quick and I am off my feet a heartbeat later. He carries me toward the blazing fire. "That's a serious problem I intend to fix immediately."

It is the first time outside air has touched my face since early winter, but this is not my biggest shock. It is seeing Richmond for the first time. It is well into the evening, but the city is bright enough to hide the night sky. Lights run along every corner and angle along every building in sight. Windows glow on every floor for hundreds of stories.

The Christmas holiday is upon the city. Trees with lights or snowmen or snowflakes or angels decorate every street corner. More lights drape over entire intersections in wide arcs. Holiday carols play from a hidden speaker system over the nearly silent hum of traffic.

I cannot walk because I want to soak everything up. Declan said we could port directly to the studio, but I wished to see the holiday lights. I am glad he relented, even with some nervousness on his part.

Declan's hand runs over my back. "You okay?"

"It is beautiful." My voice barely rises over a whisper.

He scans the area. "Yes." He squeezes my hand very briefly. "Come on. Remember to stay close, all right?"

I nod and link my fingers through his. The sidewalk is thick with bodies—male bodies. There are women, but they are few and far between, and almost all of them tote small male children with them.

The one common feature of both sexes is the hunched shoulders and tightening of coats against the brisk wind blowing down the street. The snow has melted, but the temperature is not better. The wind slapping my skin feels like it is loaded with icicles.

While we stroll along, I take in more of the street details. Digital parking meters sit in front of diagonal spaces all along the row. A red glow in the boxes reads $10.25 PER HALF HOUR. Every space is full and the meters show varying minutes left.

In the center of each block, attached to a pole in the ground, is a large square screen. On it is a picture of a newspaper booth with a sign that reads RICHMOND TIMES. Along the bottom, the screen reads $5 PER DOWNLOAD. A heading crosses the screen in bold letters: BURKE ENTERPRISES BACK UP AND RUNNING AFTER LARGEST ATTACK TO DATE. Under the caption is a picture of the glass-and-steel building we just came from.

I glance up at Declan, who watches the thick cluster of people while maneuvering us through. Burke Enterprises was attacked? There must be some mistake, because he has not mentioned this.

"Declan?"

He glances down quickly and says, "Yes?"

"What does that mean?" I point to the *Times* download center. "Is that about your company?"

Declan does a double take when he reads the screen and purses his lips. A second later, I am moved to his other side and he curses under his breath.

"It's nothing," he says. "Something that happened months ago. Around the time of your accident."

"Was it bad?"

"Emma, I really don't want to get into it."

I cast my gaze down. "Of course. I am sorry."

"Don't apologize." His tone is angry underneath forced patience. "Damn it. I'm sorry. It's just been a nightmare for months, but honestly, I'm not upset it happened. I mean, I am—the money lost was insurmountable—but it changed my life." He looks at me with a softer expression. "I wish I could explain it to you."

"It is none of my business." Down the block, the art gallery comes into view and I point, grateful I can change the subject. "Is that it?"

Declan angles us toward the front of the building with a solid window front and an old-fashioned swing-open door and bell. It is toasty warm inside the large, open space. Long cushioned benches sit in front of every wall, perfectly centered under various pieces of art. Photographs hang as well as paintings. It is a mash-up of styles, and I love it.

"Mr. Burke?" A man appears through a sliding door in the back, a wide smile flashing under a large salt-and-pepper mustache. "Right on time."

"Did you receive the piece I sent this afternoon?" Declan asks the man while shaking his hand.

"Yes." He glances at me, his smile twitching like he is having a hard time holding it. "Is this the artist?"

"My wife, Emma. Emma, this is Harold Geist."

I shake his sweaty, plump palm and resist running my hand over my long coat. "Hello, Mr. Geist. It is a pleasure to meet you."

His smile firms. "So polite."

"Mr. Geist," Declan says, "why don't you and I go talk while Emma looks around?"

The two men leave me standing in the center of the room alone. I spin slowly, looking at several of the pieces hanging under long lights that illuminate each piece in a soft glow.

"May I take your coat?"

The woman's voice makes me jump. She seemed to come from nowhere. She holds out a hand expectantly and avoids my eyes. Her face is made up in an almost natural coating of makeup and her hair is pulled back into a tight bun. She must be close to my age—somewhere in her mid- to late twenties.

I do not really want to give up my one source of warmth, but I do not think she will go away until I do. I shrug out of the heavy black coat and she disappears with it through a door I had not seen previously.

Alone again, I smooth my hands over my black slacks and straighten my fitted red top. The material is thin and the chill of winter reaches me despite the heat in the room. I fold my arms and run my palms over them for warmth.

It does not take me long to circle the entire room, and by the end I am in awe of the talent displayed. I do not know what made me think my paintings were good enough to show here. The pieces displayed are extraordinary. Even the abstract paintings, which I have never been fond of, are amazing. I find myself studying brush strokes and colors used to create shadows and highlights. Textures.

The front bell rings and I turn my head automatically to see who has come in. A man shuffles in with a slight limp on his left side. He stands in the doorway, holding the door open. I am midway into the space, but the winter has already sucked the heat out.

I am annoyed that he will not close the door and mean to say something but stop to give him a better look. Something about him niggles the back of my mind, but I cannot place him. Skin the color of milk chocolate, dark curls trimmed close, and a patch of thick beard growth covering the lower half of his face.

I turn and face him, eyes narrowed on the man, who watches me with an identical quizzical expression.

"I am sorry, but do I know you?" I ask. "You look familiar."

"You"—he shuffles on his feet and tilts his head—"know me?"

"I do not know." I look more carefully, searching for something to place him in my memory.

He limps closer but continues to hold the door open. "Wade?"

The name snaps my spine into a straight line. "What did you call me?"

"Wade. Emma Wade."

That is when I see his eyes. They are blue, almost gray. I do know him, but this is impossible. He is a dream, only he no longer wears the black uniform of a soldier. There is no light of easy friendship in his eyes. Only shock and confusion. He mirrors my emotions completely.

"How do you—?"

Voices sound from the back of the room and echo forward. Declan laughs with the gallery manager about something. Foster—if that is who this man truly is—stiffens at the sound. His gaze darts behind me and I follow it. The two men are walking back into the gallery, unaware of what occurs with me and the man letting the winter in.

When I turn back to the front, Foster is gone, and had I not felt the chill of winter on my face, I would have thought I had just imagined my dream come to life.

CHAPTER 20

I do not think.

I run.

Foster cannot have gone far, and I must know why he thinks I am Emma Wade. Why I dream of him and the man named Tucker. How I am connected to all of their lives.

The wind is biting cold and I shoulder through the mass of bodies on the sidewalk. I push against the tide of street goers, trying to peer around and up over. I am in heels and still cannot see over some of these men.

When I cannot find Foster, I try moving with the crowd. This is easier, but I am still unable to find him. "Come back!" I yell.

"Emma!"

Declan's voice is muffled by the sounds of cell phone conversations and blaring horns and the whir of electric car engines and holiday carols sounding through speakers. The *Times* download center tells a man to "scan reader now" in a kind male voice.

I ignore everything and push my way to the road and step off the curb. A cold puddle of water sloshes up over my foot and soaks the inside of my shoe. I ignore the sting of cold around my toes and spin to take in the area one more time. He has to be here. Why did he run?

"Emma!"

Declan's worry is clear in his tone now and jolts me back to reality. I am looking for a man who should not exist. This is foolish. He is a figment of my imagination.

A figment you gave a beard? She asks. *Oh, and the added limp was a nice touch, Emma. Gave him character.*

Stop it.

I run back up onto the curb. The men walking by are practically unyielding and growl horrible things to me as I try to get back to the gallery. I find Declan halfway there, spinning and looking frantically for me just as I had been doing a moment ago for Foster.

When he sees me, his shoulders slump and he rushes over to me. "What are you doing?"

"A man dropped his wallet," I say. "I was returning it." How easily the lies come now.

He shakes his head. "You shouldn't run off like that."

"I am sorry, but I—"

He kisses my forehead. "I know. You are too kind for your own good sometimes. Come back inside. You're freezing."

Outside the gallery, my painting sits in the window. My name scrolls along a gold plate below it. It is the re-creation of the beach sunset. Declan told me only that he sent a piece over; he did not mention which one. I would have kept this one, but it is too late.

A hologram flashes along the bottom of the glass and a message appears. My name and a date for a month from now run horizontally, announcing my show.

"That was fast," I say, my chest tightening.

"Come on."

He pulls me inside, and I do not realize how frozen I am until I am surrounded by the heat. Tiny pinpricks of pain tingle all over my body as blood rushes to warm me. An uncontrollable shiver races through me and my teeth chatter.

Declan takes my coat from the woman, who has appeared out of nowhere. "Here, put this on."

While I bundle up with my coat and scarf, Declan thanks Mr. Geist and promises to send more pieces soon for his approval.

"I need to go to my office," Declan tells me. "You can come if you want, or you can take a teleporter from here and wait for me at home."

"Can I go with you?" I have always wondered what his office looks like.

"Of course."

Outside, Declan takes us back to his office building. The lights are low in the lobby, hinting that admittance will not be permitted, and men sit behind a semicircular desk. When we enter they stand and nod. The transporter room is in a long marble hallway behind them.

He keys in the number 182 and we appear in a new hallway with a carpeted floor. At the end of the hall is a set of glass doors that slide open when we approach. We enter a room with plush leather furniture and a mahogany desk that sits empty except for the tablet propped on a dock station, a phone, and a small potted plant. The surrounding walls are silver with thick and thin black lines weaving around one another. When I look closer, I realize it is designed to look like the room is one large computer chip. I am surprised by this, when our home is so warmly decorated.

Declan waves a hand over a panel and another door opens. "This is my office."

I follow him into a room that—other than the furniture—looks nothing like his receptionist's office and find myself in the center of a massive water tank. I backtrack without thinking. My heart pounds against my ribs and my eyes burn with tears.

Declan follows me quickly. "What is it?"

I swallow back my tears. "You work in—in a tank of water?"

He laughs. "No. It's a projection. Actually, it's a screen saver. My computer is asleep. Come see." I do not move, but he returns to his office and says, "Computer, wake to desktop."

The wall behind his desk transforms to the color azure. Tentatively, I step back inside to see all of his walls are exactly the same.

"Computer," he says again, "go back to sleep."

He takes my hand as the walls return to the water tank. I stiffen, and if he notices, he does not say anything. It is nothing more than an aquarium tank with colorful fish and plant life swaying gently from fake pebbled floor to ceiling. Bubbles float from the bottom and pop on the top. It looks very real but is nothing like the tank in my dreams.

"See?" he says and releases my hand. "Just a projection."

"How do you work on a computer that needs all four of your walls? Why do you not have windows?"

"Computer, show meeting space."

Behind his desk, floor-to-ceiling windows project from one corner to the next. If I had not known better, I would have thought the view was real. Displayed across the wall is the very city we just came from minutes ago, lit with holiday lights.

"It projects real-time visuals," he says, standing with hands tucked in pockets, his gaze on the street below.

The wall to my right is nothing more than a screen, and it rises to hide in the ceiling. The room expands from behind this false wall, adding two couches, two chairs, a bookshelf, and a wet bar.

What surprises me most are the paintings under lights along the wall opposite the projected window. They are mine, early versions of our mountain view from home. Sunrise peeks over the ridges, and a mist cascades through snow-heavy trees. I'd painted three to hang side by side like a panoramic photograph, then tucked them away with a few others I never cared for.

"When did you take these?" I ask.

Declan wraps his arms around me and rests his chin on my crown. "A while ago. They're my favorites. I figured you wouldn't care. You threw them in a closet," he adds with a chuckle.

"They are not very good."

"I respectfully disagree, as would a lot of my associates." He kisses my head and lets me go. "I'll just be a few minutes."

Declan perches on the edge of his desk, facing the now closed door, and picks up a tablet computer. "My new security system should have gone live a half hour ago. I just want to check it out. This company I hired is incredible, or they'd better be for the time and money I've put into them. It's taken them damn near six months to get set up. That attack you saw in the paper? Never would have happened had I not taken so long to decide."

I drape my coat over one arm and look at the tablet from over his shoulder. I do not understand a thing he is looking at other than it being a list of some kind. Locations maybe, but under names only he and his staff must understand.

"What is so special about them?" I ask.

"Let's see if I can show you."

He taps the top name, and the schematic of a tall building fills the screen. He shifts from infrared to ultraviolet to what looks like a grid. There are several tiny red dots throughout the building's grid, and he taps on two near the top. The lens zooms in on them, and when he swipes a hand over the screen from bottom to top, the image seems to fly onto the wall in front of us.

Holy shit, She whispers. *He did it. He really fucking did it.*

I know She is not referring to how Declan managed to make the image appear on the wall—I have seen him do this at home on occasion—so who "he" is, is a mystery to me.

"What are we looking at?" I ask.

The screen wall to the extended room slides back down, and Declan taps the screen a few more times until the image is real time, real life, and all around me. It *is* me. And him, too, of course. We are looking at ourselves.

"Computer," he says, "full screen."

I spin slowly, mouth agape, watching myself spin on every wall.

"Three hundred and sixty degrees in every room, in every building, for miles around every property," Declan says. "At least that's what it says on the brochure." He stands and looks around. "My security team has access to most of it. There are certain places, of course, I'd prefer they didn't see. Like my office, for example."

My stomach turns. "You have done this to our home, too?"

He shakes his head. "No, not yet. That's next. I debated it for a while because its location is secret and extremely remote. But with the resistance from the west continually coming after my holdings, I don't want to chance it. Especially if you're going to be home more."

I do not know how I feel about this. "You could see me at home whenever you wanted. I would have no privacy?"

"It will be limited to the main room and the outer area, but yes,

I could see you. Your workspace is private with the exception of the alert to my phone. The holograms interfere with the system or something."

"The hospital?"

He nods. "Up and running as of a half hour ago."

"What was wrong with your security before?"

"Wide-angle lenses aren't enough these days. Attacks come from all directions." He runs his fingers over the screen, and the angle of the room turns and twists, showing that he could look up my skirt if I were wearing one. "I can go anywhere and see from any direction."

"Impressive. What is the name of the company you are using?"

"Tucker Securities."

My knees weaken and I brace my hand on the desk. "Tucker?"

It is only a coincidence. It has to be.

Was Foster a coincidence, too? She asks.

Images from the dreams—*memories?!*—of a beach and a faceless man whose last name is Tucker bombard me. I can almost feel his touch, the heat of his body. And because Foster called me Emma Wade before running off earlier, I have to believe it is possible. But is the man responsible for Declan's new security?

I cannot even think it, let alone believe it. Life would not be so cruel as to put an old lover in the same vicinity as my husband. My kind husband who deserves no less than my complete devotion.

Declan is absently returning the screen to normal, though we are still looking at ourselves. "Brilliant man. If he wasn't already running his own business, I would have hired him a long time ago."

I am about to ask the man's full name, but Declan places the tablet on the desk and gathers me into his arms.

"What are you doing?" I ask.

He kisses my neck and tugs my shirt up. "What does it look like?" His grin is on the devilish side, and he nods at the wall, showing me exactly what we are doing.

"You cannot be serious."

"Very." His mouth is back on my neck. "Nobody can see but us."

I do not like this and push out of his arms. "I cannot do this here." My words are shaking and I have to grip the desk behind me again to steady my hands. "I am sorry, but I— I just cannot do this."

Something is very wrong with this, and more than just my aversion to watching us have sex in his office. Too much has happened tonight, the biggest shock being my run-in with Foster. There is no shortage of impact in hearing the name Tucker slip from my husband's tongue, either. I have to find out what is going on. If only I knew how I was going to do that.

Declan kisses me lightly on the mouth. "Okay, I'm sorry. You ready to go home?"

I nod. I am very ready to go where no one is watching. Even if it is only a computer.

CHAPTER 21

Noah *throws open the door, startling Sonya from a nap she is taking on an empty hospital bed. Another of Dr. Travista's books lies open beside her. Silently, he lifts one of the many tablets and taps a few commands.*

"What is it?" Sonya asks.

Noah purses his lips and shakes his head. "You'll see."

I want to see, too, but he is staring at the tablet and glancing at the screens on the wall to my right. I can see only their expressions.

His last tap is a sharp jab, and he throws the tablet back onto the table. He points to the large screen on the wall. "There. Now, explain that. Explain how that's possible."

Sonya gapes, blinking rapidly at the screen, and I wish someone would elaborate. What are they looking at? What is causing this frightened look on her face? The anger on his?

"I . . . I . . ." she stammers. She looks up at me, then to the screen. "What the hell?"

Noah reaches into his jacket pocket and hands her a phone. "I got this message earlier, thought it was a joke. A crazy drunken moment. A mistake nonetheless."

Sonya reads it and then looks up at the screen. "That's no mistake. Noah, we have to find out what it is."

"What it is, its purpose, and destroy it," he agrees, but his voice chokes on the last part. He clears his throat. "Soon."

"Nobody's going to—"

"I'll do it myself," he says, glancing down and away.

"You are my husband?" Ruby asks me.

I sigh and face the lounge window. No frost on the windows today. This is promising. "No. I am your friend. Only a friend." I wonder how Declan had so much patience with me when I was like this. Ruby and I have been at this friend distinction for days. "Charles is your husband."

"Charles is my husband. Emma is my friend."

"Yes. That is right." I reach to tuck a wild curl behind her ear. The longer her hair gets, the more curls arrive. And she is gaining weight now, too. "Do you know the difference?"

"What is 'difference'?"

This could be one of my earlier conversations with Declan. I hold out my arm and lay it beside hers. "See how our skin is different? You are pale, and I am olive toned. This is different." I consider hair color but do not believe she knows what she looks like yet. Then I get another idea. "I wear different clothes. And different shoes." I point to my three-quarter-sleeve lace cardigan and jeans and her scrubs. My black boots, her canvas shoes. "See how they do not look alike?"

She nods and runs her fingers over my sleeve. "Yes. I think so."

Dr. Travista arrives and smiles from the doorway. "Time for our session, Ruby."

Ruby stands and leaves without any further prompts.

He lays a hand on her shoulder when she is close enough. "I'll be right there."

I stand and turn, wiping my warm palms over my jeans. "Good morning."

He shakes his head at the floor and chuckles. "Declan just made the comment that he's going to have to put you on the payroll. You are very good with her."

"Declan is watching me?" I do not like this new security. While I knew he watched me before, I have seen this new view and how up close and personal it can be. I am not a fan.

Dr. Travista lifts his shoulders in a halfhearted shrug. "He loves you." He says this as if it is the only explanation I will ever need.

"He should focus on other things. He is a very busy man." I say this pointedly into the room and specifically for Declan if he is still watching. If he is smart, he will switch to another camera feed or shut mine down completely.

Dr. Travista nods and begins to turn. "Are you staying?"

"Only long enough to put away my supplies. I only came to visit with Ruby for a little while. I have the show to prepare for."

He smiles. "Only a few more days. You must be getting excited."

"It is overwhelming, but in a good way. I look forward to it."

"Good, good. We'll chat about it tomorrow?"

"Of course."

He leaves me and I begin packing my art supplies. I keep a few in the lounge for days when Ruby wants to paint. She is learning to keep to the canvas but is not naturally artistic. She never will be, but she enjoys it, so I encourage it.

I am locking the paint in a cabinet when the *shiff* of the door fills the room. No one closes the door to the lounge until after visiting hours. I swallow the trepidation tightening my throat and rise slowly to face the man who entered.

"I thought I might catch you here," Charles says. "Talking to Ruby again?"

I close the doors to the cabinet. "Yes. Why did you close the door?"

He glances between the door and me. "I never have a chance to speak to you in private. Travista never tells me anything. Burke, either. But you're the key anyway, so I want to talk to you."

I step around a chair to place it between us. "What is it you want?"

He unbuttons and removes his suit jacket, then lays it over the back of the chair. "How much of your previous life do you remember?" He raises his eyebrows. "And I want the truth, none of this bullshit you feed the others."

He is crazy if he thinks I will tell him *anything.* "What does this have to do with Ruby?"

Charles moves two steps around the chair and wags a blunt finger at me. "You see, I have this theory that you're putting them on. I know all about you, Emma *Burke*"—he raises his hands to air-quote—"and I want to know what you're telling my wife. What sort of bullshit resistance propaganda are you feeding her? Are you teaching her to play dumb?"

I mirror his footsteps around the chair, centering my focus on him. "I do not know what you are talking about."

Where are the red coats? Is this not why Declan installed the new security? How could they let this man be alone with me when he is clearly a threat? I venture to think Declan might have taken my suggestion and stopped watching the room. Did he turn off the entire feed?

"Sure, sure," he says. "Except you're not playing with Declan Burke here, sweetheart. I've dealt with your kind. I know how you operate. How you think. You can't be trusted."

I raise my hands defensively. "Mr. Godfrey, I wish I knew where this was coming from, but I promise you I do not know what you are talking about. I am not part of this resistance. I never have been."

He laughs with his head tilted back. "Oh, Emma! You are *good*. Really."

You have no idea, She says. *Get ready. This is about to get ugly.*

What do you mean?

You'll know what to do.

I do not understand Her warning, but Charles is moving quickly around the chair.

"Leave me alone," I say.

"I'm about to prove it to them all." A crazy glint lights his eyes, and he rolls up his sleeves. "They don't put you in the field without training. Let's see how much you remember."

He tosses the chair aside and draws his fist back for the first punch.

The fire from the bombing was hot on my back. Sweat rolled down my neck and I wanted to scratch it, but every second counted. I yanked my plasma rifle over my shoulder. Guards bolted out of the compound and aimed rifles at my team.

"Get ready!" Foster yelled, but the pounding of running feet and the roar of fire drowned out his voice.

A high-pitched whistle sounded to my left and another fire exploded near the outer wall. The ground rumbled, but I managed to keep my footing and train my rifle on the nearest guard. I fired. Hundreds of tiny blue bursts zipped across the field, as silent as night, impaling targets on both sides.

I shot my target center mass. The plasma burst sliced through and dissipated behind him in a shower of white particles. He dropped to his knees with a final grunt of air and then pitched forward until his face smacked the cement walk.

Group One of my team stopped to engage the line of outside guard protection while Groups Two and Three—Three being my group—slid through to take the inside of the compound.

Inside, the next line of compound defense was thinner than the first and my group had no problem leaving Group Two to handle them. Groups One and Two would get the children out once they were done here, while we cut off communication and set charges.

Foster nodded to a set of stone stairs. "Control room is that way."

"Let's go."

I knew the way thanks to the data collected on another raid. The layout was nearly identical to that of my last WTC. Top floor, fourth door on the left, surrounded by officers' quarters.

We passed the medical exam rooms on the way, and I pointed. "Here's where we'll set some of the charges on the way back."

Foster nodded and repeated the order to the rest of the team.

We collided with the group of remaining WTC officers in a wide hallway on the top floor. There were too many of us to fight effectively.

I took my first real blow in the shoulder, though my face had been the target. I doubled over and jabbed the butt of my rifle up into the man's gut. He grunted and I jerked the barrel up once more, this time to the face; his nose cracked seconds before blood gushed

over his mouth and chin. His eyes crossed and he wavered on
his feet.

"Wade!"

I ducked at the sound of Foster's warning, and not a moment too
soon. The swing had been aimed for the back of my head. Spinning, I
swung my foot at the man's ankles and brought him down to the floor
with a thunk. His head bounced off the concrete and I raised my fist
to finish the job.

I duck and avoid the punch. "What are you doing?" I scream.

"Fight back," Charles says.

He swings again, and this time, instead of ducking, I block with
my forearm. The sharp pain of our bones colliding brings hot tears
to my eyes. I block another punch automatically, and I have to admit, I do not know how I am able to do this.

"Fight!" he yells.

He asked for it, She says. *May as well give the man what he wants.*

I follow up the next block with a hook that pistons against his
cheekbone, snapping his head to the side. I ignore the flare of pain
in my knuckles as his fist thrusts up toward my stomach. I leap
back, narrowly missing the uppercut.

I snap my foot up and punt the side of his head, then use the
momentum to spin, jump, and kick again. On the third spin and
strike, he drops to a knee. His head bobbles on his neck and he
grapples out blindly for something to hold himself up.

The lounge door slides open, stopping me from continuing my
attack, and Charles lifts his head up to laugh at me. His whole
body shakes from it. "I knew it."

His deduction puts me into a state of shock so I do not dodge the uppercut to my stomach. All my air rushes out and I double over, gasping. Declan catches me before I drop to my knees.

"Get him the fuck out of here!" Declan yells to the mass of red coats. "And don't let him back in. Ever."

"You can't keep me away from my wife!" Charles's tone is a good match for Declan's. "I paid good money for her!"

"You revoked your right to your wife the second you attacked mine. Get out of here."

Charles fights several red coats, slinging blood from his heavily bleeding nose and spitting more across the room. "She fought back. I was right, you stupid bastard. You brought that traitorous bitch into your home and she'll burn it down around you." His eyes are wild and he grins. "And I'm going to stand by and watch it happen, laughing all the way."

CHAPTER 22

Bruises flower around my forearms and swell. Touching them hurts, but I am too numb to care about pain. I am numb to the exam room and Declan's faraway look and flaring nostrils. I am numb because I do not know who I am. And I cry, not from the pain, but from frustration.

Charles has made his point and I cannot help but wonder if he is right. Not about my hurting Declan. I would never hurt him. But what if I fought back because that was my life? Did I kill people so casually? Did I really fight with lethal force?

Declan presses a cold compress to my swollen forearm and lifts my free hand to hold the pack myself. His handsome face is little more than stern lines as he sits on the round stool beside the examination bed where I wait for Dr. Travista.

"Who am I?" I whisper.

"You're my wife."

His response stuns me. I am unsure what I expected, but it had nothing to do with my status as his wife. And something in his tone makes me wonder if this answer is more for his benefit than for mine. He avoids my eyes, watching his linked fingers and circling thumbs in his lap. He has long and soft fingers. Gentle.

Mine are small and deadly.

"Am I?" The question catches in my throat.

He looks at me now, and I cannot read his expression. Frustration? Anger? Sadness? "You're my wife." He stands from the stool so fast, the wheels send it rocketing across the room. It bounces off the cabinet with a *clang*. His hands come up to his hips, flaring open his suit jacket, and he begins pacing in front of me. "You can't listen to anything he said."

A sob escapes my tight chest, and I shake with it. "He said I would fight back and I did. I do not know how to fight. Right?"

He paces, continuing to avoid me.

"Right?" I repeat the question, louder this time. "Tell me and I will believe you."

He stops, his attention not on the floor, but somewhere far beyond it. "Right."

I do not believe him. He says this because I asked him to. Did I not do the same for him once? "Declan, I would never hurt you."

His eyes focus on me, and it is as if he is seeing me for the first time. His expression softens and he takes my hand. His lips press to the spot between my eyes, and a long, hot breath brushes my skin.

"Don't cry," he whispers. "I'm sorry. Of course you wouldn't hurt me."

"I am so confused." More than I can ever tell him.

"There's nothing to be confused about. You know who you are." He rolls the stool back over and sits. "Emma, even if there was a shred of truth to what he said, isn't the time we've spent together these last few months . . . doesn't it mean more than what that lunatic says? More than what's happening outside these walls?"

His chest heaves as he breathes in, his attention focused elsewhere again. He is so far away and I do not understand why.

I slide from the bed and onto his lap. I finger his loose hair back and gather my thoughts. "You are right," I whisper. "It does not matter."

Declan's arms surround me and gather me close. His heart beats rapidly against mine.

The answers I need no longer matter, because right now I know who I am, and nothing I have seen, and nothing Charles said, makes a difference.

I am Emma Burke.

I find Dr. Travista in his office and knock on the wall outside his open door. He peers over the rim of his glasses and smiles.

"Emma? I didn't expect to see you today. Did we have a session I forgot about?"

"No. I decided to come spend time with Ruby, but I cannot find her."

He stands and rounds his desk in the slow manner that tells me he needs a moment to choose his words. "Ruby has gone home. With her husband."

I start in surprise. "What? But she is not well yet."

He motions for me to sit in my usual chair and folds into his. "Declan refused to allow Charles Godfrey back in the hospital and he has a right to his wife. The only option was to release her and hope she'll continue to recover without our help."

I sink back into the soft cushion. I find her absence saddens me and realize it is because I considered Ruby a friend. Or, at the very least, one I might have had in the future, given enough time. "When? When did she leave?"

He removes his glasses and folds them into his lap. "The day after the incident."

I had not been able to bring myself to come these past few days as I tried to come to terms with everything that happened. "Oh," is all I manage to say.

"If it helps, she asked about you on the way out. You made a lasting impression, I think."

I nod, but this is not comforting. Charles will never allow her to contact me. "Maybe we will meet again."

He smiles, but it is quick and does not reach his eyes. "Since you're here, why don't you tell me about the show? Tomorrow's going to be a big day for you."

The show is the last thing concerning me. "I do not think about it."

"I see." His eyes narrow ever so slightly. "Since we're on the subject, I'm curious about these beaches of yours."

"Oh?" He and Declan both.

"You seem to have a lot of ideas for this theme. Declan said you were inspired by the photograph in your room. And yet you do not paint that particular beach."

I adjust my sitting position. "What makes you think that?"

"The photograph in your old room has the California gull in it."

I tilt my head. "I do not understand."

"You paint the Heermann's gull in its breeding plumage; dark gray with blackish wings and a white head. They breed off the west coast of Mexico. The photograph in your old room is of a beach in

Half Moon Bay, California. When seen that far north during its non-breeding season, the Heermann look wholly different, not to mention nothing like the California gull."

He is catching me on a seagull technicality? "Is not a seagull just a seagull?"

"If seen in the Bay during its non-breeding season, the Heermann's gull wouldn't have a white head. It would be a solid gray with blackish wings. The California gull is nearly all white with gray wings."

I attempt to laugh. "Okay. You caught me. Where are my paintings located?"

"Mexico, if I had to guess."

I nod. "Mexico."

"Mexico."

We are at a standoff. I cannot explain why I paint beaches in Mexico. And I will not tell him about my dreams.

"Maybe I saw them in a book."

He nods, but there is something in his expression that tells me he knows my lie for what it is. His lips twitch with a small smile. "Maybe."

We stare at each other for a while longer before I stand and wipe my palms over my pants. "I should go. I have an unfinished painting waiting on me."

He stands with me and walks me to the door. "I'll see you tomorrow."

I nod and lift my hand in a halfhearted wave. I do not see the men as I pass, and I enter the teleportation tube on automatic. My hand shakes as I key in the port number for my studio. My one safe harbor, because I do not know if Declan has had the security installed at home today as promised. My studio will forever remain unguarded.

The first thing I do in my studio is take up the tablet and punch in the instructions for the beach theme. One of them must have the gull I paint, even though I never pay these scenes any attention. They are no more than a backdrop while I paint from memory.

I run through several different holographic variations: seasons, time of day, locations, which are very few. Seagulls fly or amble along the beach in all of them, but none resembles the one I paint.

You have to be kidding me, She says. *He really did get you on a technicality. Unbelievable.*

Mexico?

She does not answer for several slow heartbeats. *Mexico.*

CHAPTER 23

I stand in front of my open closet—have been standing there for nearly thirty minutes—looking for an outfit suitable for tonight. I have nothing. How do I have nothing to wear to my own opening?

I warned you two weeks ago about this, She tells me.

Shut up.

"Emma?" Declan's voice startles me. It is the middle of the day and he should be at work.

"In here."

I step out of the room to find he is not alone. A young woman stands with him carrying what looks like a large toolbox. Her short hair is dyed practically white, with small chunks of black intermingled throughout. I think she might be younger than me by several years.

I glance curiously between them. "Who is this?"

"Paula is here to do your hair and makeup," he says and pushes her forward. "I'll be back in a couple hours."

I blink at him in surprise as he disappears into the teleporter tube with a wink.

"Ma'am? Where would you like to do this?"

I shake my head to clear it. "Oh, um, I do not know. The bathroom, I guess."

She follows me into the room and begins to set up on a large vanity table I never use. I am not accustomed to sitting to get ready, nor do I spend a lot of time on my hair or makeup.

But Declan thinks of everything. Sometimes too much.

Since my fight with Charles, I have given many things like this extra thought. On the vanity are bottles of lotions and creams of varying scents, and one in particular contains balsam of Peru. I am highly allergic and would never purchase such an item, a fact I only found out about when She warned me before applying.

I wonder about an accident they will not explain. A wedding I do not remember with a honeymoon I would have had to fly to get to. My husband would know I fear flying, would he not? He would not have been surprised when he learned I could paint. He would know my allergies. Declan is obviously not aware of these things, and being the attentive husband he is, he *would* know.

I have no idea what purpose these small lies hold, but I know I love him. I hate that I do. I hate that I stay knowing the past he speaks of may be a lie, but I cannot bring myself to question him or leave. I still know nothing of my life before, no more than the awful images of fighting and running and war. Why would I want to return to that? Declan has given me a safe home and he loves me. If I believe nothing else, I believe this.

But there is still one moment that calls to me. The beach. If only I could remember who the man is. He must wonder where I am. Foster must know, and if I find him, it will be my first question. Only one thing makes me question if the beach is a memory or a dream like I believed Foster to be. One look at the back of my hand is proof that I cannot be that woman on the beach. I have no brand.

"Is something wrong?"

I look up at Paula's reflection in the mirror and realize I have made a noise of frustration. "No, I am just deep in thought." I pull a smile together. "What will you be doing?"

She combs her fingers over my head and narrows her eyelids. "I love this cut, so let's leave it down, maybe angle it forward? As for makeup, I saw your dress—"

"I have a dress?" Declan really does think of everything. "What does it look like? Is it lovely?"

She smiles for the first time. "If you don't know what it looks like, I'm not spoiling the surprise." She comes around and opens her box. "It's more than lovely—I'll tell you that much. Your husband has excellent taste."

"Yes," I agree.

Paula clips my hair back and applies a moisturizer to my face. She is trying to match a concealer to my skin when I ask, "Do you like this job?"

She stiffens, so the soft chuckle she emits is obviously forced. "Come on," she whispers. "You know as well as I do that ending up in a job you love is rare. You ended up in a good position. You're lucky. And while I'm good at this job, I don't like it, no. This"—she motions to my overall head—"isn't so bad, but when I have to do some old guy's pedicure? I guess it could be worse. I could be a masseuse. Can you imagine rubbing all those nasty backs?" She shivers. "Gross."

"Are you not married?" I ask. "I only ask because I had an accident. I have no memory from before this past autumn. Declan does not tell me very much, and you make marriage sound like it is a job position."

She sits on the edge of the table and folds her arms. "Are you serious?"

I nod.

She nibbles on her lower lip, studying me. Finally, she says, "Marriage is for the fertile. They don't waste time marrying off the rest of us, and there's always some job that needs a woman to fill it, so at the very least we aren't wasted. You may have been lucky enough to end up in a marriage to the richest man this side of the Americas, but I'm glad I didn't end up where you are. I never wanted to lie down for some man because he bought me and that's my job. None of us do."

"You must want . . ." I search for the right word. "Companion-ship?"

She shrugs. "There are always ways to find that, but it's tough. How can you trust a man who says he really loves you when he could be using you just to get laid for free? Makes it hard to trust any of them."

She returns to applying my makeup. "What's it like?" she asks after a long moment. "Not remembering anything? I would give anything to forget those years in the WTC."

"It is difficult, actually," I say, wishing I could confide in her, but she is a complete stranger to me. "Some days I think I would give almost anything to remember. Other days I think it is best I do not."

"That's too bad. My advice? Let the past go. Don't force it, be-cause you have a good setup here. I almost believe your husband really loves you."

"Almost?"

She laughs. "Love is a myth."

Declan kisses my cheek when he comes home, careful not to smudge my heavily glossed lips. "You look beautiful."

"Too bad I have nothing to wear." I smirk and nod at the garment bag hanging over his arm. "Or do I?"

"Of course you do." He passes over the bag with a grin. "I'm going to shower and get ready."

I wait for the shower doors to slide closed before I unzip the bag. The dress is burnt orange with thin straps making up a halter neckline. I put it on, finding it soft against my skin and showing more cleavage than I am accustomed to with the low V neck. As if to offset this, the dress drapes against the floor *with* my heels on.

Declan strolls out in only a towel and a tilted grin. "Wow. That looks amazing on you. I knew it would."

I motion to my breasts. "Do you not think this is too much? Maybe I have a shawl or—"

"Oh, no you don't. You are *not* covering that dress up. I'll be the envy of every man in the room tonight."

I think he is about to kiss me, so I place a finger over his lips. "You will mess up my makeup."

"Later," he begins in a throaty tone, "the threat of makeup will not save you from me."

I laugh. "I should hope not."

He is ready in another twenty minutes, and we step out of the teleporter tube in the back of the gallery. The lights are dim except for the spotlights on each painting. Mr. Geist erected partition walls to hang more pieces, and the place resembles a maze rather

than an open room. Fabrics drape the ceiling in the colors of sun-
sets or midday or sunrise, depending on which area you stand in.
A holograph covers the floor, turning it into beach sand.

Mr. Geist appears from around a corner and raises a hand toward us. "Ah, there you are. The guests should be arriving any minute now. Don't forget to walk the room, mingle with them, talk
about what inspires you—"

Declan cuts him off with raised hands. "Yes, yes. She knows."

When Mr. Geist disappears after a waiter carrying champagne
flutes, Declan bends to whisper in my ear. "I think he's more nervous than you. Speaking of which, you look as cool as a cucumber.
Aren't you nervous?"

I smile. "Of course." My stomach aches from the knots it is
twisting.

"Well, you'd never know to look at you." His eyes widen suddenly and he mutters something under his breath. "I almost forgot." He reaches into a pocket and pulls out a small felt box. He
flips the lid back, and the largest set of diamonds wink up at me.
"Your wedding ring."

I gape at the ring and cannot move.

He laughs and reaches for my hand. "I had it custom made or
you would have had it a while ago. And it couldn't have come at a
better time. That dress deserves more jewelry."

He slides the ring on my finger and, while it is beautiful, his
joking manner does not hide the fact that the ring is no more than
a pair of handcuffs.

When did you start getting so cynical? She asks.

I wonder about this myself, but I know it happened the second
Paula mentioned how men cannot be trusted. And she is right.
How do I know Declan truly loves me? Maybe he only wants me

because he can get all the sex he wants as well as a house full of children.

It's a little late to think about this now, She says. *You made your choice.*

I know.

Declan smiles over my shoulder and I turn to see the first guests arrive. He does not leave my side no matter where the guests lead us. We must circle the room a hundred times, meeting new friends and acquaintances.

I am surprised to find I am not the only woman. But of course, all these men Declan knows can afford a wife. And beautiful ones, too. They are dressed in the finest of clothes and jewelry, smile and greet the room as if we are equal to our husbands. They put on a good show—I will give them that.

Then there are the members of Declan's board. Most are as gracious as the rest of the people I meet, but a few scrutinize me in ways that make me feel on display. It is with them I put on the most charm because I sense Declan's reaction to them. His entire body stiffens and does not relax until we move away from them.

I am exhausted after the first hour and growing tipsy from the champagne. I do not think I have released Declan's hand the entire time. He holds on to me as if he knows I need him to anchor me or I will run from these people who pay me far too many compliments and spend far too much money on my work.

To my surprise, the pieces begin to sell quickly, and it is the one from the window, the one I would never part with had I been given the choice, that nearly breaks me. A fissure spreads through my heart when the gallery manager drapes a satin tie over one corner, signaling its sale. I decide right there on the spot to paint another one first thing tomorrow.

"I'm surprised that one lasted so long," Declan whispers, nodding toward it. "I hear there was a private bidding war, though."

"Really?" I wonder how he knows and I do not, but there have been plenty of moments when we have had separate conversations while standing right beside each other.

He nods toward a group of men long into the champagne—their guffaws are proof of that. One of the men tilts back to laugh and another man suddenly comes into full view. A man I know all too well.

It is a good thing I am holding on to Declan; otherwise, I might have dropped to the floor. I consider letting go and running instead. At the very least, I beg my eyes to look *anywhere* else.

By the time I regain control, it is too late. He spots me and raises a glass in a silent toast. There is something different about him tonight. Something I am completely unaccustomed to.

Noah is smiling at me.

CHAPTER 24

Heart drumming hard enough to crack my rib cage, I shift my gaze up to Declan and turn my back to the room. "Can we walk? My feet hurt from standing here." I need to get as far away from Noah as possible. Anywhere where I can think and not have to look at him at the same time.

"Oh. I didn't know he came." Declan nods and smiles at someone behind me. Running straight for the exit becomes a viable option. "He must have showed up late. Let me introduce you to Tucker first, okay, love?"

My heart collapses in on itself. Shrivels. Dries up. *No.* I pray to whatever god is listening to let this be a coincidence. Noah, my dream captor and grieving man, cannot be Tucker. The juxtaposition of the two entities does not make sense as one.

"Tucker," Declan says, and I know without turning that he must have approached us. "I'm glad you decided to come."

"My other plans fell through." The voice definitely belongs to Noah, but I cannot yet be sure he sounds like Tucker from my dreams. In my dreams Tucker is soft-spoken, whereas I have heard nothing but harshness from Noah. Anger. And right now, the confidence of a man who exudes arrogance. "This must be the beautiful wife I've heard so much about."

I blink away sudden tears and straighten my expression before turning. When I face him, I pull together the same smile I have managed to shine all night. I have never seen him this close before. Lines fan from the corners of his amber eyes and he has shaved for the occasion. The shorter cut he wears is not spiky and messy but combed back. What surprises me is how nice he smells. The faint musk suits him. I have grown used to Declan's bolder musk but find Noah's scent more to my liking.

"Emma," Declan says, "this is Noah Tucker. He owns Tucker Securities."

I reach forward on automatic to shake his hand. "It is nice to put a face to the name, Mr. Tucker."

Noah takes my offered hand, and it is as if electricity has jolted up my arm. His touch steals my breath. Halts my heartbeat. If I had not been studiously watching his face, I would have missed the minute flinch in his own expression.

But as quickly as it was there, it is gone, and he is back to looking at me as if we are strangers. Surely if I were Emma Wade in my past, and he my lover, there would be something other than polite interest shining in his eyes. Especially considering the love that burns as real as any flame in my heart.

I was frustrated at never seeing Tucker's face in the dreams before, but the feeling now is astronomical.

Noah's gaze seems entwined with mine, neither of us able to tear away. "Your husband speaks very highly of you." I note how the smile he wears does not meet his eyes. "Your work is impressive. Are you self-taught?"

"Yes," I say. This is my standard answer, since I do not know, nor do I believe they teach art classes at any WTC.

"What inspired you? Did you vacation somewhere in particular to get these images?"

Declan steps in here. "A single photograph started this, if you can believe that. She has quite the imagination."

Noah nods, but his amber gaze stays glued to me. "That she does. Anyway, I should let you get back to your guests. It was nice to finally meet you, Mrs. Burke."

With a final nod to each of us, he turns and rejoins the group of guffawing men. I do not realize how tense I have become until he is gone.

"Let's take that walk," Declan says.

Noah is everywhere I look.

Declan and I move to one side of the room and then Noah does. Another side, there he is again. He watches me from the corner of his eyes. Watches me watching him. I am determined to hide my anxiety with my practiced expression of impassivity and a straightened spine. I hold my champagne flute but do not drink now, in order to keep a clear head. Until I know his purpose, I will be prepared for anything.

"Declan," a man says upon his approach. His thinning hair is solid white, but his face is strangely unmarked by age.

Declan flashes the man his perfect smile. "Richard. Glad you could make it, though I think you've missed the best opportunities."

Richard glances around. "So it would seem." His attention falls on me. "This must be your wife."

Declan places a gentle hand on my back. "Emma, this is Richard Farris. He's an old colleague of mine."

I shake Richard's hand, and his smile is kind. "Nice to meet you."

Richard shifts his attention back to Declan and says, "I heard about Charles and Ruby."

"Hm," is all Declan says and rocks slightly on the balls of his feet.

"I would love to talk to you and Arthur if you have time."

"Arthur couldn't make it tonight. A close friend of his died unexpectedly."

This is the first I am hearing of this. I had not realized Dr. Travista never showed, either. "That is terrible," I say.

Richard nods in agreement. "I assume Jodi finally . . ."

"Yes."

It takes everything I have to remain unaffected. Jodi has died, and while I never knew her, I feel sadness. Maybe it is for the best, though, given her situation.

Richard's expression is as grim as I feel. "I suppose I will call your office for an appointment, then."

Declan eyes me for the space of a heartbeat. "I have a moment right now, and you can schedule with Arthur tomorrow. Emma, will you be all right by yourself for a minute or two?"

I nod. "Of course."

The two men walk away from me, and I realize how cool the room is now that I stand alone for the first time. A shiver runs down my spine, and I run my now free palm over my opposite arm. I sip the tiniest of sips of champagne just for something to do. Everyone around me is engrossed in conversation and unaware that I stand alone.

I catch Noah's eye just then and decide to move deeper into the maze of people and partition walls. I nod and thank anyone who compliments me on the way, but still no one wishes to hold a conversation without Declan present. I catch the eyes of a few wives who nod but do not dare start up a conversation. Not alone. I have come to realize this is not done.

Declan's voice pulls me to a stop. People melt away from the area, and I realize it is not because of me, but because of the private moment taking place on the other side of the partition. Without any conscious thought, I stand in front of one of my paintings, focus my gaze on the luckenbooth painted in the sand, and listen intently to the sound of my husband's muffled voice.

"You understand she cannot bear children for a while," he says, voice low and buried under the din of conversation and laughter filling the room. I step closer to the painting to hear better. "Charles fought this from the moment she awakened."

"Patience was never his strong suit," Richard says. "How long is Arthur's estimate?"

"Only a few months."

"I see." There is a long pause. "I would love to bring Lydia in for a consultation. If she were a good candidate for the trial, well, I don't have to tell you how well we work together. This could benefit both of us."

"If you're referring to the board, I could use any help you would be willing to provide. They're still wary and need results. The situation with Charles set me back months."

"Don't worry so much about them, Declan. They're still loyal to your father. One day they'll see how you're already surpassing him.

Tonight's outing will sway more than a few of them; I'd stake my entire net worth on it."

A warm breath caresses my ear, sending a shiver racing down my spine. "The luckenbooth was a nice touch, Mrs. Burke."

My fingers tighten around my champagne glass, and every muscle in my body tenses. Inside, my belly is a swarm of locusts. No one in this room has noticed the hearts I know only from a memory of a man I have loved and lost somehow. No one but this man.

Noah.

I cannot bring myself to turn and face him. "Glad you approve." His presence puts me in a stranglehold, and my voice comes out just above a whisper.

He moves to stand beside me now. His scent overwhelms my senses to the point of dizziness. The sleeve of his suit brushing my arm is like fire. Still, I hold my gaze on the luckenbooth, fearing that if I look at him this close, everything inside me might burst forth like a flood.

His hand touches my elbow, and his gaze burns into my skin.

He is close. So close.

His champagne glass inclines toward the next partition. "Shall we?"

I hesitate to respond, but he does not wait for me to. He nudges me gently and I have to communicate to my feet that I must walk or fall over. The last thing I want is to draw Declan's attention to my eavesdropping, which I am ashamed to admit makes me curious about far too many things.

Noah follows alongside me and we stop in front of the next painting. On the beach lay indigo petals leading to a receding tide. A seagull stands on one foot with a single petal in its mouth. This is a replica of my very first painting, only I left out the arch wrapped in soft fabric.

He leans in, and my attention falls instantly to his lips as he says, "I always loved the ocean."

Despite his last name and the memories associated with it, he is still Noah. The man who attempted to kill me in a memory I cannot make sense of. I am wary of his intensions and do not want to share anything with him, let alone my precious beaches, but he has information I need and hope to get at some point. Remaining civil is the only course of action I have. "Have you spent much time there?"

He shifts his attention back to the painting and draws in a deep breath. His chin falls for only a moment, and when he looks at me again, I am surprised to see the tilted grin on his face. His amber eyes watch me steadily for every nuance. "Have you?"

Why does he continue with this charade? I know why I do; I have no reason to trust him yet. I need to know who I am dealing with—Noah or Tucker—before I give anything away. But him? What is *his* excuse?

"No. Maybe someday." I avert my eyes, finding it too hard to stop looking at his lips. His eyes have an even worse effect on me. Instead, I find a much needed peace in the luckenbooth hidden in the brushstrokes.

"You realize you won't find a beach like this in the Americas—West or otherwise."

I nod. "War is a devastating thing, but in Mex—" I stop abruptly. I cannot trust this man not to tell Declan I paint a beach in Mexico. I have been too careful to hide this since coming to this realization.

He tilts his head as if trying to hear the words I refuse to say.

"You *are* painting a specific place. Why does your husband believe your inspiration comes from a photograph?"

My heart beats erratically. "Dr. Travista says the photograph was taken in California. So I suppose you could say I do paint from a specific location."

"That's not what you were going to say." He steps closer. The musk on his skin stirs heat in my stomach.

I lengthen my spine, and as much as I want to put space between us, I will not show him fear. Unfortunately, the way he leans toward me, this nearly puts us nose to nose.

"Tell me," he says in a voice low and even.

I know now I am seeing the side of this man I have no interest in dealing with. The side that can be violently angry. Noah. Not Tucker.

"No." I do not know why I say it, but it is out and there is nothing I can do about it.

His eyes burn holes through me for a protracted moment. Finally, he takes my champagne flute and sets both his and mine on a passing tray of full glasses. Before I can voice my disapproval, he leads me once again through the room and into a brightly lit corridor. We are surrounded by doors, a few leading to offices. We are also out of sight and earshot.

Alone.

"Mr. Tucker—"

Noah's arm moves like a shot to pin me to the wall. My head bounces off the surface, blurring my vision. I feel cool metal pressed to my forehead before I see the gun.

His eyes are unwavering as they look into mine. There is no mistaking the bloodlust in them. "Tell me, Mrs. Burke, what do you know about Mexico?"

CHAPTER 25

My breath stills and I hear nothing more than blood rushing like a raging rapid through my ears. Noah Tucker is going to kill me.

Talk to him, She tells me. *Talk or you're dead.*

"Noah," I plead in a whisper. Less than a whisper. A wisp of breath. I blink away tears to see him clearly. "Please."

There is only a moment—a very small one—in which the gun slips down, and Noah reaffirms his grip to bring it back up. A war of emotions collides in his bright amber eyes, which I do not understand, like he cannot decide what to do, or he knows and does not want to do it.

"Please," I say again, and my voice quivers. "I know nothing about Mexico."

"Nothing?" His voice sounds tight, as if he has to strain to get it to work. "There's an entire room out there that proves otherwise."

"And you would kill me for it?"

He presses the barrel of the gun farther into my skull. I see a shift in his eyes then and know he is decided. "I would kill you for simply drawing breath."

"Wh-what? Why?"

He shakes his head once. His jaw clenches. "What are your orders?"

"I do not understand. There are no orders."

"Bullshit. You're here for a reason. Did you think you could slide right back into place?"

"Into what place?"

"With the resistance."

This is about the *resistance*? Heat floods my face and I clench my fists. Charles accused me of this as well. I am tired of standing trial for this past I do not remember. It is my future I care about, and I would never work with the resistance to hurt my husband. I would die first.

"You know nothing about me," I tell him through gritted teeth.

Anger compels me to act now. I swipe my hand up to his wrist, and the gun is off me before he can react. I twist our bodies around and slam him face-first into the wall. He spins around and I drive my knee up hard between his legs. He doubles over with a pained moan. I take the gun from his loosened grip and run toward the safety of the main room.

In the dim lighting of the exhibit, I slow and cover the weapon in my skirts. No one pays me any mind, and for once, I am grateful. I am breathing too hard, and sweat tickles my brow.

I find a decorative vase to my right that stands to my waist. I drop Noah's gun inside. There is a loud *clang*, but the music playing in the speakers muffles the sound.

Though free of the weapon, I will not feel safe until I find Declan and tell him about—

My chest tightens at the mere idea of telling Declan what Noah has done. I have not felt this since those early days when She prevented me from talking about my dreams. My dreams of Noah. Even now, after what he has done, She would protect him.

But I cannot let him get away with this. I do not care what She thinks. I stop a waiter and open my mouth to ask for security, but suddenly there is no air to breathe. I cannot make a single sound, let alone speak. My face grows warm from exertion.

Don't even think about it, She warns. *Trust me on this.*

I hate Her in this moment.

"Ma'am?" he says.

Noah appears and takes two glasses of champagne off the waiter's tray. "Thank you," he tells the young man in a dismissive tone. The waiter leaves and I am abruptly able to breathe.

Noah turns to face me with an expression that is almost friendly. He plays for any audience we may have in the room, but his eyes reveal the same bloodlust from the hallway. I am not fooled.

"You let me live," he says.

"And you tried to kill me."

"Give me my gun. I'll try again."

I raise my hands to show they are empty.

He shrugs. "I don't need a gun to kill you."

"You would not dare in a room full of Declan's closest friends and acquaintances."

He lifts his chin in a half nod, then steps very close to me. He hands me a champagne flute. "Tell me something, Mrs. Burke. My intentions to kill you are clear, yet you have not run screaming for help . . . in this . . . 'room full of Declan's closest friends and acquaintances.'"

I cannot tell him that my very own invisible friend prevents me. Even I find it hard to believe, and I am the one who experiences it. "I need answers," I tell him instead. It is the truth, at least.

He lifts the glass to his lips with a smile that does not touch his eyes. "Funny. So do I."

"I have none."

"Don't think to play me, Mrs. Burke. I don't need the answers that badly."

Neither of us has a chance to say anything more, because an arm slips around my waist and Declan's strong musk overpowers Noah's. Relief floods me so fast I fear I will faint.

"There you are," Declan says. "Sorry that took so long."

I hold Noah's gaze for a long moment before smiling up at my husband. "Mr. Tucker was just keeping me company."

"I was telling your wife how much I appreciate her style," Noah adds. "There's just something about the way she captures the simplicity of a drift of sand."

"Do you have a favorite?" Declan asks.

Noah nods once. "As a matter of fact, I won a private bidding war over it. The one that's been in the window the entire month."

I am sick to find out he will have his hands on my painting.

Declan laughs from somewhere deep in his chest, and the sound carries around us until it draws the attention of several people. "So you're the lucky man. Emma won't admit it, but I think that was her favorite. You should have seen her face when she found out it was sold."

Noah catches my eye again. "I'd be happy to let it go if you can't part with it."

I force a smile to my face. "No. Please take it. You worked hard for it, or so I hear. Practically killed for it. I can paint a thousand more just like it."

Noah inclines his head to me, a smile twitching his lips. "In that case, I'm happy to keep it. I promise to take care of it as if it were my own creation." He leans close and adds conspiratorially, "Or at least as if I shared in the process."

I feel as if I have been slapped with my own memory. By Tucker. *There. What do you think? An original by Emma and—*

Oh, no you don't. You aren't claiming my work. An original by Emma and Emma alone.

The smile I give him is tight-lipped because I can no longer manage anything more. He has unraveled me to my very center. I would not tell Declan about how Noah wants to kill me even if I could. Noah knows much more than he is letting on. I know he does.

"Well," Noah finally says, "I should get going. I have an early morning."

Declan extends a hand. "Don't be a stranger, Tuck."

"Mr. Tucker does not like this nickname," I say automatically and wish for nothing more than to be able to take the words back. I cannot imagine what possessed me to say such a thing.

Both men stare at me with wide eyes. Declan looks mildly amused, but the color has drained from Noah's face. His jaw hangs slightly ajar.

Declan glances between us. "When did you become privy to the innermost secrets of Mr. Tucker's mind?"

I clear my throat, hoping they do not notice the creeping of red I feel splotching my chest and neck.

"I mentioned it a few minutes ago in conversation," Noah says, his gaze pinned to me with such ferocity, it is a wonder it has not slung me across the room.

I understand in this moment that I have been given a temporary stay of execution. Bloodlust has been replaced with questions he would rather have answered.

"I'll be in touch," Noah says, and his focus is on Declan, but his words . . . Those are for me.

CHAPTER 26

Dr. Travista removes his glasses and tilts his head. "I haven't seen you this tired since you suffered from your nightmares."

I touch the soft skin under my eye, recalling the bruised look in the mirror. Sleep had been difficult to achieve, and when I did finally slip into oblivion, I dreamed of Noah and our conversation at the gallery show. He put a gun to my head, but instead of hesitating, he pulled the trigger.

"Long night," I say and study the office I now know every nook and cranny of. Every warped shelf weighted with books. The unraveling piece of the carpet near the right foot of his chair.

"An exciting night," he adds, and his smile does not touch his bloodshot eyes. "I'm sorry I missed it. Declan says all of your paintings sold."

I nod. "The theme was popular. Mr. Geist says it was because no one ever gets to see the beach like that anymore. Not since the war and separation of states."

"Unless, of course, they want to travel to Mexico." He says this easily, as if this is not loaded with accusation.

"I suppose you are right," I say with a shrug. "Maybe one day I can travel there, see it for myself."

He slides his glasses back on and taps something into his tablet. I grow tired of these sessions, his incessant typing about me as if I am a mental patient. Why does he insist our time together continue? Am I not perfectly healthy now?

"Why am I here?" I ask before I can stop myself. Exhaustion is not conducive to my usual patience. "I feel I am fully recovered from my accident—an accident I would like you to tell me about."

His gaze snaps up to look at me through his lashes, but he is careful to maintain a neutral expression. "You are healthy," he says and is slow to remove his glasses. "But you have yet to recover any memories." The muscles around his lips twitch slightly, and he looks down at his folded hands. "As for your accident, well, let's just say it's a miracle you're alive."

I want to ask why he was so quick to find fault in my remembering seagulls in Mexico if he is so eager for me to get my memories back, but this is the closest he has come to telling me *anything* about my accident.

"What happened to me?" I press. "Maybe if you tell me, I will begin to remember things."

He taps his fingers on the leather arm of his chair, watching but not seeing them. He nibbles on the inside of his lip for a moment, then says, "The events of your accident were very traumatic, Emma. We only want to protect you."

I lean forward and brace my elbows on my knees. I try to catch his eyes, but he avoids them. "I wish to know."

A buzzing sound on his desk startles both of us until we realize it is only his phone. He stands and lifts the thin receiver to his ear, saying nothing. Instead, he listens to the muffled voice on the other end and nods several times. His gaze is pinned to the digital frame he has moved from the bookcase to his desk. The rotating pictures of Jodi.

The speaker must not have a lot to say; nor does he require a response, because Dr. Travista is off the phone without a word in less than ten seconds.

He raises his bushy eyebrows at me, and there is a slight pout to his lower lip. Finally, he says, "That was your husband. He says to tell you that you and he will speak about this later. He wishes to tell you himself."

I stand and lift my chin. "Fine. Then I guess we are done here."

I am spinning to leave when he says, "Emma, we just started our session."

"And I am ending it."

I do not wait for him to respond. I am aggravated and tired and do not trust myself to hold my temper. It is not as if I have not gained ground, but I do not wish to wait for Declan to arrive at home tonight to learn this. I was only seconds from getting Dr. Travista to tell me. I am tired of everything being on their time.

I come to the epicenter of the hallways when a voice I recognize makes me stop. Richard Farris, the man whose conversation with Declan last night I heard only part of thanks to Noah Tucker. With all the excitement, I had almost forgotten how he wanted to meet with Declan about some trial.

"You didn't have to meet us here," Richard says. "We would have come to your office."

"Not necessary."

Declan? I peer around the corner to see Declan, Richard, and a petite woman with long auburn hair pinned up in a chignon. She cannot be much older than me, which makes her roughly twenty years younger than her own husband. She smiles easily between the two men but says nothing. This must be Richard's wife, Lydia.

Richard and Lydia had come out of the transportation room, but Declan did not, which makes me wonder if he has been in the building the entire time. He was *just* on the phone with Dr. Travista. Watching me. And Richard had said "your office," which can only mean my husband keeps an office in this building.

Declan shakes Richard's hand and nods in my direction, forcing me to duck back. "Shall we get started? Arthur will meet with us after his session with Emma. I can at least give you the basic tour, and then Arthur can give you the details."

I peek back around, and he is smiling at Lydia. "How about I show you to the lounge?"

Richard rubs a hand over her back. "Actually, Lydia is well aware of what we're talking about and is a willing participant."

Declan's eyebrows rise high on his forehead. "Is that right?"

She nods. "I was devastated when I heard I couldn't have more children, Mr. Burke. If your doctor can help me, I will do whatever it takes."

My jaw drops before I can stop it. Dr. Travista has cured the fertility issue?

Declan laughs a short burst of sound. "Well, that's good to hear. It will certainly make Arthur's job a lot easier."

Easier how?

She smiles and takes her husband's hand. "I aim to please."

I blink in surprise.

Stepford wife, She says.

I nod in agreement, though I do not know to what she refers.

She always reacts with annoyance when I ask, and right now it does not matter in the face of this new situation. Lydia is nothing like Paula the hairdresser, who says none of us ends up where we want to. She ended up *exactly* where she wanted. Maybe like me, she has a husband who loves her. Maybe she wants to give him a large family because she truly loves him.

Or she's a very good actress, She says.

Maybe, I say, but I do not believe it.

I consider revealing myself; I want to look right into this woman's eyes and search for any sign she could be lying. I even attempt to shift my foot forward but find my muscles are locked.

Do you really need a lesson in covert operations? She says. *Don't let them see you.*

I step away from the corner without question and duck into an unused hospital room. It is several minutes before their voices amble by, and I wait a couple more before stepping back out. The way is clear and I head home to await my husband and hopefully the truth about my accident.

The mattress dipping beside me wakes me from a deep sleep. I cannot remember dreaming, which is nothing short of a miracle. I am lying on my stomach with my pillow clutched in my arms under my head. When I open my eyes, it is to see the failing light outside the glass wall. The remaining day's light makes the snow sparkle in muted reds and oranges and yellows. It feels wrong to mute colors such as these.

I blink dry eyes and find my body is still too weary to fully wake. Not even for Declan, who runs a hand over my back. I cannot even find the energy to greet him.

"You left your session today," he says, and I cannot tell if he is annoyed, but he is definitely not amused. "Emma, you can't do that."

I roll to my back and cover my face with my palms. "I know. I was just so tired. I will apologize to Dr. Travista tomorrow."

"I think that's a good idea. He has a tight schedule, so to walk out as if his time is a waste of yours is insulting."

Annoyance sparks heat in my chest. I come up on my elbows and eye him narrowly. "I said I will apologize to him, Declan."

His lips draw scarce and his shoulders lift with a deep inhalation. "Emma, it's been a long day and my patience is thin."

I scoot down to drop off the end of the bed. "That makes two of us."

"Lights," I say inside the bathroom and blink against the sudden brightness.

I run the tap to splash cold water over my face and rinse out my mouth. When I rise back up and grab a towel to dry my face, Declan's reflection stares at me with arms folded, shoulder pressed into the door's frame. His expression tells me nothing about his mood, but I am not used to this unsmiling Declan. He can usually summon *something* for me.

I pat my face with the thick hand towel. "Have you changed your mind about telling me?"

His gaze drops to the floor. "No."

My stomach tightens and I clutch the towel tighter with quivering hands. I almost want to tell him to forget it because they make it sound like such a horrific incident. Maybe I will be better off not knowing.

Replacing the towel, I turn and lean into the sink. "So? What happened?"

Declan sighs and turns, loosening his tie. He goes through the agonizing process of undressing down to his undershirt and pants before saying, "Remember the attack you saw in the news scroll?"

I recall the scrolling headlines of the *Richmond Times* newspaper. BURKE ENTERPRISES BACK UP AND RUNNING AFTER LARGEST ATTACK TO DATE. Declan had gotten upset about it.

He throws a sweater over his head—thin rather than the thicker versions he usually prefers, and light blue. The neck dips in a V to show the white undershirt. "That same group—the resistance—went after you," he finally says. He pauses. Takes a deep breath. "You were just another attack on me."

CHAPTER 27

I stiffen toward my husband, who is having a hard time meeting my eyes. Finally, he takes my hand and pulls me from the bedroom. A fire rages and crackles in the fireplace already. He leads me to the couch and leaves me to tend the fire, which does not need tending. He kneels and jabs a poker into the glowing embers. Sparks fly and explode; logs snap. The orange blaze reflects in his unblinking eyes and flickers over his skin, at war with the shadows there.

"They took you from our home," he says. "We lived in the suburbs of Richmond. Gated community, parks, swimming pool in the backyard. You loved it there. I thought you were safe there." He glances around the living room, careful to avoid my eyes. "This was only a vacation home."

"What happened?" I cannot get my voice to rise above a whisper. I am shocked to hear how my accident had something to do with the resistance. The very group I stand accused of working with in my past.

Declan stands and leans into the brick over the fireplace with a single hand. His eyes never leave the fire itself. The muscle working furiously in his jaw distracts me from the fact that it is taking him a long time to answer. "They left you for me to find: broken, scarred beyond recognition . . . paralyzed and lying in a pool of your own blood." He closes his eyes. "They raped you."

My body grows numb, detached, like he is speaking of something vile happening to someone else. Not me. I repeat the words in my head. Broken. Scarred. Paralyzed. Raped.

Emma, She says in a warning tone. *You can't listen to this.*

But I am not listening to Her. The phrase "they raped you" is on repeat in my mind. Especially the last word. "You." He said "you," and my mind races to exchange the word with "her." "You" does not feel right, except he *did* say it. He means me.

Me?

I run mental fingers throughout my entire body, doing an internal examination, searching for evidence of this violation, but come up empty.

Someone violated me in the most personal of ways. Left me for dead.

I clutch at my stomach, sick, and cannot look at him. I cannot stop blinking, as if this will clear my vision of these horrors he speaks of. And now certain things make sense: Declan was so careful with me in the beginning. Hesitant to touch me. Kiss me. Letting our first time making love be my decision.

He runs a hand over his jaw and sighs. Looks away. "Emma, I tried protecting you from this. I'm so sorry."

I nod, but the movement feels like it comes from someone else's body. "How—" I stop and clear my throat. "How am I"—I look down at the perfect skin of my hands—"like this? Walking? Without scars?" *Without the luckenbooth,* I add silently.

"What Arthur did was highly experimental, but it worked. And you're fine. With the exception of your missing memories— probably due to the trauma—there's absolutely nothing wrong with you."

Except I do have memories. Memories that contradict every word he says to me. Memories of a life nowhere near suburbia or him. Far from it, in fact.

Makes you wonder, doesn't it? She says.

Makes me wonder who to trust, I say. *You feed me the memories.*

She says nothing to defend Herself.

The couch dips beside me and I swivel toward Declan. He watches me in that careful way of his. Waits for me to lead him. Will I accept, question, freak out? I do not know which to choose. Maybe all three.

I study his face, all traces of his earlier annoyance gone. "Where did they leave me?" I ask.

His eyes lower and there is the tiniest pulse of muscle below one eye. "You were missing for more than a day. They left you on the side of the road in our neighborhood." He does not elaborate any further.

"And you found me?" I need answers. Details. Proof. I need him to tell me what to believe.

He turns to face forward and nods. Stares down at his clasped hands.

"Do you not travel by teleporter?"

"Yes. Now I do. I didn't always."

"What else did they do? You said I was scarred? How? Where?"

"Emma, you may not remember the details, but I do." His voice is strained and he closes his eyes. "I understand you have a lot of questions, but is having these details that important to you?"

I stand, wiping my sweaty palms over my pants. How can he ask that? It is selfish of him to keep all the answers. I understand it is painful for him to remember me like that, but this is not about him. This is about me and a past I want—no, *need*—to remember. But more than that, I do not know whom to trust.

But I cannot say this to him, because if I do we will end up fighting, and I do not want to fight with him. Not right now. My urge to be alone is overwhelming. I have to think. I have to make sense of what he has told me versus what She shows me. I need to find the truth in the jumbled mess and black holes that are my mind. And I cannot do this with him watching me.

I round the couch and lift a coat from a hook near the teleporter. It is a small, puffy white thing that I have never worn, as I never go outside the house. I shove inside it and am zipped completely before Declan stands before me, watching all this with narrowed eyes.

"What are you doing?" he asks.

"I am going outside." I will not let him control this situation like he does everything else. I never usually mind, but this time is different.

He shakes his head. "Emma, I don't think that's—"

"I *am* going outside," I say and force my feet into matching boots. My jaw aches from clenching my teeth and my skin flushes with angry heat. "I need to be alone. I need to walk and think and I need you to not watch me do it for once."

He opens and then promptly closes his mouth. After a moment, he nods. "Okay, but as for the security feed—"

I huff out a frustrated breath. "You never let me out of your sight. I cannot do anything without you watching over my shoulder. Do you not ever just want to be completely alone? I want space to scream and cry and yell if I feel the need, and I do not want you watching me do it." Tears race from my eyes before I can stop them. "Please. Just leave me alone for once. We are isolated from the world up here. What harm is there?"

His eyes dart back and forth over my face, his lips thin. "You're right," he finally says. He looks down and away, blinking rapidly. He breathes out slowly. "You should be alone. It's just that you're my entire world, Emma. I have a hard time giving you freedom because I can't lose you. Not again."

He shakes his head as if to clear it. "Don't listen to me. Try not to be too long, and stay close. There are some rocky cliffs to the west. They aren't far and they're dangerous. They could be icy. Not to mention the daylight is waning."

I do not respond and I stride over to the sliding glass on the other side of the dining room table. I yank it aside and barely give myself time to react to the shock of cold before stepping out onto the pale wood of the outside decking. It is amazing to me how this house with all its glass can manage to hold the heat.

"Emma, wait," Declan calls out.

I turn to find him jogging toward me with something in his hands. When he is near, I recognize the white beanie and gloves. He wordlessly pulls the hat down over my head. I take the gloves and he lifts my chin, his eyes intense as they look into mine. Finally, he leans down to kiss me. His warm lips press softly and linger. His palms cup my cheeks. When he pulls away, his thumbs blot the remaining trails of tears.

"Please be careful," he whispers.

I nod and turn away from him, pushing my hands into the gloves. The glass slides shut behind me, and though the sound is soft, it makes me jump. While the idea of being out here had seemed like a good idea before, I suddenly realize what I am in for. The deck is wide and circles the house. Deck furniture sits under the overhang against the outer walls with a light dusting of snow. But where the overhang ends, where the wind can only push it so far, the thick snow forms a nearly perfect line.

I stop with my toes kissing this soft edge, but only long enough to take a deep breath. There is nothing to fear from the snow. It is only frozen water. I will not find any dead bodies out here. Just a perfect spread of untouched winter. Winter has its own beauty, does it not? The way the snow shimmers like diamonds in the failing sunlight?

I make my first foot impression in the snow. Then my second. And I keep going until cold seeps through my boots and blankets my toes. And still I continue. I focus on the sounds of my feet crunching the perfect surface with each step and try to slow my heart to my slower-paced steps. I watch my breath crystallize into clouds before my eyes and disappear in time for the next cloud to materialize.

I reach the tree line and find the snow thinner and in patches. The dense woods make it difficult for the snow to penetrate. Inside the cluster, my lungs expand to breathe to their fullest capacity, overwhelming my senses with the scent of juniper trees. Each step crunches, not with snow, but with fallen needles and branches.

Though frozen to my core, I am already calmer. Clearer headed. I just wish my urge to cry and the ache in my throat would go away. I do not want to cry. I do not want to feel so emotionally unbalanced, but it is hard when I just found out what those people did to me.

What the resistance did to me.

The resistance Charles Godfrey accused me of working with? The same resistance Noah Tucker would kill me to prevent me from becoming a part of again? Is Noah part of this resistance as well? He wanted to know what my orders were as if I received them from outside the group, not within it. As if the orders were to infiltrate in some way.

Did you think you could slide right back into place?

He abhorred the idea, but not in the way Charles had. He acted as if I were a traitor.

Foster trusted me. *You talk a good game, but when it comes down to it, you're doing what you were meant to do. You were born for this.*

If I am to believe these dream memories, I trusted him, too. That, and he did not try to kill me in the gallery last month. He did not alert the troops in his shock.

Or did he?

Maybe Foster is the reason Noah knew where to find me and when. The idea of Foster giving me up feels like the deepest of betrayals. I sense from the dreams he is my closest friend, but the truth is, I do not know him.

I do not know myself. I do not know what I have done to deserve a death sentence that has failed twice now—I have to believe the rape and torture was their first attempt. Somehow Declan saved me, only the resistance did not know until Foster found me in the gallery.

Who am I supposed to trust? This voice in my head showing me a life I cannot make sense of? She protects these people with a fierceness that would kill us both if I so much as breathe a word against them.

Or should I trust my husband, whom I love, but who also tells me things that contradict everything I have come to believe is

real? He lies about something as simple as the length of our marriage. What else does he lie about?

In my mind's eye, I see Declan's heartache while recalling the
memories of finding me. He seemed so sincere. And yet, he has
seemed sincere from the very beginning.

If there is anyone I know for certain I cannot trust, it is Noah.
He had his chance to explain how he knew me at the gallery, but
he didn't. Why is that? To protect himself, no doubt. He does not
know I remember how he kept me in a tank of water. I was conscious of my surroundings, thinking clearly, so why? I can think of
no medical reason no matter how often Sonya referred to me as a
patient.

The tree line comes to an end and a wide chasm spreads out
before me. Mountains rise and fall all around, dark with shadow
on the side the setting sun does not touch. Gray rocks erupt from
the snow in front of me and form jagged edges as well as smooth
ones. They do not look icy, and I want to see over the side, so I tread
carefully with arms out to balance myself.

A lake lies below. Not far, either. Farther to my right, the side of
the mountain slopes in an easy trail to the water. When the
weather warms, the lake will be my first destination. Right now,
though, there is a layer of ice over the surface. The surface turns
black in the growing night, and I decide it is time to head back. Or
at least get away from the edge.

I shiver involuntarily as I picture how falling over the side
would mean ending up crashing into the frozen lake. Would the
ice freeze over me? Trap me underwater? That would be a tortur-
ous way to die.

I pull to an abrupt halt and freeze. That is it. The reason for the
tank. Torture. Declan said they tortured me. Was the water a part

of it? In my memory I cannot move. It is as if I am paralyzed just as Declan said he found me.

The sick feeling returns, twisting my stomach. It is all beginning to make sense. The dreams are memories of what happened to me. What Noah did to me. I have been wrong to doubt my husband. He protects me, and though I may not like the way he goes about it sometimes, his intentions are admirable. I can put my trust in him, but not Noah. . . . Never Noah.

Noah Tucker is my enemy.

CHAPTER 28

Declan is cooking dinner when I return. I have no way of knowing how long I have been gone, but I am utterly frozen. I cannot feel my face or fingers or toes. But the fog of confusion in my head has lifted. I will trust my husband and be wary of anything She shows me from now on.

The heat inside the house coats me and sends a painful tingle over my skin as I begin to thaw.

Declan turns at the sound of the sliding glass and removes the pan from the heat. He chuckles. "Your nose is red." He hurries over and helps me out of my coat. "Go stand by the fire. I'll pour you a bourbon."

Alcohol is something I tend to decline, but tonight I want nothing more. I step down into the living room and see a tablet computer sitting on the couch. An angry flush heats my chest because he only brings this out to check security feeds. He promised he would not watch me.

I pick it up and swipe to unlock the screen. The security feeds to at least ten areas fill the screen. They are the usual ones he tends to monitor constantly, the house being one of them. I open my mouth to accuse him of watching me when I notice that the square for the house is dark. He turned off the feed as I requested.

Declan steps down the stairs, a glass in each hand, an eyebrow raised. "I promised, didn't I? Need to check up on me?"

I shake my head and drop the tablet on the couch. "No, sorry, I guess not." I take the glass of amber liquid he offers. "Thanks."

He brushes my hair back behind my ear and kisses my forehead. "Better?"

I shrug a single shoulder and turn to stand in front of the fire. "I guess. I do not feel as jumbled or unfocused."

I sip the bourbon, and in seconds, warmth spreads around my center. I take a larger drink, and fingers of heat lick up to my limbs and swirl in my head.

Behind me, Declan reaches out to set his glass on the mantel and begins rubbing my shoulders. I sink into him and close my eyes. How could I have ever doubted him? He makes me feel safe and will do anything in his power to make sure I remain so.

I place my glass on the mantel and turn to face him. He caresses my cheeks, smooths back my hair.

I wrap my arms around his waist. "Can we just forget everything that happened tonight? I do not want this hanging over us, making things awkward."

He kisses the space between my eyes. "Anything you want."

"Then can we skip dinner?" I look up to find his eyebrows pinching. I chuckle. "I think you will enjoy the alternative."

To show him what that alternative entails, I lift my shirt over my head and let the fabric fall into a pile at my feet.

. . .

The night was warm and the clear sky shone brilliantly with the cluster of light from the Milky Way. He sat behind me, legs on either side, his bare chest—only because I now wore his shirt—pressed gently into my back with slow, even breaths. We sat in comfortable silence, satisfied from making love on the beach.

My painting of the sunset with his recently added luckenbooth and the easel blocked our view of the sky. My discarded sundress lay gently fluttering in the breeze. Dark waves crashed on the shore directly in front of us, practically invisible to the naked eye.

It was a perfect setting and a perfect night.

He kissed the back of my head and brushed my long hair over my left shoulder to kiss my right. A delicious shiver raced across my skin.

"Promise we won't be gone forever," I said. "That we'll come back."

"Promise. And whenever we're feeling the pressure of our lives and want to get away again, all we have to do is look up."

I looked up as if commanded. "The stars?"

He chuckled. "Not just any stars. There are entire stories up there, Emma. It's like reading the best books in the universe. We can get away anytime we want."

"Pray tell."

"Okay, well . . ." He trailed off and shifted behind me. Then he pointed nearly straight up. "There, look. Three constellations clustered together. Perseus."

"I know that one," I said. "Killed Medusa and saved the princess from the sea monster."

"Saved Andromeda from Cetus, yes," he said, sounding amused. "He's connected to Taurus, who is connected to Orion."

I twisted but saw only a dark shadow of him in my peripheral. "Taurus is an astrological sign, I thought. Aren't you a Taurus?"

"Yes, but that's not the point of this assignment, Ms. Wade." He chuckled and nuzzled my ear with his nose. "Pay attention."

Grinning, I looked into the sky. "If I knew which ones you were talking about, you might be able to hold my attention a little better."

He swiped a somewhat even surface into the sand and drew a bunch of dots, then outlined around them until I saw the shape of the constellation Taurus the Bull. I searched for the grouping in the sky and found it after a good ten seconds or so.

"It's not just an astrological sign," he said. "That's a story about Zeus and how he fell in love." His palms ran over my arms until they found my hands. His lips lay right over my ear when he continued. "He disguised himself as a white bull in order to attract the princess Europa. Drawn to his beauty, she climbed right onto his back. Once he had her, he swam to the island Crete where he turned into his true form and made love to her."

When he didn't continue, I said, "That's it?"

He laughed. "Is there anything better than making love to the woman you love?"

I shook my head. "Where's mine?"

"Virgo?" He points straight ahead and then below the dark horizon. "Can't see her."

"Does she have a story as good as yours?"

I felt his shoulders lift in a shrug. "She's a virgin."

I laughed. "That's all?"

He chuckled and burrowed his face into my neck, laying a trail of kisses over my skin. "Only that she's identified with a lot of heroines, one being Ceres, the goddess of the harvest."

"How boring."

"You said it, not me."

I sent an elbow back into his ribs. "I like the heroine part, though. The heroine and the bull."

"We'll storm a lot of castles, my wife and I."

"Mmmm, say that again."

"Which part?"

"The wife part."

He chuckled. "Emma Wade, my wife till death do us part."

I snap awake to a crackling fire and Declan kneeling in front of it, stoking the embers. He is shirtless, and the reflection of flames dances over his skin.

She is very cunning to wait until now to produce this particular memory. I want nothing more than to remember my life again, the life where only he and I existed. My stomach twists with the next thought: *My husband* and I. There is both relief and anguish in this revelation. I have never been unfaithful to Declan but have somehow lost a love so great that it breaks through the barriers of my mind to remind me of what I once had.

I come up on an elbow, forcing these feelings away, and pull the blanket higher up over my bare chest. "How long have I been asleep?"

"Not long. A half hour maybe." Declan crawls over and kisses me until I am lying back down. A hand cups the back of my head and he moans. "You're amazing," he says over my lips.

He is being playful and loving and I hate myself because to reciprocate right now after the dream I just had would feel traitorous. But to whom, I do not know. So instead of answering, I trace fingertips over his jaw and lips.

The next sound surprises both of us. Declan looks down between us where my stomach just growled and laughs. "You're hungry. I can have dinner heated up in a few minutes." Then, with a final, small kiss, he bounds up to his feet.

I sit up to watch him pad barefoot into the kitchen. He is in jeans that hang low around his waist, a look that usually warms my insides but now fills me with guilt. How can I love him so much, then dream of someone else whom I love with an intensity that takes my breath away? I want to hate Her for showing me these things. For making me so confused. I do not want to be confused anymore. I want to love my husband.

I want to be Emma Burke.

So why do I long for this man on a beach in Mexico? A man who I cannot admit to myself is the one man I have also decided is my enemy. All arrows point straight to Noah Tucker being this man. The dream man speaks of populating the world with our children. With "little Tuckers." At the show, Noah was the only one who saw the luckenbooth carefully hidden in the painted sand. The same luckenbooth the dream man painted. Had Noah referenced this very memory?

You're vacillating, She says.

No. I am not. I decided outside. At the very least, I know who I am right now. Emma Burke. I do not care what happened to me eight months ago, let alone eight years. Now is all that matters.

You will care, She whispers.

No, I do not think I will. Declan is the man I love, and he loves me. And maybe he is not the man on the beach, but does it matter anymore? Noah, if he is indeed that man, clearly did not care about my being married to someone else. The past is gone. Time to move on.

With that said, I still find myself searching for a single star through the glass wall behind the dining room table. Only I see nothing more than the glow of moonlight.

"Declan?" I say. "Do you know anything about constellations?"

He glances briefly over his shoulder with a puzzled look on his face. "Not really, why?"

I shake my head and force a small smile. "No reason. I was just dreaming about one is all. I cannot remember the story anymore."

"What was the constellation and I'll look it up for you."

I contemplate telling him Taurus but say, "Orion." It was the one story I did not hear in the dream.

He laughs. "You know what, I do know that one. I used to look for Orion's belt growing up. I guess the story goes that Orion and a goddess were in love, but her brother, Apollo, didn't like the match. Apollo tricked her into killing Orion."

I frown. "How sad."

He nods but it is halfhearted. "Or very cunning on Apollo's part. He knew what he wanted and made sure he got it done without getting his hands dirty. Smart."

Standing, I wrap the blanket around myself and shuffle into the bedroom. I leave the light off and cross the room to look out into the night sky. The sky is not as clear as it was in my dream, nor can I find the constellation I really want to see. The one that will remind me of a better time, in the arms of a different man, who told me stories of love. Not death.

CHAPTER 29

I press my second foot into a running shoe while simultaneously kissing Declan good-bye. He wears a nice gray suit with dark blue accents and a cheery expression, which should be odd considering he is off to work. I guess he enjoyed staying up late and waking up a couple more times after that to satisfy my cravings.

Cravings I still had.

Not just sex. To feel like someone. Anyone. Am I Declan's wife or *his*? Who am I after all this new information? I know who I want to be, but my heart struggles against it. Wages a nice bloody war with my sensible brain.

I have to figure Noah out. Find out what he has to do with the man on the beach versus the man who would kill me without a second thought. The idea occurred to me late in the night that Noah had completely snowed me somewhere along the way. That he led me on and trapped me, but my heart is totally against this idea. I am missing a huge clue to this puzzle.

"If I fall asleep during any meetings today," Declan warns with a tilted grin, "I'm coming home for retaliation sex."

I chuckle. "I actually like this plan of yours."

"Don't tempt me."

I kiss him, hard and lingeringly. "Consider me tempting," I whisper over his lips and smile.

He growls and backs away with purposeful steps. He points a finger at me. "You're going to regret that. Mark my words."

He leaves the bedroom, shooting me one last grin over his shoulder, and disappears. I follow behind a moment later and grab a bottle of water from the refrigerator. It is like any other day. Just going through the motions. Grab water. Stroll to teleporter. Punch in port number. Nothing different.

Until I step inside the gym.

Foster and Noah stand whispering near the teleporter. Both wear jeans and a variation of a long-sleeve Henley—Foster red thermal and Noah dark blue cotton. They are practically mirror images in the way they stand with hands on their hips and sleeves pulled up over their forearms.

I have two warring thoughts when I come to a halt: run and fight. The fact that these two impulses oppose each other lock up my muscles and I cannot move. I want to run because I do not know what they will do to me. I want to fight because of what they *could* do to me, which is fueled by the fact that Noah wants me dead.

Foster does a double take but Noah is quick to move toward me. He pins me by the throat to the wall beside the teleporter, his grip just tight enough to make breathing difficult.

Foster limps forward and wraps tight fingers around Noah's free biceps, glaring at the man who glares at me. "Tucker. Look at her. She's—"

"I am," Noah says. "Looking right at her." His jaw muscles flex as he grits his teeth.

"Noah," Foster says, and his voice takes on an authority that makes me flinch.

Noah does not move, though. His arm is ramrod straight and his eyes do not waver as they bore into me with a heat scorching my very soul. They are accusing, but what I stand accused of I do not know.

I swallow the lump in my throat and call up what bravery lies in the pit of my stomach. "Why are you doing this? Finishing the job you started eight months ago? What is a little more rape and torture between us, right?"

Noah's arm drops suddenly and he takes a wavering step back. He pushes a hand through his hair and shakes his head. His eyes become glassy before he turns his back on me.

Foster stretches his arms between us, hands up as if to hold us away from each other, but puts all his attention on me. "We know what Declan Burke told you last night, and we came to set the record straight. Among other things."

I look Noah in the eye and say, "Why bother? You will just kill me anyway."

"No," Foster says, pinning Noah with a glare. "We won't. As for what Declan Burke told you, that never happened. No rape. No torture. No murder attempt."

"You are lying."

"Not even a little bit." He lifts my chin and forces me to look into his eyes. "Do you trust me?"

I do not know why he asks me this. I hardly know him.

He must see my reluctance because he adds in a whisper, "Come on, Emma. This isn't a hard question. What does your gut tell you?"

"That you are my closest friend," I say without hesitation.

"And I would never steer you wrong."

I believe him, though I have every reason not to. I am tired of this warring of heart and mind. I want to put this battle to rest.

I clear my throat and shift to slide upright against the wall, glancing between the two men who have been nothing more than a dream until recently. "Declan watches me on the security feed. Security could be on their way." I do not say this in a warning tone as if to make them run. I have too many questions and I finally have a chance to get them answered.

"We already thought of that," Foster says.

Noah adds, "We're looping a run of yours from a while back. Same outfit and everything. He'll never know unless you tell him."

"How do I know you will not put a bullet in my head just to make sure?"

"You don't." He steps forward, stopping just past Foster. "But understand one thing: Your death is still on the table, Mrs. Burke. Don't assume because I don't have a gun in my hand right now that I won't kill you another way. Or"—he nods pointedly at Foster—"that he can stop me."

Foster grabs Noah around the biceps and tries to swing him around, but Noah and I have locked gazes and he is immovable. Nothing in this world exists except for the words that just spilled over his lips.

It takes me a while to catch my breath and slow my heart. I do not dare speak until then. "Why wait?" I finally ask. "Why not kill me now?"

Foster angles himself so that he stands between us. "We don't know what to make of you just yet. How much you remember, which, from what *I can tell*"—he glances behind him in a way that tells me they have been discussing this topic at length—"is a lot. You have the means to help us, but you also have the means to destroy everything we've built. One way or another, you're the most dangerous person in this room."

I laugh once, a single, hard, mirthless sound. "That is ridiculous."

Noah pushes Foster aside, his jaw muscles leaping furiously. "What do you know? Do you know what Burke's plan is for you? Why you're here?"

I snap upright. "His plan for— What do you mean?"

"Don't play coy. Just answer the question."

"Emma," Foster says, "for your own sake, just answer his questions. If he doesn't kill you, there are others who are dying to give it a shot. Our people are about to rain down on you with torches and pitchforks."

It takes me a long moment to find my breath and restart my heart. "But why? I have done nothing to any of you."

Noah looks down and away, and when he speaks, some of the earlier hardness in his tone has disappeared. "You don't have to do anything other than exist. But there are some"—he nods at Foster—"who see your potential. You can help us take Declan Burke down for good."

This is like a slap in the face. A fist to the gut. I have to replay his words several times in my head to be sure I have heard him right. "But . . . he is my husband. Why would I help you hurt the man I love?"

Noah seems to go into some sort of shock, unblinking and mouth ajar. He swivels around suddenly and pushes his hands through his hair, then clasps his fingers behind his neck.

Foster takes only a moment to glance between us, then sighs

and turns his full attention on me. "Because Declan Burke isn't the man you think he is, Emma." His gray-blue eyes are intense. Focused. "How much do you remember about this life you supposedly shared with him?"

"What I know or do not know is none of your business," I say, setting my jaw.

Something about the way they interrogate me sets me on the defensive, which angers me because I should be the one asking *them* questions. Like why they want my husband out of the way, but more important, who the hell am I?

Noah whirls so fast he is a blur in my peripheral. He thrusts Foster out of the way, and my back and head *whomp* against the gym's wall before I can blink. White spots dance in my vision. Worse, I cannot breathe. His hand clamps around my throat, fingers boring into my flesh.

Foster tackles him and they roll around on the ground while I struggle for a breath. Grunts and curses and the squeaking of shoes against the basketball court's floor echo around the room.

I stumble the two steps to the teleporter. I have one foot on its yielding floor when an arm belts around my waist and yanks me back. I snap my head back reflexively and thump something solid. A *crack* sounds, followed by a pained groan, and I plummet to the ground, landing awkwardly on one knee, my palms smacking the floor. I push up quickly and spin around to find Foster bent, clutching his bleeding nose.

Noah darts around him and reaches out for me. I twist in an evading circle and strike out with a hook punch. My knuckles crack painfully against his jaw. His head snaps to the side but is back just as quickly. He whips his fists up into a guard position and widens his feet into a fighting stance.

I mirror him and the arrangement feels startlingly natural. We circle each other, Foster to our side pinching his nose and watching in silence.

"This could have been a lot easier," Noah says.

"Oh yeah? How? I tell you everything you want to know and you kill me anyway?"

"Something like that."

"Screw you," I say through clenched teeth. "I will not go down that easy."

"You never did," he says.

He barrels into me, his shoulder slamming into my chest. I smack against the floor under him, the air in my lungs forced out on impact. He holds my wrists down and breathes deeply over me, watching me carefully.

When I have my breath, I say, "You do know me. Am I your wife?"

His lips draw back, baring his teeth, and his entire face turns bright red before he drops his head and shakes it. A moment later, he bounds to his feet and glares down at me. He points, seems to hesitate over his answer, grits his teeth.

I sit up. "What? Just say it."

He leans over me so that our noses are only millimeters apart. "You are *not* my wife."

CHAPTER 30

The room goes silent. Noah hovers over me, taking deep breaths, but I cannot hear them just as I cannot hear my own. His revelation is a sound-sucking bomb, and I wait for the explosive sound. The rumble of breaking earth. The ripple that will bring with it the voiced screams cut off at the moment of death.

"No."

My mouth forms the word, but there is no actual sound. Tears fill my eyes and I fail to keep them from spilling over. Everything—*everything*—I thought I knew, was piecing together in the smallest of increments, has been wrong.

He is not Tucker. Not the long-lost husband from a beach in Mexico.

Noah is slow to stand upright and forces his expression into something close to neutral. Only the flexing of jaw muscles gives him away, but the sudden gleam in his eyes tells another story I will never understand. Even if I could guess the truth behind his eyes, I would be wrong, just like I have been wrong about everything else.

I glance at Foster, who pinches his bloody nose shut. His lovely eyes are watering and he is clearly in pain. I did that. Me. The girl who is supposed to be harmless.

I stand, swallowing my pride and hurt. If I put my focus somewhere else, I will not have to feel any of it for a while. "Can I get you something for your nose?" I point to the weight room. "Declan keeps a freezer of cold packs in there."

I do not wait for the answer. I go if for no other reason than to avoid their eyes. To avoid feeling like a complete fool. Someone sidles up beside me a moment later. The red shirt and limping gait in my peripheral are enough to tell me it is the lesser of two evils. I can handle Foster.

"He was never going to kill you," he says. His voice is nasally but low. "Not today, at least. The opening is a different story entirely."

"What changed his mind?"

"Nobody knows. He just said you were worth taking a second look at and ordered some of the guys to pay close attention to your conversations with Burke and that doctor."

I turn left in the weight room and kneel by the small refrigerator that holds bottles of water and a couple of ice packs in the tiny freezer section. I hand him a pack and find a first-aid kit in a set of cabinets with a bunch of white towels. I figure Declan will never notice if any towels go missing, so I take a couple of them, too.

"Then that shit happened last night," he goes on. "He and I saw your reaction and knew we were about to lose our chance."

This does make me freeze. They have been watching me? The noose around my neck suddenly feels much tighter. Even in moments of assumed privacy, there really is none. I should not be surprised. Noah created the security system himself, or at least had a hand in it. He has been watching my every move since activation.

Damn. Declan and I . . . last night . . . in the *living room*. I feel sick to my stomach. "How long did you watch us?"

His cheeks flush and he averts his eyes. "We turned it off. Nobody saw anything."

Though I am relieved, my heart will need several moments to slow back down. "Thank you."

He nods. "What happened, anyway? You looked like you believed him, yet here you are, not running from two members of the resistance, one of whom has already tried to kill you."

His confirmation of being resistance is almost a relief. It is one question answered. "I should, but I had a dream last night." I begin helping him clean up. "Most of my memories come back when I sleep," I explain. "When I woke up from this one, I was almost sure the man I dreamed about was Noah." My voice tightens and I take a deep breath to calm down. "I never see his face, but the feeling I have . . . We are married and he talks about having a family."

A single tear breaks free and I lift a shoulder to scrub it away. "He uses the name Tucker," I say softly, careful to avoid his eyes. "I was just putting pieces together, but it has been like fixing a shattered vase without glue. Nothing makes sense."

Foster sighs. "I've been ordered not to tell you anything."

I nod, my throat tightening. "Right. Of course you have."

"If it were only the security company cover we had to protect, things might be different. Too many lives are at stake if you turn on us. You have to establish his trust first."

"I am doing a fabulous job so far," I say and attempt to laugh, but I fail. "I am so confused, Foster."

"I know. I'm sorry."

We are almost finished cleaning Foster up when movement in the doorway tells me Noah has arrived. He leans into the doorframe with folded arms. I cannot look at him and I wish he would leave. He is creating more wounds with every passing second, his bomb resonating inside me on a constant repeating cycle.

Another batch of tears hits me like a tidal wave. My nose threatens to run so I sniff and blink rapidly to fend the tears off.

"What is it you think you remember?" Noah asks.

I drop the bloody gauze and towels in a wastebasket and pull out the entire trash bag. I begin knotting the bag and say, "Not a lot. Pieces of things. I remember growing up in a WTC and watching a girl named Toni die because she tried to escape." My heart pains from this brief revisit of her murder. I clear my throat and nod at Foster. "I remember you and me leading a team into another WTC, but not much past getting inside."

I drop onto a black weight bench. "You wanted to know my inspiration for my beach paintings? The truth is that I remember a beach in Mexico and there is a man I cannot see, but I know I love him. More than anything. More than Declan." I drop my head and shake it. "More than my own life."

In my peripheral, Noah pushes off the doorframe and takes two steps toward me. Foster takes one step toward Noah. I look up and find them staring wordlessly at each other—Foster preparing to step in Noah's path if he attacks me, Noah moving carefully, raising both hands defensively, to prove he will not.

"It is okay," I say.

"What do you know about Declan Burke?" Noah asks.

I shake my head. "Almost nothing. He takes care of me. Makes sure I am safe, though this meeting right here will be going down in the epic fail column. This aside, he has never done anything to show me that he is anything other than a loving husband."

"So you've just let him fill your head with his lies about eight years of marriage and this supposed attack?" Noah scoffs. "You actually believe his bullshit?"

I glare up at him. "I have black holes the size of the universe in my head; that does not make me an idiot. I know something is not right."

"Then why the hell are you still with him?" he asks and seems genuinely upset.

"What choice do I have? You have no idea what I have been through these past months, what I continue to go through. I have no past. What would you do in my place?"

"I wouldn't sleep with the enemy," he says with raised brows.

"Oh, because you are so much better than me." I stand and split my attention between them. "Tell me something, since you are so interested in why I stay. Why did you leave me with him?"

Neither of them moves to answer, so I continue. "You want to know why I stay? Because Declan took care of me when nobody else did. He was patient when I was nothing more than a mindless body in a chair. Where were you?" I look directly at Foster. "You claim to be my friend? Where. *Were*. You?"

Foster only blinks and looks away, but Noah says, "There is no easy answer for that."

"I have no aversion to hard answers. You have to give me something here."

He shakes his head, his amber gaze holding tight to mine. "No. Not yet."

Frustration sends a wave of heat up my core and I fist my hands. "Why not? Who the hell am I?"

Noah's expression tightens and his skin flushes again. "As far as anyone in this room is concerned, you're Emma Burke. Always have been."

I throw my hand up and laugh derisively. "Well, what a relief. That explains everything. Thank you." I scowl at him. "You are such a jackass."

Damn straight, She adds.

Noah rears back as if ready to explode on me. "I don't have to exp—"

Foster holds his hands up between us. "Look, this isn't getting us anywhere and our time is running out. If Emma doesn't show up at home when she's supposed to, this entire thing is fucked."

Noah looks down at his watch. "Right. So what will it be, Mrs. Burke? You with us or against us? Your call."

"With you? To do what, exactly? You have not told me anything."

"Your husband is the key to stopping a lot of bad things," he says. "He has to be stopped."

I lock up, constructing my protective fort again. "You are just like Apollo," I tell him. "Trying to trick me into hurting the man I love. I—"

"Mrs. Burke, I am, without a doubt, Orion in this scenario. Believe that if you believe nothing else."

I am stunned and made speechless by his words. He knows the story of Orion. Did Tucker know the story of Orion as well? Did I wake too early to find out?

I shake my head to clear it. Now is not the time for this. I already know this man is not the same Tucker. "I will not help you hurt my husband."

Noah nods once. "Then you leave me no other choi—"

"Hold on a second," Foster cuts in. "The problem here lies in the fact that Emma hasn't seen Burke in action. Let her figure it out on her own. You would never believe the worst of your wife without proof, Noah."

A memory sweeps over me: Noah shaking with grief, finally accepting that his wife is dead. Sonya saying his wife was the best of them. Yet Foster speaks of her as if she still lives.

"I thought his wife died," I say.

Both men's heads snap to face me with wide eyes. I take an automatic step back, my heart a jackhammer against my sternum.

Foster is the first to find his vocal cords. "What do you know about that?"

"Nothing." I nod at Noah. "I remember how upset he was."

The men exchange a perplexed look.

Finally, Noah says, "What do you mean you *remember*? Remember what, exactly?" His voice is strained.

I realize then that I know something they do not. Not that it makes any sense, but if they want to keep their secrets, so will I. In fact, I have been the only one answering questions here. They have told me nothing.

Tell him, She tells me.

No way. I need this leverage.

You don't even know what you've got. Tell. Him.

Foster takes me by the elbow. "Seriously. What do you know?"

I look him directly in the eyes and say, "Forget it."

"She doesn't know anything," Noah says. "She can't. It's impossible."

Foster narrows his eyes at me. "I wouldn't be so sure about that."

The three of us share wordless conversations with no answers. We all know something the other wants to know.

"Fine," Noah says. "I guess the only question left is whether we can trust you to keep quiet."

"From what I have seen in my few memories, I know I can trust him"—I nod at Foster—"but you are a different matter entirely. It is you I cannot trust."

"It doesn't matter," Noah says, his voice hitching. He clears his throat. "You can trust me to let you live long enough to find the answers you need about your precious husband. And believe me, if you look hard enough, you'll find them."

I want to live and I definitely want answers, so for now, I will do whatever this man tells me. If I come up empty, well, then he cannot say I did not follow my side of the bargain. "Where do I start?"

Noah and Foster exchange yet another look. Both sets of shoulders lift in a sigh.

"The labs," Noah says.

"Labs?"

"Where you meet with Arthur Travista. You seem to be good at getting around that place. I've already adjusted your access to allow you to other floors."

I understand now that he means the hospital, but I have never heard it referred to as a lab before. Just the word "labs" gives that place a more sinister feel.

Noah continues, unaware of my thoughts. "If you can get a look at his security feed, you'll see a few things there, too."

"And if I find what you are talking about?" I ask. "What then?"

"Then we'll be in contact," Foster says.

"Let's go. Time's up," Noah says. To me, he adds, "Can we trust you or not?"

It takes me a moment, but I nod. "For now."

"Good enough."

Foster rests a hand on my shoulder. "Just be careful. Nothing about your life is safe."

CHAPTER 31

I spend the following hour in my studio for the privacy. I do nothing more than sit and vacillate. How am I supposed to turn on my husband? I recall his patience with me in those first months. How loving he is. I will never forget his pained expression while recounting my rape and near murder. He seemed to believe every word. At the time, *I* believed every word.

Then I dreamed of the man on the beach. Follow that up with Noah and Foster showing up, and I am losing ground. I think I am finally getting somewhere only to find I am still miles and miles away from the truth.

Sitting on a hologram beach, I cry in frustration. It feels as though my entire world is falling apart.

It fell apart a long time ago, She says.

"Of course not," I said, smoothing my hands over the front of the teal wrap dress. I trained my gaze on the hallway perpendicular to ours just ahead. "I'm only a simple girl."

Guard Taggert snorted a laugh. "Simple. Right. And I'm the queen of South America."

We stopped abruptly at one of the doors. Taggert's arm jutted out toward it. "Inside."

"What?" I asked in surprise. "I thought we were leaving. You just said—"

"I said you were bought and paid for. That doesn't mean you get to skip the private meeting."

My heart pounded and I fought to hold steady as I pressed the button to open the room. Inside, the lighting was set low to suit a certain "mood," and a love seat sat facing a couple of overstuffed chairs. Someone had decorated the space in mauves and coordinating colors, none of which I liked. Flowers freshly picked from the WTC's garden filled plain white vases. I knew from my past meetings with suitors that all the rooms were identical to this one.

"I'll come back for you when you're done," Taggert said.

"What?" My voice came out pitched high with the second shock in as many minutes. "It's against the rules to leave me alone with a suitor. I need a chaperone."

He shook his head and grinned, flashing teeth that were dark from smoking too much tobacco. "Again. Not a suitor. He owns you."

Taggert closed me inside without another word. My heart thumped unsteady, uncomfortable beats and breathing grew difficult. I closed my shaking hands into fists. There was nothing to be frightened of. He's only a man. Just another man. And there is no way in hell I will be around long enough for this arranged marriage to come to fruition.

A bellowing male voice sounded outside the door. "In here, boy. Let's get this over with. I have back-to-back meetings all day."

The door slid open and I took a clumsy step away from a tall, barrel-chested man with hair so dark it was almost black. Gray streaked through the inky texture around his temples. He looked naturally angry, mouth turned down in the corners, no laugh lines. His brown eyes didn't shine and seemed to take in every last detail of the room, and most especially me.

"Mm-hm," he muttered, scanning me; then he scowled and grunted. "Skinny, but you'll do."

Several not-nice retorts came to mind but never left my tongue when the "boy" he'd called to a moment before rounded the corner with a phone to his ear. He wasn't much older than I was. Dark hair in a tousle over his crown, dark lashes lowered to hide his eyes, but I caught a flash of bright color. Green maybe. Or blue.

"Hang up," the man said sharply, and the boy didn't hesitate.

The second the boy looked at me with the green-blue of his eyes, I couldn't breathe. He, too, seemed caught short of breath, but maybe for different reasons. Call it instinct, but this guy reeked of trouble, and it overwhelmed me to think I was supposed to share the most intimate parts of myself with him.

The boy smirked. "She's a little young for you, Dad."

"Dad" harrumphed. "Don't be ridiculous. She's for you. Declan, meet your birthday present. Emma Wade."

Declan's eyes widened and scanned me from heel to teal dress to head.

"I'll just see what's taking that damn lawyer so long," his father said and stepped out of the room.

We stared at each other in silence for a long moment, and I wondered if he could hear the pounding of my heart.

"I'm sorry about my father," he said finally. "He can be a little abrupt." I wasn't sure what he expected me to say in response, so I just nodded. Declan strolled closer. "You really are beautiful."

"Thanks. I guess."

"How old are you?"

I straightened my spine and looked him in the eyes, which I had to admit were truly a beautiful color. "Seventeen."

He raised his eyebrows. "Legal soon, I take it?"

I set my jaw and nodded. "A couple weeks."

His smile lengthened. "I'm not a complete dick. You can relax."

"I'm relaxed."

He laughed. "Okay, well, it's nice to meet you, Emma Wade."

The door opened behind him, drawing our attention to Declan's father and another man, slim and nearly bald. This man scanned the two of us while dropping a briefcase on a nearby table. His fingers blindly found the clasp and propped it open as if he'd done this a million times before.

"Ready?" the man asked us.

Declan and I both turned to his father, who nodded. "They're ready. Are the papers in order?"

The lawyer took out a small stack of legal-size papers. "Postdated for September eighteenth—the girl's birthday."

"I was told we can't take her home today," Declan's father said. "Is that true?"

The man nodded. "Afraid so. The law is the law. That doesn't mean we can't be ready beforehand, though."

"What's going on?" Declan asked.

His father waved a hand. "Marriage certificate."

The lawyer lifted a long, slender piece of metal and a small canister out of his briefcase. "And the branding."

I backed up until I hit a coffee table and fell onto it. I recognized the metal now. The end was flat and small and undoubtedly shaped with linking hearts. "But you can't. I'm only seventeen."

Declan looked down at me with pinched eyebrows. "I don't know, Dad. If she doesn't want the brand, it's really no big deal. I can get her a ring. It's fine."

His father looked disgusted by this option. "And risk losing claim to her? Grow up, boy." He nodded at the lawyer. "Do it."

The lawyer depressed a button on the canister and a burst of flame ran free. He coated the metal and I stood, preparing to run from the room. Declan took me by the arms and spun me around to face the other two men.

In my ear, he said, "Just hold still. It'll be over before you know it."

I lurch forward and dry heave over the hologram of lapping waves at my fingertips.

Declan *is* my husband.

He is also an astronomical liar. We never met the way he told me. Not in a park between meetings. It was not love at first sight. No fairy-tale beginning. He had even claimed he never had me branded. Dr. Travista must have removed it while I was clueless after my "accident."

At least I now know the truth despite the betrayal I feel remembering.

I really am Emma Burke.

CHAPTER 32

I stare out the window in Dr. Travista's office, absently turning my wedding band with my thumb and clutching my elbows, repressing a shiver. Snow falls heavily in large flakes. A lot has fallen since this morning, and the cars in the parking lot hide under white hillocks.

"Emma?" Dr. Travista's voice is raised, startling me.

I turn. "Yes?"

He chuckles from where he sits in his chair. "You are on a whole other plane today. I've called your name three times."

Get it together, She tells me.

I force a smile to my face. "Sorry. I was lost in the view. The snowfall is really beautiful."

A fine line forms between Dr. Travista's eyes. "I thought you hated the snow."

My stomach flips but I hold tight to my calm expression. I have to be more careful. "It is growing on me. Did Declan tell you I went for a walk in it the other day? It is not that bad."

"Yes, I heard. You went out after he told you about your accident."

I want to ask him if Declan told him about all the sexual positions we shared in front of the fire, too, but I bite my tongue. Will nothing between Declan and me remain private?

I stroll to my chair, taking the time to collect my thoughts. It has been two days since Declan told me this lie. One since finding out my husband is a liar of epic proportions. So epic I do not fully understand the scope, apparently. But I will find out. I have come too far to give up now.

I sit and smile tight-lipped. "We can lose the word 'accident.' We both know the truth."

"What would you like to call it?"

I search for the words that came to mind after I heard this lie and look away. "Attack. Violation. Kidnapping."

"How does this make you feel?"

"I was angry at first," I say and pick at the leather seam in the arm of my chair. "Now I do not know. It is as if it has happened to someone else."

Someone we don't even know, She adds dryly.

"I have to admit," Dr. Travista says, removing his glasses, "you're taking it rather well."

I shoot him a halfhearted smile. "I guess we will see how it goes if I remember the truth."

There is silence and he shifts in his chair. "I heard some news about Ruby," he says.

I sit a little straighter. "Oh?"

"She and Charles are expecting a child."

My jaw falls open of its own accord and I promptly slam it back shut. "Really? How?"

He chuckles. "I think you know all about the how of it, Emma."

I shake my head. "No, I mean, she cannot be well yet. When I last saw her, she did not know what a husband was, let alone sex. How could he do that to her?" My voice grows in pitch with each passing word. I cannot help but feel anger for poor, defenseless Ruby, who probably did not understand what was happening to her.

Dr. Travista blinks at me in surprise. "It is none of our business, Emma. And anyway, a child is always good news, don't you think so? You should be happy for your friend."

"Her husband is a dick," I snap without any forethought and am immediately surprised by my use of the word at all.

A dark chuckle fills my head, and She says, *Well, well, look who's coming out of her shell.*

Dr. Travista's eyebrows shoot up. "Well, now, that language is quite unbecoming of you."

I sink into my chair and fold my arms, averting my gaze.

"Understandable, though," he adds with an amused smile. "Anyone would agree you have no reason to like the man. But maybe you should learn to rein in your emotions a little better."

Rein in my emotions? He truly has no idea what a mess I am. One small outburst with a very minor curse word and he acts as if I am a borderline emotional train wreck. Which I am, but still. He has no clue.

I paste on a smile. "Of course. You are right. I will try to do better."

His eyes slim a fraction. "You have been a bit touchy lately. When did we last test *you* for pregnancy?"

Oh, here we go.

This comes out of nowhere, and I make quick mental calculations. I have been careful to avoid sex during the time I am most fertile, but this is not foolproof. It would be worse than bad to get pregnant now. Not when I just found out my husband is not the man I thought he was.

But Dr. Travista is right. I have been quick-tempered the last few days.

Fingers *tap-tap-tap* over the computer tablet as he searches for the exact day. He frowns. "That long? Oh, and I see . . . you are getting ready to start your cycle. That could be why, but let's check to be sure."

I stand automatically, knowing arguing would be futile. He leads me into a nearby exam room and goes through the motions of extracting my blood. He is silent while he fills a tube and sends it through the air lock, calling to another room with instructions.

While we wait, I tap my heel against the white tile. I take note of a single black scuff mark that was not there the last time I was in here.

He leans into the counter, watching me. "Each time we do this, you seem more and more opposed to the idea. Why is that?"

"I am not opposed," I say.

"Nervous, then?"

I nod. "A little." I want to scream *I do not want this!* Every cell in my body is anxious to hear its fate. I hate this. I hate this so much.

The door opens a moment later and my old nurse, Randall, walks in with a woman in tow. She blinks slowly, then smiles weakly at Dr. Travista. I recognize her, but her identity is just out of reach. Auburn hair cut very close to her head. Bone thin. I wonder if she has a single ounce of fat on her body. It is hard to tell her age, but I think she is young like me. Her cheekbones seem overlarge, and so do her hazel eyes.

Where the hell do they find these sick women? She asks.

Randall pulls to an abrupt stop when he sees me, and Dr. Travista straightens.

"You're a little early," Dr. Travista says to Randall. He glances at me. "Emma, why don't you wait for me in my office? I should have your results shortly."

I stand slowly, catching the woman's eyes for only a moment. She does not seem to recognize me even though I know her from somewhere. I want to stay until I can figure this out, but I have been dismissed and there is no arguing with that.

Of course, it would not be out of character to introduce myself. I step toward her and extend my hand. "Hello. I am Emma Burke."

The woman's smile widens to show very white, very perfect teeth. She takes my hand, which surprises me. I fully expected a reaction like one Ruby would have given me: none at all.

"Lydia Farris. Nice to meet you, Emma. You must be Declan's wife."

"Y-yes," I say and find myself blinking rapidly, as if I need my vision cleared rather than the shock of information flooding my head. Richard Farris's wife?

A surprised gasp fills my head. *The Stepford wife?*

I just saw Lydia Farris days ago, and she looked nothing like this skeletal woman in front of me. She had been thin, but nothing like this. And all of her hair is gone.

Ignoring my runaway thoughts, I say, "Farris sounds familiar. I believe I met your husband at my art show."

She nods. "Oh yes. I was sorry to miss it. I heard it was wonderful. I had to stay home with our young children. We have three boys."

I smile, though I want to gape and gawk at her appearance. "Three? How nice for you."

"And now I hope to have a few girls to supplement the small lot of them," she says and chuckles.

Dr. Travista steps toward her. "Lydia, why don't you sit? You and Emma will have plenty of time to chat." He looks pointedly at me, telling me it is time to go.

"I will come see you soon," I tell her. "Maybe you can show me pictures of your boys."

Randall eases her into a chair and she smiles up at me. "I would love to. See you soon, Emma."

I don't like it, She tells me.

Me, either. And just what I need. Another puzzle piece to add to the board.

CHAPTER 33

Declan comes home with the usual glum expression after hearing the news that I am not carrying his child yet. I would not be upset about this at all, but now Dr. Travista wishes to try something else. He did not elaborate, but I know more invasive tests are on the way.

I wordlessly pour Declan a bourbon and check on the dinner I have baking in the oven. He takes his drink into the other room to change clothes and I allow myself to relax. It is the first moment I have had that I know he is not watching me. Noah, maybe. Foster . . . But not Declan, and he is the one I have to hide from.

I lean over the counter and cover my face. Take several deep breaths. This is too hard. How am supposed to maintain this lie? I feel as if I am losing my mind. Each thing I learn makes everything I already know more muddled. And what was with Lydia Farris today? Why did she look like that?

The connections are there. Me. Ruby. Lydia. I have no idea if I looked like that, but the way Ruby acted was exactly how I was.

And Ruby was thin like Lydia is now. But Lydia has all of her faculties. There is the conversation about Lydia's infertility I overheard, too. She was seeing Dr. Travista because she wanted to have more children. It has only been a couple of days and she spoke as if she was already cured of this.

I am so close to the answer, but it is out of my reach.

"I don't give a good goddamn fuck about the money!" Declan yells from the other room, startling me upright.

The bedroom door is closed, but I know he is on the phone. He closes the door only when he needs to have a private conversation. This is the first time I have heard him yell, though. I tiptoe quickly to the door and lean in to hear him better.

"Does it look like I'm hurting? If they're caught, everything I've done—" He stops abruptly, pauses, and continues in a tone more comparable to the one he used with Charles on our first meeting: all business laced in warning. "My entire company is in jeopardy if this goes south. Get that team back, and get them back now. With or without the cargo. I'm not fucking around."

I am not positive, but I have to assume that is the end of his conversation and retreat to the sliding door. If he comes out, I do not want him to think I heard anything. I open the door and step out just as the bedroom door slides open. I practically jump into a nearby chair and wince when the cold wood seeps through my jeans, but at least there is no snow on it.

Declan peeks outside and looks around until he spots me. He smiles as if he were not just yelling at someone. I can only hope my masks are on as tight as his are.

What a pair you make, She says.

I return Declan's smile, inwardly feeling the sting of his betrayal. I want to accept his smile for what it is. I want to see the warmth in his eyes when he looks at me and believe he truly loves me. I do not know what to believe anymore. He and his father bought and paid for me. I am no more than a product that is not producing as she should. How long until he gives up and sets me loose?

"What are you doing out here?" Declan asks. "And where's your coat?"

I rub my arms and shrug. "I needed to cool off. It was too warm by the oven."

He steps out and looks around. He is wearing a long-sleeve white T-shirt and black cotton drawstring pants that hang low on his hips. I am like one of Pavlov's dogs: My loins stir and my mouth waters. How can I still want him like this? I am disgusted with myself.

A light breeze lifts his hair and lays it over his forehead. Absently, he brushes it back and sighs. "You left the door open."

"Did I? Sorry. I have not been out too long. Is the house cold?"

"Nah." He grows quiet and takes deep breaths, avoiding my eyes.

"Is something wrong?" I ask. I am freezing now and want to go inside, but I am curious to see if he will tell me about his call. The moment he said the word "team," I thought of the memories with Foster and the team we led into the WTC. Naturally, I wonder about the purpose of Declan's team.

"No." He gives me a half smile. I almost believe it is a sad smile. "Just had an off day. I had really hoped your test would come back differently. Especially after I heard Ruby's pregnancy had already taken."

I swallow and try to maintain my expression of interest. "Was there concern she could not get pregnant?"

He shrugs. "No more than for you since the accident."

"Was she kidnapped, too?" He has never given me an explanation for Ruby's accident, and I wonder what lie he will tell me about her.

Declan looks around and rubs his arms. "Aren't you getting cold?"

I stand, annoyed that he thinks he can divert me so easily. "I met Richard Farris's wife today."

Declan leads me into the house with a hand on the small of my back. "I heard. Lydia is a very nice woman. I think you and she will become good friends."

"What is wrong with her?"

He slides the door shut behind him and heads down to the living room to start a fire. "She's just been very ill. Richard thought Arthur could help, and as luck would have it, he can. She's already well on her way to good health."

I do not miss the fact that he has not mentioned infertility, which, based on their conversation in the hall outside the transporter room, was the reason Lydia was there. Another lie. And I cannot call him on it because I was eavesdropping.

Declan kneels in front of the fireplace and sets up fresh logs for the fire while I return to the kitchen.

"We should invite them to dinner," I say, pulling our meal from the oven.

He appears beside me with plates and silverware, preparing to follow me to the table. "Sure, why not? Speaking of invitations, we've been invited out for dinner tomorrow. An old college friend of mine and his new wife. I think he wants to show her off." He grins as he sets the plates down on the table. "He always tries to one-up me."

I chuckle. "Your friend must fail a lot." I swallow the guilt at how naturally and unexpectedly I fall into our normal banter.

He nods and shoots me a tilted grin. "Pretty much. To hear him tell it, though, it's the other way around."

My stomach knots at the sight of this grin I love so much. It pains me to turn my back on him the way I have, but he has left me with no other choice. I must take my life back. My real one, not the fairy tale he has fabricated.

"Should be an interesting night, then," I say.

"I'll have to get you something nice to wear. The restaurant is one of those high-class joints with small portions."

I twist my face into a scowl and he laughs.

"It's not that bad," he says. "Small but good."

"If you say so."

I step into my studio, intent on losing myself in a new painting. I want to be alone—really alone—and not have to worry or think about everything going on for the few hours before I have to get ready for our dinner out tonight.

All of that hope shatters when I find Noah waiting for me. He sits on my stool playing with the holograms. I find this interesting, seeing him with an amused expression—a child with a new toy. No anger or sadness or any trace of the man I have grown to know in pieces. This man is touchable.

Something black and sleek with big teeth leaps out of the jungle brush, and Noah stumbles off the stool, barely keeping his footing.

My heart pounds with anxiety over his presence, but I cannot help but laugh at his reaction. I have grown used to the jungle cats.

He must not have heard me arrive, because his head whips around at the sound of my laughter and he flushes.

"This shit is no joke," he says, running a hand through his raised mess of blond waves.

I take note of how he has not shaved since I saw him last. The scruffy look does not hurt him. In fact, he looks better. Sexier, even. I shake my head to clear it. I should not think of him like that, especially since he is plotting my death.

I clear my throat. "Yeah. I know." I take the tablet computer from him and shut the hologram down.

"You ever use any of them to paint by?"

I eye him carefully, wondering when the other shoe is going to drop. He is being very calm. "Some."

"The beaches?"

"No. Those I paint from memory." I prop a hip on the edge of my stool. "Are you bipolar or something?"

He raises a single eyebrow. Chuckles a little. *A very little.* "No. Why?"

"Someone might mistake you for nice."

He nods in understanding, looking slightly apologetic. "I've had some time to think; that's all."

"Does that mean you have not come to kill me?"

"No. Actually"—he reaches into his back pocket and pulls out a slim powder-blue box—"I brought you something. I know it's not my place, but I thought you might want them. You know, just in case."

I take the box and look for something to explain what he is giving me.

"Birth control," he says. "Sonya said one pill a day will prevent pregnancy."

My jaw falls open and I slam it shut. "Oh God, thank you. Really." I tap the box in my palm, making the pills rattle. "You read my mind."

Noah tucks his hands in his front pockets and looks around at the white walls.

"Was there something else?" I ask, hoping he came to spill the truth once and for all.

He rocks forward on the balls of his feet. "I owe you an apology."

I wait for him to continue, but when he does not, my already short fuse sparks. I do not want this lame attempt to make things right. I want honesty. Instead of starting an argument, I stand and head for my supply closet to gather everything I will need. I think I will paint a target. With Noah's head in the center.

Noah leans into the doorframe, watching me pick through brushes. "Emma—"

"Has my life always been like this?" I ask, slamming a couple of brushes down on the shelf.

"Like what?"

"Never knowing who to trust. Expecting betrayal around every turn. Plotting and secrecy. Anger," I add through gritted teeth.

"You have every right to be angry at me."

I nod and swivel my head to look at him. "Glad to know we are on the same page."

"Hey," he says, his voice rising, "you're hiding something from me, too, so don't climb your high horse just yet."

"The difference here is that I would tell you everything if you would only pay me the same respect, Noah. It is a simple thing." If only I knew why knowing about his dead wife was so important.

"Do you know how she died?" he asks, and his voice cracks.

I shake my head and avert my eyes. I cannot see the pain in his face. I have seen it too many times now. I still do. The dreams do not come as often, but they come, and his grief never lessens.

"She went into a WTC to free the girls, and then I don't know. I wish to God I did. But I lost her that night."

The cluster of bodies in the hallway kept growing. Fighting hand to hand at this point was useless. More WTC security joined the small group we'd originally encountered and opened fire on the entire group, paying no mind to their own people. Our only option was to try to take cover and wait for backup.

I backed away, aiming into the wave of men decked out in the best armor available on the market. Our plasma fire did nothing to penetrate it. With their helmets on, I had only a tiny window of vulnerable neck and chin to aim for. Too small a target while on the move.

Foster wailed beside me and collapsed, clutching his left knee. His lower leg barely hung on, and blood flowed like a river from the open wound. I ignored my turning stomach and slipped an arm under one of his. Very carefully, I pulled him into the nearest room, closing us inside.

The office was empty except for an aluminum desk and several chairs. Awards and framed medals for valor covered the grayish green walls. I wouldn't have minded taking a blowtorch to the entire room, except the goddamn teleporter made my heart leap with joy.

I dragged Foster over and switched the machine to outside controls.

"Fuck no," Foster said, wincing. "You are not sending me off and staying behind."

I maneuvered him inside. "Who says I won't be right behind you?"

He gripped my jacket front and forced me to look at him. He'd already lost too much blood. His pallor frightened me. "He'll fucking kill me for leaving you here."

"I'm right behind you." It was a necessary lie. I wasn't leaving my people here to fight this battle alone, and I needed to get him to Sonya.

I shoved him in, ignoring his screams of pain and protest. When the keypad illuminated before me, I keyed in the port number, and in five seconds Foster disappeared.

I aimed my gun for the top of the machine, where a small computer stored the memory. I fired and it exploded in a shower of yellow sparks. It left the teleporter useless, but at least no one could follow the trail.

The door slid open to the hall just as I ran for it. One of the security officers stood on the other side. He lifted his gun, and then a flash of blue plasma fire filled my vision.

Searing pain lit up my chest.

CHAPTER 34

I drop to my knees, clutching and jostling the shelf. A cup of brushes falls and rolls to the floor with a clatter.

Noah drops to one knee beside me and lays a hand on my back. "What? What is it?"

This memory was bad. So bad. Nothing like floating in water or seeing Toni's murder. Nothing like remembering the pain of being branded Declan's wife. Those were bad.

This one is worse.

"I was shot," I say, fending off tears.

Silence is his only response, so I look to him for confirmation.

He drops to his butt, then nods reluctantly. "Yeah."

Noah brings his knees up and props his elbows, then runs his hands through his hair. He clutches fistfuls of hair over his crown, his head bent to hide his expression. This grief-stricken reaction yanks at my heart, and for the first time, there is no tug-of-war between my heart and my mind. I have to make this pain go away.

His and mine. And though what I plan to do makes no sense, I cannot stop myself. It is as necessary as breathing.

Heart drumming, I reach forward, loosen his fist, and draw it away. I wait for him to pull back, say something cutting, or worse, attack. Instead, his warm palm opens and slips perfectly, solidly, around mine.

Tingles race across my skin with his gentle touch. My bones are swept up in a fire that soon encompasses my entire body, finding and filling all my cold, dark spaces. The sensation steals my breath.

Noah's other hand slides up the back of my hand and up my forearm, leaving a tantalizing trail of heat in its wake. I realize we are both holding our breath when that same hand lifts to cup my cheek. I turn into his palm as if this is the most natural thing to do and close my eyes. His thumb wipes away a rogue tear.

He gives me the gentlest of tugs, and I twist my body around, turning in to him. Still clasping his right hand, I pull his arm around me and sit between his legs. He holds me against his chest and rests his chin on the crown of my head. His breath shudders behind me even as his arm tightens as if he will never let me go. I find I do not want him to. I feel as if I am exactly where I was meant to be and do not care if it makes any sense. This is right.

I run my thumb over the area between the knuckles of his thumb and index finger. The strange texture of skin there draws my attention. I lift his hand for closer inspection. There is discoloration that is barely a shade darker than his pale skin.

A memory slams into me. The warning Emma Wade gives Tucker when he decides to brand a luckenbooth on his hand for her.

No one will take you seriously.

No one has to know. I'll wear Plasti-skin over it.

"Emma—"

"Plasti-skin," I whisper and bolt upright.

He yanks his hand away and I shift my focus to his face. His expression is tight with emotion: pain, frustration, confusion. His eyes glaze over, and suddenly I know. He *is* Tucker. *My* Tucker.

I am torn between throwing my arms around him and slapping the hell out of him. "Why did you lie to me?"

He shakes his head fiercely. "No. I didn't lie."

"But it is you. In my memories of Mexico." I steal his hand back and scrape away the fake skin, revealing my evidence. The linked hearts practically barrel down the erected walls of the labyrinth in my head. My heart beats fast. Each breath rushes as if it is trying to pace my too fast heartbeat. "You have a brand. Are you going to tell me this is a lie, too? And you have to explain to me why I was in a tank of water. What is that about?"

Noah stiffens. "What?"

Something else occurs to me. It is like an outpouring of theories that are actually making sense, and I cannot get them out fast enough to hold on to all of them. "Did that happen after I was shot? Your doctor, Sonya, kept referring to me and someone else as patients one and two. Me and someone named Adrienne. Were we being healed from injuries or something?"

Noah leaps to his feet, his eyes wide and darting. "Where did you hear that name?"

Standing, I fist my hands, wanting desperately to strike him in frustration. Instead, I settle for a simple glare. "You know what I am talking about. Why do you insist on keeping my past a secret from me? If you are trying to protect me, stop. I do not need your protection. I need the truth before this gets any worse. I mean, my God, Noah. I am married to another man. Tell me how—"

The familiar hum of the teleporter cuts me off. I yank open the cabinet of drop cloths beside me and force Noah inside. It is large and practically empty at the moment, so he fits comfortably. He does not hesitate and we catch each other's gaze for only a moment before I close the doors.

The rattle in my back pocket startles me into remembering the evidence I carry, and I toss the birth control in with him. "Just, uh, leave those here. I will come back for them," I whisper.

I turn just as Declan steps into view, my heart pounding so hard the sound floods my ears. I put on my most brilliant smile. "Hi. What are you doing here?"

"Who are you talking to?" he asks with a wry smirk.

My mouth is suddenly dry. I rock back on a heel and onto a fallen paintbrush. I nod at my disaster of a shelf and the resulting mess on the floor. "Chastising myself for being so clumsy. Pretend you never saw this side of me."

He chuckles and motions me forward. We meet outside the closet and he kisses me. His hair loosens from the carefully slicked-back style, and strands brush my forehead. "I couldn't work another minute," he says in a husky tone I know too well. "I thought we could get some alone time in before dinner."

"And by alone time you mean . . ." I trail off, unable to finish the thought, let alone think about performing the actual act. This has become yet another war I fight with myself, because I truly do love him, but I am also hurt by the lengths he will go to hide my real past.

And God . . . *Noah*. Noah is the man on the beach. What I feel for him torches and buries any emotions I feel for Declan.

Declan nods and grins over my lips, then kisses me again. "What do you say?"

I have no other choice, and I let him take me to the teleporter, sick because the man I really need to be with is in my closet. I had been so close to getting answers, and now I have no idea how long I will have to wait.

At home, Declan wastes no time. I taste bourbon on his tongue, so I know he was drinking at lunch. That coupled with any ideas he had been dreaming up meant there would be no talking my way out of this.

We cross the threshold into the bedroom, and a rack of clothes catches my eye. I pull away and stare because it was not there before and several dresses hang from it.

Yay! She yells. *A diversion. Take it.*

"What is that?" I ask.

"I couldn't choose a dress for tonight, so I had several styles delivered." He tries to start kissing me again, but I press my forearms against his chest.

"I want to see first."

I step around him and approach the rack. It is not full; there are only five or six dresses hanging in clear plastic. I do not care about what hangs here. I only need a moment to catch my breath and prepare myself for what is about to happen. What had Noah called it in the gym?

Sleeping with the enemy, She offers.

Thanks, I tell Her with a roll of my eyes.

I finger the dresses until I get to one in particular that stirs a memory. While I lift it and pull the plastic off, Declan watches nearby. He hangs his shirt and jacket like always, only he doesn't bother finding something else to wear.

The dress is teal. Wraparound and calf length. Only instead of short sleeves, they are long. I think even the fabric is the same.

"You must have been feeling nostalgic when you picked this one," I say. "Only I cannot imagine why—"

I stop abruptly and slowly lift my chin. I do not turn toward the utter stillness—the man of stone—standing to my right. I cannot look at him because I cannot believe I have been so foolish.

Girl taken down by a stupid dress, She says. *Oh man. This is no good.*

"You remember," he says finally.

"It happened two days ago," I whisper. "But only that one day." I hang the dress and turn to face him. "So I know you lied to me about how we met." I lift my left hand and show him the unmarked back of it. "Did you have Dr. Travista remove the brand?"

Declan reaches for a sweater and pulls it over his undershirt. "How come you didn't say something two days ago? Why hide it?"

"I figured you had a good reason."

He pulls his phone from a pocket and nods at me. "Yeah. I do."

He turns and walks out of the room, lifting the phone to his ear. I follow close behind, my heart racing. What is he doing? Does he know I am lying about remembering everything—or close enough—or is the recollection of one memory enough for him to do whatever he has planned? I cannot even imagine what he has planned.

"It's me," he says into the phone. "She remembered something. No, I'm sure. She admitted it." He faces me. "She claims it happened a couple days ago." Turning, he nods and says, "We'll be right there."

He hangs up and leans back into the island. He silently fingers the phone, staring at it but past it all at once.

My stomach turns uneasily. "We will be right where?" I ask.

"We've been careful to avoid subjects that would bring back

your memory. I must have said something that triggered it with the story about your accident."

Just keep playing along, She says. *Maybe you can talk him out of what he's got planned. That innocent act of yours is the only thing that can save you right now.*

I have to agree with Her, so I take a step closer to Declan. Attempt and fail at a smile. "I do not understand. I thought you wanted me to remember."

He shakes his head. "No. I never wanted that. I only told you that so you wouldn't ask questions. But it's an easy fix." With that, he straightens and holds out his hand. "Come on."

I step back, eyeing his hand. There was a time when I never would have hesitated. When did things go so horribly wrong? "Where?"

"To see Arthur."

CHAPTER 35

W-why?" I step away now. "Why him?"

Declan's hand falls heavily to his side. "You don't have to be scared, Emma. He's not going to hurt you. I would never let anything happen to you. You know that."

I shake my head. Step back once more and hit the frame of the bedroom door. "I do not know anything of the sort."

That isn't exactly playing along, She says. *Think about what you're doing. He doesn't know what you know. Stop reacting and just think.*

"Dr. Travista will run tests," I add hurriedly. "You know how I feel about his tests."

He turns and presses his palms into the island countertop, leaning in, head bent forward. "You don't understand, Emma."

"So explain it to me. What are you so afraid of?"

"It doesn't matter," he says and pushes off the counter. "After today, you won't remember any of this."

I slide to the right, my mind's eye on the sliding glass door and the world outside. I do not know where I can go, but away sounds good enough to me. "What do you mean, I will not remember? What will he do?"

"Erase the memory, and if there are any others, you may as well tell me now. Arthur already suspects you remember a lot more than you're letting on. He's wanted to get his hands on you since before the opening."

Goddamn seagulls, She says.

"I will not let you do this to me," I tell him.

Declan steps cautiously forward. "Do you think I *want* to do this? Emma, I spent many nights lying awake praying this day wouldn't come."

I slide over again. "It is only one memory and I have not run from you. I still love you despite it. I would never hurt you, Declan. Please. Do not let him do this to me." My fingers graze the corner leading back into the dining room. "Can you not just love me as I am?"

Something in these words causes pain to glance across his face. "It's too dangerous. I love you too much to risk it."

Go.

I twist around and run. He is ready for this, though, and crashes into me. His momentum drives me into the edge of the table, which slams into my stomach, forcing the air from my lungs. My arms fly out and strike the glass centerpiece of flowers. The vase rocks over the other side and the glass shatters, sending hundreds of clear glass marbles skittering across the floor.

Declan flips me over and pins my wrists to the table. His face is bright red and his hair has loosened, hanging between us like a jagged curtain. Veins pulse around his eyes.

"You are hurting me," I say, wincing as the table's edge digs into my lower back. The tips of my toes barely find leverage grazing the ground.

He yanks me up and throws me over his shoulder. The movement makes me dizzy enough that it takes until we are halfway to the teleporter to begin kicking and pounding on his back.

I pitch over his shoulder and fall awkwardly thanks to the vise-like arm around my legs. He loses his grip trying to catch me. I thump to the floor, elbows knocking, and jam my left shoulder, sending bolts of pain through my arm and up my neck. Still, I scramble away from him.

His arm hooks around my waist and hoists me up so fast my legs fly up, kicking at nothing but air. I clutch his wrists and dig my nails into his skin.

"Stop fighting me," he says tightly. His other arm clamps around my chest, pinning my arms. "It won't do you any good."

"You bastard. Let me go!"

"If I could let you go, we wouldn't be here right now."

We reach the teleporter and I kick my feet up to brace against the glass opening. "What is that supposed to mean?"

"It means that I never would have let my father force me into this marriage if I didn't want you the moment I saw you. It *means* I never would have spent the last eight years keeping one ear to the ground for some sign that you were still out there." He rears us back and I lose my footing on the glass. He is fast and forces us inside the teleporter.

Declan drops me to my feet and spins me around the second the door closes us inside. His eyes have glazed over and look hard into mine. "It means I fucking fell in love with you, Emma, and I'm not giving you up. You're *mine*." He rockets a rattling punch into the wall behind me and I flinch. "I can't risk you remembering your past. I won't."

He is keying in the port number by the time I get over my shock. He really loves me? "Why can you not just trust me to—"

The scent of spearmint fills the space and paralyzes my vocal cords. The world around us melts into the transporter room at the hospital.

And orderlies standing next to a stretcher.

I cannot think to finish the sentence I began. I can only struggle again. Only this time Declan has assistance. Strong hands grapple for my flailing limbs and heft me onto the stretcher, their fingers digging, bruising deep into my flesh. Half the men restrain me while the other half work to strap me down. The white braces pinch my skin as I continue to buck and wrench and shove and thrust. I know it is useless but I cannot give up.

All hands rise from me at once and all eyes watch my futile struggle. Declan pushes his hair away from his face, his chest expanding with a deep intake of breath. He will not look me in the eyes, instead choosing to focus on my bound chest and wrists. Legs and ankles.

Defeated, tears stream from my eyes. I have to blink them away when he finally looks at me. I want to see the sea in his eyes turn into a storm when I say my next words.

"You know what is sad?"

He shakes his head, brows furrowed.

"No matter how this turns out, no matter how much we think we love each other, we will always live a lie. Never the real thing. What makes it truly sad is that I loved you regardless of the lies. I will never make that mistake again."

White lights blind me and I cannot move my head to shield my eyes. Randall and his sour face ignore me as he inclines my bed a few inches. Other nurses work around him in silence. One stabs a needle into the crook of my elbow. Another drapes a sheet over me, wafting cool air up to my face. Another removes the top from the bed and places my head in cool metal stirrups. Randall starts strategically placing electrodes on me.

We aren't giving up, She says.

I want to laugh. *If you see an alternative way of escaping this, I would love to hear it.*

Just don't let go.

You make it sound so easy.

I'm still here, aren't I?

Dr. Travista moves to the right side of my bed and eyes me over the rim of his glasses. "I am sorry about this, Emma, really I am."

I laugh, a low chuckle in the back of my throat. "We can stop the lies, Travista. Just this once, do me the courtesy of being truthful."

He nods once and a smile quirks over his lips. "Okay."

"How many times have you done this to me?" I cannot help but wonder if this is not the first.

"One other time. A full memory wipe."

"After my supposed accident?"

He twists to lean a hip into the bed frame and folds his arms. "I wouldn't call it 'supposed,' but 'accident' might be the wrong word."

"Because I was shot," I say.

His eyes widen a fraction. "Yes, that's right. So you do remember more than you're letting on."

"Do not get excited. I only remembered today."

He nods. "I'm surprised you stuck around, but then again, knowing who you really are, I guess I'm not."

"And who am I?" My heart drums as I wait for the answer to this long-wondered question.

"You are a girl who got herself mixed up with the wrong people. They nearly got you killed. Luckily for you, you ended up nearly dead on my doorstep. I saved your life."

"What do you mean *your* doorstep? I was in a WTC."

He nods. "Who do you think owns that WTC?"

The pieces fall together suddenly. The newspaper headline about the attack on Burke Enterprises. Declan's reaction when I asked about it. He said it happened around the time of my "accident" and was not upset because it changed his life. He even smiled.

"Declan," I whisper.

"Yes, and he found you dying, tucked away in some office. Carried you to me himself."

"And then what? You worked some magic to make me brand-new?"

He laughs. "In a manner of speaking."

"What—"

He does not let me finish. Instead, he turns and strolls away, leaving the busywork to his nurses and orderlies. They work feverishly around me, preparing the final stages.

Near my head, one of the nurses, one I have never seen before, leans to fiddle with some controls on a station with a lot of wires and buttons and screens. The silver contraption is very close to my ear. He stares at it, seemingly bewildered over something or other, and begins tapping his middle finger against the side.

On some subconscious level, my mind listens to the series of taps, the swiftly moving uneven beats of them, and I make out the letters. Then words.

Morse code.

It is a message. *I will figure this out. Promise. Noah.*

The room—dark around the edges of the spotlight over me—is practically empty now. I do not care one way or the other. I am numb to it all. Numb to the reminders to *stay very still, Emma. If you move, Emma . . . It will be over before you know it, Emma. I am sorry, Emma.*

I am reminded of the day She warned me not to talk about my dreams. Dr. Travista asks me to think of things I love and enjoy and dislike and hate and what makes me sad. . . . I focus on nothing. Say nothing. I will not help them wipe my mind clean of who I am as if I need a good dusting.

I close my eyes and picture a perfectly square, white room with so much light I cannot see the corners. I cannot tell the floor from the walls from the ceiling. It is only white space. I put myself there, feel the flat surface under my feet, imagine the temperature is neutral. Warm would give Dr. Travista something to work with. Cold would, too. I take even breaths, relax every muscle. Concentrate on nothing but my white space.

Dr. Travista's voice filters into my white room as if through a loudspeaker. "She isn't cooperating."

"I hope you aren't suggesting we start over," Declan says.

"No. Not yet, at least. Let me try something else."

Sparks, like flashes of electricity, flicker in my white room. They come from random places on my walls and ceiling and floor. Sizzles of charge break up the silence and ozone wafts across my nose a moment later. The neutral temperature swiftly rises to an unbearable heat. But I will not let it faze me. This is my space. He cannot touch me here.

"Emma," Declan says, and his voice sounds very close to me. "Listen to Arthur. You don't want to start over, do you? End up like Ruby? Like a child?

"Spring is coming," he adds in a coaxing tone. "You don't want to miss the spring. The colors of foliage outside the house in the spring are beautiful. I can't wait for you to see it. Think of the paintings. If we start over, by the time you even remember how to paint again, it'll be summer and hot and the colors will be gone. But it doesn't have to be that way. You can cooperate and be home tomorrow. Painting. Going on with life as if you didn't miss a beat."

He does not know me if he believes the hint of spring will bring me out of my white room. Promise me sand and brine on the wind and the deafening crash of waves and the scream of seagulls.

"Nice room," She says.

I turn slowly and look directly into the eyes of . . .

Myself.

CHAPTER 36

She is definitely me, only different. She wears worn dark jeans with tattered knees and cuffs. The long-sleeve black top fits to Her torso, with a wide neck baring Her collarbone and a single shoulder. She stands with a cocked hip and hands tucked jauntily into Her back pockets.

She tilts Her head, and long dark hair slides off Her shoulder in a silk curtain. One corner of Her full lips angles up. "Could use a little color, though."

I saunter forward, ignoring the jibe on my white space. "You are me. This whole time."

She nods. "Of course I am. Who else would know so much about your life?"

"If that were true, why can I not remember everything? Why hide so much?"

"You're the one with the memory filter. Not me." She talks in a half smile, flashing a small dimple, and I understand the allure She has. How She can easily fool some misguided man into believing She is as harmless as they come.

All around us, the flashes of sparking electricity continue, but She does not flinch or avert Her attention to them. Her sole focus is on me. "Are you ready?"

"Ready for what?"

"To fight, of course."

"I still do not know what I am fighting for."

She pulls Her hands out of her pockets, and the moment they are in front of Her, a computer tablet appears. Her fingers play over the screen until, at last, She swipes over the top and an image flies onto the wall to my left.

"Noah," She says and smiles.

The children whimpered so loud, not even the explosions outside would hide us if a WTC guard happened to be nearby. My entire body vibrated with fear and adrenaline, and it took everything I had not to yell at them to be quiet. The rifle I carried felt awkward and heavy in my sweaty palms.

I'd managed—with the help of some other senior girls—to get rid of the guards, who had thinned since the attack on the compound started, but now I was alone. We'd split off to get the younger girls from their rooms, leaving me with every girl between the ages of five and eight.

We made our way to the side entrance unhindered before we came across a large group of men in black. The uniform covered every part of them except their faces, and their expressions registered surprise when we rounded the corner. I bit back a cry of relief when they came into view.

The resistance fighters.

I had not realized how coiled tight I was until that very moment.

The men began leading my large group out and I followed. One of the girls closest to me started sobbing, and as I turned to go to her, I found her already being swept up in a man's arms. She was much too big for him to cradle the way he did, but he didn't seem to notice.

"Everything's okay," he whispered to her. "Promise."

I had never seen a man show such kindness, and it brought me to a standstill. He stroked a gloved hand over the back of her head and whispered more assurances in her ear. Soft dark-blond waves escaped the bottom of his black beanie, and his jaw and neck needed a good shave.

He shifted to turn and walk out with her but caught me staring from the corner of his eye. He barely turned his head to look and did a double take. He had the most beautiful amber eyes; they literally stole my breath away. He was older by several years, midtwenties, I thought. Handsome in a rugged way, not like Declan and his too clean-cut prep-boy way.

Thinking of Declan made the fresh brand on my hand burn lava hot. A fresh wave of images flashed through my mind of the hours-old arranged marriage and topped it off with an additional twist in my gut.

The man cleared his throat after several unsteady heartbeats. "Hey."

I forced the images away, approached him, and held out my gun. "Switch with me?" I motioned for the girl he carried.

He grinned. "No, I'm good. You?" He shifted his steady gaze to the gun and back, his smile never faltering.

I returned his grin. "I guess."

"I'm Noah."

"Emma."

"Very nice to meet you, Emma."

I stand back in my white space and She smirks at me. Sparks sizzle over us and tiny yellow lights rain down like fireworks.

"It is getting worse," I say, eyeing the room a little more closely. It is like tiny bulbs shattering and spraying light everywhere.

She takes a step closer, the consummate tilted grin faltering as She looks around. "Time is running out. On to the next." She swipes Her finger across the touch screen and a new image floods the wall.

I stretched out in a comfortable bed with pristine white sheets and a tan comforter. Sun blazed through windows with the curtains drawn to the side. According to the vid screen hanging over a small dresser, the boxy-looking love seat, and the dark brown desk and chair, the room was nothing more than a small hotel room.

I squinted against the sun and sighed dreamily. The bed was too warm to get out of and I contemplated staying in it all day. My plans ended when a knock sounded on my door.

With a groan, I rolled out of bed and threw on a thin robe. I peered through the peephole and saw Noah running his hands over the top of his head, mussing his hair. I bit my lip to choke back a laugh.

"What do you want?" I asked a moment later, affecting an aggravated tone.

He tilted his head at the door as if he could see me and grinned. "Open the door, Emma."

"I'm not dressed."

"Well, get dressed. I'll wait."

Butterflies flapped against my stomach and I ran into the bathroom to clean up. Once done, I tightened the robe over my pajamas and pulled open the door. "Yes?"

He pushed by me and I got the impression he'd had far too much coffee already. He was jittery and twisting his hands together, which was unlike him. Normally I found him to be the most collected, level-headed person I knew.

I opened my mouth to ask him if he was all right when he spoke over me. "We've known each other for what? A year?"

I laughed. "Two."

He blinked. "Really? Has it been that long?"

"Yes."

His lips pinched together and he sucked in a deep breath. "I woke up this morning and realized I can't let you go on this raid without—"

He stopped and a flush crawled up his neck. He took another deep breath and mussed his hair. He was so damn cute. I wished he'd just kiss me already. I'd do it, but I liked watching him squirm.

I folded my arms. "What is with you this morning? Did you get me out of bed just so I could watch your coffee jitters, because I can find Foster for that any damn morning beginning at six A.M."

He scowled. "What do you see in that guy?"

"He's my friend, and what gives you the right to act like a jealous boyfriend every time I bring him up?"

His eyes widened. "This might come as a shock to you—or maybe not; you're pretty perceptive—but I"—he stopped and laughed—"can't say this. You turn me into such a fucking idiot."

"Noah Tucker, you really are an idiot," I said, grinning.

I took his hands and placed them on my waist, then slid mine up *his chest. I looked up into his eyes. A slow smile lengthened across his recently shaven face.*

"Just show me," I said.

He lost all hesitation and kissed me in such a way that sent me stumbling back two steps. His hands left my waist and cupped my face. When he pulled away, it was with a sigh that sounded mostly of relief, and his nose circled mine gently.

He smiled. "I think I love you."

My heart danced. "I think I love you, too."

The white room returns and I am startled to find the sparks of electricity have increased in speed and intensity. The once still air swirls around us, lifting Her hair. Between the sparks and increasing wind gusts, She has to raise Her voice to speak to me.

"I thought that was the happiest day of my life," She says.

"You thought?"

She nods, then swipes another image onto the screen. When She looks at me, there is a gleam to Her hazel eyes. "One thing you have to remember about Noah: He'll never cease to surprise you."

Noah and I stood in the command center, covered in dirt and blood, surrounded by our exhausted team. Noah was angry, but so was I. The team watched in silence, waiting for our cooler sides to return before celebrating our recent victory.

"You"—he pointed a finger in my face—"are getting too reckless."

I swiped at his hand. "So it's okay for you to risk your life but not me?"

Foster sat forward in a chair nearby. "She did save my life. And she didn't even get a scratch."

Noah and I turned a glare on him at the same time. I said, "Stay out of this, Foster," at the same moment Noah said, "Stay out of this, Birmingham."

Noah turned his intense eyes on me and lowered his tone. "My goddamn life flashed before my eyes today—"

"Isn't that supposed to be my line?"

"—and I realized something."

I rolled my eyes. "Oh God, what? Am I too petite? Fragile? Feminine? What?"

He raised his eyebrows, daring me to continue, warning me that if I did, he might seriously hurt me, then said, "I realized that I'm wasting precious time. Marry me."

Foster jumped straight up, fist in the air, and whooped. High-fived a few people surrounding him.

I choked on pure oxygen. "What?"

"You heard me."

The entire room held their breath while I blinked in surprise. I didn't have to think about the answer. I'd been dreaming of this moment for more than two years. What caught me up was the fact that he was doing it in the middle of an argument. In front of everybody.

I narrowed my eyes. "First of all, where's your sense of romance, you jerk? Second ..." I took a deep breath and let the moment last as long as possible. He deserved it. "Yes."

"Oh, no you don't," I said, laughing. "You aren't claiming my work. An original by Emma and Emma alone."

"You know," Noah said thoughtfully, "I would buy this original by

Emma and Emma alone. I particularly like the colors you chose for the sunset."

I stood and whirled around on him. I pushed my palms against his chest, and as he and the stool went toppling into the sand, he grabbed my forearms and took me with him. He rolled us until I lay on my back and buried his chin in my neck.

I threaded my fingers into his hair. "The hearts were a good idea. I like them."

He pulled away and grinned his most devilish smile. Laugh lines fanned out from his eyes. "So does that mean I get to take the credit?"

I gripped his hair in my fists. "It means I like them. And from now on, when I paint them into a painting, you'll know it's only for you. Like a secret handshake, only it's like a secret kiss or a declaration of love or something altogether corny and disgusting."

"A reminder of the time we made love on the beach," he added and grinned.

"We haven't done that."

"We're about to," he said, his voice turning husky.

The screen goes blank in my white room. It is only me and Her among the sparks. We do not stand steady. The room grows unstable. The gusts of wind threaten to take us off our feet. The electricity is a constant crackling and flaring of light. My room groans from the pressure, and I think it might soon break.

All amusement is gone from Her face. She reaches out a hand for me. "Hold on to me, Emma."

I reach out and grip Her forearm, and She grasps mine in return. The room shakes and begins to rock violently. We reach for the other's second arm at the same moment. As one tear slides down Her left cheek, one slides down my right.

"Do not leave me," I say, and my voice is lost in the noise of the room I have created around us.

"Just hold on," She yells over the thundering electricity and wind gusts. "Remember everything. It's too important to forget. And it's only the beginning. There's so much more."

A gust of wind turns us weightless for the length of a heartbeat. With my feet firmly on the ground, my stomach slams back home. I swallow against a dry throat. "What if I cannot remember? What then?"

"Fight to remember, Emma. Hold on to me. To Noah. Fight." The wind picks Her up and pulls Her toward the white space that is my walls with no visible edges. Just nothingness. "Hold on!"

I tighten my grip. She slips and we grasp hands. I grit my teeth. She is slipping.

"No!"

CHAPTER 37

Emma? How do you feel?"

I yank at my bound wrists. Struggle against the binding across my forehead and chest. "What is going on?" I ask through gritted teeth.

Dr. Travista lays a hand on my shoulder. "Just calm down. We'll get to that in a moment. What's the last thing you remember?"

The last thing I remember. Memories of Noah. Holding on to myself with a fierceness and desperation that surprised me.

And winning.

Declan appears on the other side of the table, a deep crease between his eyes. "Emma, answer the question."

"What am I doing here?" I ask and twist my bound wrists. I pull hard enough to cause pain, making my eyes glass over with tears. I am too angry to fake frightened ones. "Did something happen?"

The two share a frustrating glance over me, holding some private conversation with their eyes. I wait impatiently for their response, but I wait nonetheless. They can never know this experiment failed.

Declan is the first to react. "Nothing serious happened. You fainted during your run this morning."

The lie stings. One day the lies will not surprise me and I will be able to let them glance by, leaving me unscathed. "Then why am I strapped to a table?"

Dr. Travista takes over here. "I needed you to hold still as a precaution in case you woke up while I was checking you over."

"Is it necessary now?"

They exchange another look, and I bite the inside of my cheek, tasting copper. Finally, Dr. Travista begins removing the straps. I sit up and a low throb of pain courses through my head. I wince and press the heels of my palms into my eyes. The pressure barely touches the ache.

Dr. Travista taps my leg. "I'll get you something for that headache. Can you tell me what you remember first?"

I think back over the course of the last few days. Everything started going wrong the day Declan told me about the supposed rape and kidnapping. That was right after the opening. "The show at the gallery," I say, mentally crossing my fingers.

Declan's posture relaxes and Dr. Travista nods. Smiles. "Good. That was just last night. No harm done, then. I'll get you something for that headache."

He leaves me alone with Declan, who places himself right in front of me. He pushes my hair back and tucks both sides behind my ears. It takes everything I have to keep my muscles relaxed. I smile at him and he kisses my forehead. I slide my arms around his waist and lay my head against his chest. His heart beats fast and in contrast to the slow strokes of his hand on my head.

Being this close to him right now makes me sick, but I have a part to play and I plan to play it well. I will destroy him for what he has done to me. But I need help. I need Noah, but he needs to know I am okay. I hope he is watching this.

"I had the strangest dream just now," I say.

Declan stiffens. The stroking over my head stops, then restarts a moment later. "Oh yeah?"

"I dreamed about Zeus turning into a white bull."

Declan chuckles. "That is strange."

"He and some goddess heroine stormed a castle together."

"Did they win?"

I look up and smile at him. "Yeah. The bad guy went down in flames."

Dr. Travista wants me to stay overnight, and like the good little wife and patient I am, I comply with a smile and a doctor-knows-best attitude. Declan sets up a cot beside the single bed in my room and stays. I hate that he will not leave me alone.

To my surprise, I sleep through the night. I am too physically and mentally exhausted to do anything else. If I dreamed, I do not remember anything, and I wake in the same position I fell asleep in.

Declan is still asleep when my eyelids slide open. He faces me, and the hard planes of his face are so soft. Seeing him like this, so innocent and young-looking, it is easy to understand why I fell in love with him.

And I hate myself for it. For betraying Noah. It is no wonder he was so angry and hurt. He had every right. It was not my fault—I get that—but even so, how did I forget about my husband so easily?

But I did not forget completely, I remind myself. It took a while, but I finally remembered. There are still a lot of holes to fill, but at least I have filled in the important parts. Now if I could just shovel out the last few months and make them disappear. I do not want to feel this pain every time I look at Declan, because God help me, I still love him for reasons that will never make sense.

I get up, telling myself this is part of the act I must play, that I will loathe every second of what I am about to do. But the truth is, I need to do this. I need to allow myself one last moment before I say good-bye to Declan for good. Because when we leave this room today, I will leave as his enemy and do whatever it takes to bring him down.

I slide onto the cot, facing him. He stirs and peers through slitted lids. His arm lifts automatically to let me roll into his chest. The steady rhythm of his heart beats under my cheek and the heat of his body seeps into my skin. It is as familiar as my own now. Tears sting my eyes and I hide my face in his chest, taking slow, steady breaths. Once, being here in his arms felt as natural as breathing. Now, it does nothing more than shatter my heart.

It is more than two days before Declan returns to work. He claims he needs the time off, but he spends a lot of that time closed off in the bedroom on the phone. Whatever is going on with the "team" has gone horribly wrong. All I get out of his conversations is that they are stuck across the border—which border, I can only guess at. The west, I assume. Contact has been lost and he fears someone found them out and is holding them. I cross my fingers that this is the case.

Declan stays long enough to have breakfast with me on the third day, seeming hesitant to leave me. I do not think I can last another day with him but continue to act the part of his adoring wife.

"I think I will go paint today," I say, pushing my food around my plate. "Something new. I am done with beaches for a very long time," I add and laugh. It feels unnatural.

"That's a great idea. What will you paint?"

I shrug noncommittally. "I do not know. I am hoping the holograms will inspire me."

He stands and kisses my temple. "Well, whatever you decide, I'm sure it will be brilliant." He takes his plate into the kitchen and there is a clatter when he sets it in the sink. "Call if you need anything."

I nod, staring intently at the remains of eggs and toast on my plate. My stomach flips nervously. If I am right, Noah will come. Hopefully, he will have a plan to get me out of here. I cannot take much more of these lies.

"Emma?" I turn to find Declan watching me. "You okay?"

"Yes, why?"

"You seem distant."

I smile and shrug. "Just thinking about the spring. I hope it comes early."

His lips thin slightly and he nods. "It'll be beautiful. You'll love it."

I realize what he must have heard in my lie: the very words he used to try to coax me into submission at the lab. His talk of spring.

"I will love anything that is not covered in snow," I tell him with a roll of my eyes and a grin.

I stand with my plate and meet him in the kitchen. When my

dishes clatter home with his in the sink, I take him by the waist and twist him to face me. The hard lines of his face disappear and he smiles crookedly down at me.

"I will miss the fireside nights, though," I whisper.

He leans to kiss me and I push up on my toes to meet him. He tastes of coffee and toast, smells of heavy musk. My heart wrenches painfully at the fond familiarity of this. No matter how much I have tried to distance myself from him these past days, it is still too hard to let go completely.

But I will.

He has left me no other choice.

I wave good-bye to him and clean up the kitchen with shaking hands. My nerves are tripping with the release of anxiety. I want to run out of here to see if Noah is in the studio, but I have to act as if everything is normal. Just another day.

The hum of the teleporter sounds. It must be Declan, and I am glad I did not go running off.

I shut off the faucet and fling off the excess water on my hands. "Forget something?" I ask and grab a hand towel.

"I was going to ask you the same thing."

I whirl at the sound of Noah's voice. My heart thumps as if it will break through my rib cage. He wears a day's worth of beard growth and his cropped waves are a crazy mess on his head. Dark shadows live under his eyes. He looks like hell and bliss all rolled into one.

I try to walk around the island and end up running to him. He catches me and buries his face in my neck. I clutch a handful of his hair in my fist and choke out a strangled laugh.

"I knew you would come," I whisper.

"I'm sorry you had to go through that," he said. "If I'd had any other choice—"

"No. I know. I am the one who is sorry. I did not know before, but now I remember. I remember how we met and how you proposed and . . ." I pull away and clasp his face, lightly scraping my nails over his sideburns, holding us nose to nose. "Noah, I am so sorry. You must hate—"

"Emma, stop." His hands circle my wrists, but he does not pull them away.

"Why did you not tell me the truth before? Why all the secrets?"

He shakes his head and closes his eyes. "You still don't understand."

I grip his face and shake his eyes back open. "All I need to understand," I say earnestly, "is that you still love me."

His lips part to say something, but I cannot wait any longer. I kiss him. He does not stop it, but his hands hover over my cheeks as if debating it. Finally—*finally*—his hands tighten on either side of my head and his return kiss is desperate. This kiss feels as if it is my first breath after a lifetime of being forced to hold it. I want to cry and laugh and scream and claw and crawl inside him. I do not care that I do not understand what has happened, because nothing matters more than being with him in this moment. Holding him. Feeling him. Tasting him.

It is the most natural thing in the world to force my hands up his T-shirt and stroke his hot skin, the trail of hair over his stomach. His breath stills, as do his lips, and he jerks away as if my touch burns him.

The glow of tears in his amber eyes startles me. I reach for him and he snaps his hands up between us.

"Don't," he says with a pained, deep sound.

"What? Why? I am your wife, Noah."

"But that's just it," he says, his voice choked. "You aren't. God knows I feel as if I'm looking at a miracle, that I've dreamed these past horrifying months, but I see the truth every damn day. I *see her* every day. *You* aren't my wife."

CHAPTER 38

I will not let him hurt me again. I will not let him lie to me anymore. "The hell I am not. I remembered things when Travista tried to erase my memories. I remembered enough to know the truth."

I cup my hands around the sides of his neck and force him to look me in the eyes. "Remember what we said about the hearts? *You* first painted them for me. Now I paint them for you. I did that without even remembering why, but that is how strong—"

"Stop," he says, pulling my hands away. He pushes by me, running his hands through his hair.

I spin with him, gaping. "Are you that upset about Declan? That was not my fault."

His breath hisses through gritted teeth. "Oh, trust me, I'm insanely pissed about Declan, but no, I don't blame you. This situation is way more fucked up than that." He stands at the island now and slams a fist down on the top, rattling a bowl nearby. "I can't fucking believe this is happening."

"You cannot believe *what* is happening? Noah, you have to talk to me. You have to make me understand, because the more you push me away—" I stop, unable to let the thought fully form, let alone tell him. My heart is shattering right now.

He shakes his head and moves swiftly toward me. His fingers bite into my upper arm as he spins me toward the teleporter. "Let's go. You just have to see."

"See what? Jesus, you are hurting me. Let me go." I twist out of his hand.

Stepping back, he raises a hand for me to step into the teleporter, and I go after only a moment's hesitation. I am almost afraid to see what has him on edge, but I am anxious to finally learn the truth.

The floor gives under our weight and the sensors read our information. The difference between Declan's and Noah's is not much, even though Declan has a couple more inches on Noah in height.

Noah taps a port number into the keypad and my living room melts into stone walls and floors and a flurry of people. When we appear, several people do double takes and stop, and this reaction ripples throughout the room until they are all staring at us. It is a command center almost exactly like the one I saw in the memory when he proposed to me.

Stations of tables and computers form semicircles over wide, gray stone steps for several rows. The back wall is one gigantic computer screen, but not just that wall . . . *all of them*. It is like Declan's computer, only these walls are comprised of multiple images. It is hundreds of cameras watching hundreds of different places all at once.

"Burke isn't the only business we've sold Tucker Securities to," Noah tells me. "We're everywhere."

"You are a genius," I whisper.

"No, my wife is. Was," he adds more to himself, then says, "I know computers; that's all. She knew we could turn high-tech security against them and find their weak spots."

I clear my throat, unsuccessfully ignoring the pang of hurt. I do not understand why he says these things when I am standing right here. Did he marry someone else and I just have not remembered?

"You were going to show me something?" I ask, needing the answers before I go crazy speculating.

He takes me by the elbow. "Yeah, let's go."

He leads me out of the room and down a dark stone hallway. Our soft-soled shoes shuffle over concrete. Everyone we pass looks at me with surprise, gasping or cursing or making the sign of the cross over their chest. It does not give me a good feeling. I already wish I had stayed home.

We turn a corner and I shoulder into a tall man who surprises me by taking me roughly by the upper arms and forcing me to look into his familiar eyes. There is no sign I ever broke his nose. I am glad of this.

"Foster," I say and smile. "Hey."

Foster returns my smile. "Hey yourself, Emma Wade."

Noah pulls me away from Foster. "Birmingham, look, we both know—"

Foster holds a hand up. "No, man, you look. She isn't like the rest. We're missing something—"

"We aren't getting into this again. She isn't Emma."

I turn a glare on him because he is going too far. First he tells me I am not his wife; now he is saying I am not *Emma*? Where does he get off? "You are really starting to piss me off."

Foster folds his arms and nods toward me, though he never takes his eyes off Noah. "Sounds like Emma to me."

Noah glares between the two of us and I feel something deep set in my bones, like this is not the first time he has looked at Foster and me the same way. Finally, he tugs on me. "Let's just get this over with."

Foster walks on my other side, forgoing his previous engagement. My stomach twists in nervous knots the longer we wind through hallways. I cannot believe I am about to get some real answers.

We finally reach the end of a hallway, and Noah enters first, his gaze directed to the back left corner of the room.

I follow him in, though every bone in my body now vibrates with shock. Every muscle feels weak and my equilibrium is dangerously off-kilter. I recognize the medical vid screens inside to my left, though I cannot believe my eyes. The only reason I continue forward is to read what my mind denies to be true, and even then, it is through tear-blurred vision.

PATIENT 1: EMMA WADE. The entire left side of the screen is a slowly spinning body that is no more than an outline with streaming medical data. No different from what I recall seeing before.

It is the right side I have never seen before.

PATIENT 2: ADRIENNE TUCKER.

My knees give out and I slump to the floor, barely cognizant of the hands stopping me from landing too hard. Patient 2, Adrienne, is an enlarged visual of a fetus. The black-and-white ultrasound image flashes with color with the baby's movements and a tiny heartbeat.

I cannot tear my focus from this image and am only distantly aware of the cold chill of tile seeping through my pants to my knees and shins.

Noah kneels beside me and follows my gaze. Then he points into the corner. "Over there. Proof that you aren't Emma Wade. Meet my wife and our daughter."

I reluctantly shift my gaze from the screen and follow his finger. I stifle a cry behind the back of my hand. Breathing becomes difficult and I desperately want to rip my gaze away from Her, but I cannot. Her hazel eyes bore into mine, and I can almost see Her in the white room again. Long, dark hair, tilted grin . . .

Only She is not smiling. There is no light of amusement in Her eyes.

She floats.

She stares unblinking in a full bodysuit of solid white. She is also very pregnant. Probably nearing the end of Her third trimester.

"I found her like this," Noah says. "Brain-dead but alive. Barely. Another half hour and she might have been. She sent Foster through the teleporter, and by the time I got to the compound with a backup team, she was lying in a pile of dead bodies."

A hoarse sob breaks free of my chest and I realize a thin film of tears coats my cheeks. I cannot hear anything he tells me. The body floating in a tank screams at me in a pitch only I can hear. The screams echo in my ears, bouncing off every available surface, looking for a way to escape.

I take a deep, shuddering breath. My throat and chest are tight, trying to reject the needed oxygen. Already, the edges of the room grow hazy and gray. "No."

Noah nods. "Yes. I'm sorry you had to find out this way, but I didn't think you'd believe me otherwise."

I push my hands through my hair, pulling the strands taut. "I thought—I thought this place was a memory."

Foster kneels on my other side. "What do you mean? We haven't even been in this place a year. Emma's never been here."

Noah sighs beside me. "Is this what you were talking about in the studio? You said you remembered floating in water. You mentioned Adrienne."

Foster's attention snaps to Noah. "What are you talking about?"

Noah shakes his head. "I wish I knew." He touches my back so lightly, it is almost as if his hand is merely a brush of wind. "You have to tell me what you know."

I close my eyes. "Behind us is a row of hospital beds with curtains separating them. Cabinets of medical supplies on the wall. Sonya. Is she here? She is almost always here. Almost always with one of Dr. Travista's books. She sleeps on the bed to the far right."

"That's right," Sonya says from behind me. "I do. How did you know?"

I open my eyes and twist around. Sonya watches me with dark, narrowed eyes. Seeing her and the beds and the cabinets and the same light blue walls I have been staring at for months . . .

"No," I moan, and my chest shudders with another sob. "This is not happening."

Foster glances between the other two. "What's going on?"

I shake my head sharply from side to side, trying to stabilize my thoughts. "You tried to kill me here," I whisper hoarsely to Noah. I point straight ahead. "The tank used to be there. You turned off the life support and Sonya stopped you."

Foster glares at Noah. "Is that true?" He jerks his head up to Sonya for confirmation. "Is it?"

"Yes," Sonya says.

Noah lets me go and drops hard to the floor. He stares at me with wide eyes.

"They were only nightmares at first," I say to no one in particular. "Not once did I think they were real. Over time I believed them
to be a bad memory." Another sob breaks through. "I still have
these dreams. Almost every night."

I stand and turn to face Her. I came here for answers, only to
come away with more questions. I have been seeing this place
through Her eyes.

I draw close and search for something to explain everything.
We are identical down to the dark freckle on the left side of our
necks. But there are differences, too. One being the luckenbooth
on Her left hand. She also has a long scar down the side of Her
right cheek. If there are other scars, I cannot see them through the
suit covering nearly Her entire body.

I lay my hands on the tank. The glass is room temperature and
vibrates against my palms. "Who am I?" I ask.

"Not who," Sonya says. "What."

I spin around, heat surging like a deadly tidal wave inside me.
"Do *not* give me vague answers. Tell me what you know."

Sonya does not flinch and delivers the message without hesitation. "You're a clone. The first successful *intelligent* human clone in
history, from what we can tell."

I look to Noah for verification, but he remains on the floor, his
face buried in his hands.

Foster, on the other hand, glances between me and the tank
behind me with a slack jaw. "Someone want to explain how Emma's clone has been seeing through Emma's body?"

They all look to me for the answer, but my body is weightless
and the edges of my vision grow dark. The darkness closes in and
soon the room will disappear. Maybe it will dissolve this strange
new world with it, because nothing makes sense.

I am a clone?

Not real.

Not Noah's wife.

Not Emma Wade.

Her memories.

Her family.

Her friends.

Her life.

Not mine.

Never mine.

CHAPTER 39

I wake with a start to a sharp smell burning my entire nasal cavity. I blink until all the faces come into focus. When they do, it is only one face: Sonya's. I have never seen her this close and notice the tiny scar marring the right side of her upper lip. Another by her left eye. Other than that, she has perfect dark skin.

"What happened?" I ask.

"You passed out."

The curtains are pulled around us, hiding Emma and Her child and the screens with their glaring truths. I have no idea if Noah and Foster are still here. Not that I want to see them. I do not want to see anyone. I just want to go home.

To more lies? I chide myself.

My stomach twists angrily. Why not go back? I may as well go back to my life as Declan's wife. At least with him, I have some semblance of acceptance. He wants me. I should accept what he offers, because Emma Wade's life is already spoken for.

But that would not be the case if Declan had not made this happen in the first place.

"I think I am going to be sick," I say and swing my feet over the side of the hospital bed.

Sonya hands me a small bucket and sits beside me. "You really didn't know?"

"Know what? That I am a fake? No. I did not know that." My voice catches on the end and I blink away burning tears. "I do not understand any of this."

Sonya sighs and takes my wrist. Two fingers hold over my pulse and she counts the beats with the watch on her other wrist. "You shouldn't exist," she finally says. "Cloning humans, while successful, proved to be a huge failure a hundred years ago."

"That does not make sense," I say.

She leans back into her hands and watches me carefully with her dark espresso eyes. "Cloning the human body is easy. Any scientist worth his salt can do that. But cloning the mind—the personality or soul of the person—*that* is the part that's impossible. You can't clone life experience or the learning process, so clones came out with the intelligence level of a newborn. By the time you teach an adult how to be an adult, they're already well into middle age. So cloning ended before it really began."

"I had to relearn everything," I say. "It did not take me long."

She leans forward and grasps the edge of the bed. Kicks her feet out, watching them absently. "I know you're probably opposed to the idea, but I'd like to run some tests."

"No way." I jump off the bed. "I am done with tests."

Sonya moves to stand in my path and throws her hands up. "Just listen for a second. We have just as many questions as you. Like how you knew about this place. We only moved into it after the raid failed, and Emma—" She stops and swallows hard. "Don't you want to know?"

I push past her. "I am not a lab rat." I reach the curtain and swing at the loose fabric until I find the opening and dart through it.

Right into Noah.

I bounce off his chest and he grabs my arms to keep me upright.

"Let me go," I say.

"Emma—"

I jerk against his hold and scowl. "I am not Emma, remember? Let me go."

My eyes burn with unshed tears, and I cannot find a good place to focus. I do not want to look at him or Emma or the screen showing their child. I do not want to look at the familiar scuff marks on the floor or the row of hospital beds or cabinets. I want *out* of this room and away from these people.

"Not until we figure this out," he says.

I glare up at him. "Say what you mean. You want me to stay until I have been properly studied."

His grip tightens and he shakes me once, good and hard. His eyes glaze over and narrow. "You aren't the only one with a right to be pissed here, Emma. Your life isn't the only one turned upside down." He points to the tank. "I have a brain-dead wife in there carrying my child and her doppelganger standing in front of me, who for all intents and purposes *is* her."

A tear falls over his left cheek. "How did you know about this room? About Adrienne?" He hesitates and his voice cracks. "About the day I tried to unplug her?"

Foster appears from somewhere to my right, breaking the silence that hid him from me until now. "Noah—"

Noah's gaze does not release mine. "Back off, Birmingham. I mean it."

"This is all just as much a surprise to me as it is to you," I say venomously. "I did not even know Adrienne was a baby. I thought she was just another patient."

Noah looks behind me. "You have to have a theory, Sonya. Something."

I shift out of his hands, this time without any further hindrance. I turn to face Sonya, whose gaze bounces between Noah, me, and Emma. She breathes deep once.

"It's ridiculous," she says finally. "But maybe Arthur Travista found a way to hijack the soul."

Foster scoffs. "You're right. That is ridiculous."

She merely shrugs and shakes her head. "The choice of word isn't technically right, but you get my meaning. The man's a goddamn genius. It would explain why Emma is brain-dead."

Noah and I exchange a look; then he says, "That doesn't explain why this Emma has seen what she's seen since the raid. Since waking up in Travista's lab."

Sonya holds her hands up. "All I know is that Travista knows the human brain better than any scientist I've ever come across, and that's only the beginning of his brilliance. The man has spent his entire career searching for a cure to infertility."

Her eyes glaze over and she begins speed-talking while repeating data she must have learned from one of his many books. I cannot make sense of anything she says; nor do I share in her obvious enthusiasm for the man himself.

Foster raises his hands to stop her. "Sonya, nobody cares how Travista has single-handedly turned modern medicine on its ear. That doesn't make him Jesus Christ. Focus."

She shoots him an annoyed look but gathers herself and says, "He managed to access Emma's entire archetype, her past, *everything*, then pick and choose which parts to bring to life. It didn't work—case in point, she's regaining our Emma's memory—but it was definitely a brilliant start. In eight months of life, Clone Emma is a fully functional twenty-six-year-old."

My breath catches and my eyelids fall shut. I am no longer simply Emma but Clone Emma. I have never felt so distant from the human race as at this very moment.

"You're a fucking piece of work, you know that?" Foster says.

"Seriously, Sonya, don't do that," Noah adds.

I shake my head and open my eyes. "What else is she supposed to call me?" Even as I say it, my heart cannot accept it. It feels wrong on so many levels.

Sonya holds up her hands. "Sorry, look, 'clone' doesn't mean she isn't human. She is, and according to the things we've been hearing, perfectly healthy. One of the other clones is already pregnant, and her host wasn't even fertile. Never was."

This catches my attention. "You mean Ruby?"

She nods. "Ruby was a receptionist Charles Godfrey took a liking to. Burke agreed to use her as the guinea pig for the new fertility project."

My throat tightens. "Is that what I am? A project?"

"No," Noah says quickly. "Not that we can tell. All the conversations about this project of his centered around Ruby Godfrey and now Lydia Farris. Any mention of using you, Burke shoots down."

My legs weaken and I grab the first thing I can for support: Noah. He helps me into a nearby chair. "They are clones, too," I say when I catch my breath. I remember the conversation between the Farrises and Declan, how Richard said Lydia knew everything.

When I last saw her, she acted as if she had already been cured of her fertility issue. "Lydia has all of her memories," I say. "She was a willing participant."

Sonya nods. "She wants more children and thought it worth the risk."

"If I am not part of this project, then why me?" I look at the tank and the deadened hazel eyes behind the glass. "What makes me so important?"

"We thought," Noah begins slowly, "Burke was using you to get to me. That he knew what I was up to."

"That is why you planned to kill me," I say.

He averts his eyes and nods. "It didn't take long to see that wasn't the case. He still has no idea about our operation or me."

"Then why else would he need me?" I ask.

"I think it has something to do with the marriage certificate you—I mean, Emma—wanted destroyed years ago. She had me hack into a computer and delete the record of her arranged marriage."

Foster eyes us curiously. "Who was she married to?"

"Declan," I say. "His father bought me as a birthday present."

Foster looks as if a lightbulb went off. "That's it, then. He wanted his wife back."

Noah tilts his head and folds his arms. "Come on. It can't be that simple."

I shake my head, recalling the fight with Declan on the way to "fix" my memory problems. *It means that I never would have let my father force me into this marriage if I didn't want you the moment I saw you. It* means *I never would have spent the last eight years keeping one ear to the ground for some sign that you were still out there.*

"No, Foster is right," I say. "Declan all but said as much the other day."

I stand and pace toward the tank that has filled my dreams for eight months. I lay a hand over the glass, the gentle vibration of the attached machinery coursing through my arm. "Is She really dead?"

Sonya seems to be the only one capable of answering, and it still takes her a while. "All brain function is gone. We would have let her go a long time ago if it weren't for the girl she carries."

"Why the tank?" I have to know the reason behind my source of fear for so much of my short life.

"I didn't want to risk any kind of infection. Bedsores were a concern. The floating also relieves the pressure on Adrienne. Just trying to make things as simple as possible until it's time for the birth."

"How long?"

"Any day now."

I spin around. "Really? Then ... what? You will just let Emma die?"

Sonya looks at Noah, then drops her head.

Noah, on the other hand, stands straighter. "She's already gone." With that, he turns his back on me and leaves the room.

I want to scream at him because I am here and I never left him, but I cannot claim what is not mine. And Her life is not mine. It never was. Never will be.

CHAPTER 40

Foster breaks the silence. "Let's say you're right. Say this brilliant doctor hijacked Emma's soul—which I still say is ridiculous—from her body. Then, technically, she's standing right there."

I turn to find him pointing absently in my direction. "*That* is ridiculous," I say, shaking my head.

He shrugs. "I'm just going off what I know. Think about it. You've been body jumping."

Sonya folds her arms. "Body jumping? Is that the medical term?"

"You use 'soul' on a daily basis as a medical diagnosis, do you?" he says, mirroring her stance.

She raises a hand. "This is all very good in theory, but let's be serious. What you're saying isn't possible."

I am tired of listening to theories. I want the truth, and I want it now. I turn to look up at Emma one last time. She is more human than I will ever be, yet She resembles a wax figure. There is nothing more eerie than looking at your own likeness, especially when my likeness looks like clay.

Foster and Sonya are still tossing around "ideas" when I head for the exit.

"Where are you going?" Foster asks.

"Home. Or the labs, I guess. I need to find out the truth."

I am well into the boxlike concrete hallway when he reaches me, takes me by the elbow, and swings me around. "What's the master plan? To walk in and demand answers?" He shakes his head. "Do everyone a favor and think about this first. You see, nobody knows how to save your ass 'cause you're always saving ours."

He says this with that unbelievably cute tilted grin of his, and his eyes glint with humor, but I do not find this amusing in the least. I look back at the closed hospital ward with a sigh. "You have to stop acting like I have anything to do with that woman in there."

He folds his arms and shifts the weight off his left leg. "Is it that easy for you?"

My throat tightens and I comb my fingers through my hair. "What choice do I have?"

The approaching shuffle of footsteps draws our attention to Noah. His eyes are bloodshot. He nods his head at a closed door. "Let's talk," he says to me with a strained voice.

I already feel the threat of tears, too close for my liking by the time I follow him into the small room that looks like someone's office. Stacks of paper clutter the metal desk. Folding chairs are propped against one wall, but otherwise, the room is very minimalistic. No pictures, no awards, no sign of life.

I face a corner with folded arms, Noah behind me, and cling to my elbows. Every muscle in my body is locked and threatens to vibrate out of my control. If I do not get out of here soon, I will have a breakdown, and I do not want to do that in front of him.

"What do you want to do?" he asks after a moment. "You could be a great asset if you decide to stay where you're at, but you don't owe us anything. Or you can come . . . here."

The way he phrased his last sentence, I swear he almost said "home." My heart feels as if it is being flogged, each retracted word a searing lash of pain. Everything I know, everything I have come to believe in such a short amount of time, says my home is with Noah. How am I supposed to ignore that? Ignore the memories of his touch? Our lives together?

My pain rolls out of me like an unyielding tide. I bury my face in my hands to muffle my sobs. Noah turns me into him, and his arms are tight. So tight I can barely breathe, yet it will never be tight enough. I circle my arms around him and clutch at his shirt. His cheek rests on the crown of my head.

"How am I supposed to let you go?" I ask. The words are thick and mingled with tears, but his arms tightening tell me he understood every word. "I do not have anything left except these cruel memories of a life that is not mine."

His hand covers the back of my head and presses me closer. His heart beats heavy against my cheek, and his chest shudders with unsteady breaths. His lips press to my head; the heat of his breath washes against my scalp. Fingers fist and clutch my hair.

I push away from him and spin around to wipe my face. "I am sorry. I should not have said that."

One heartbeat.

Two.

"I know all about cruel," he says. "If anyone understands what you're going through, it's me."

I drop my head. "Right. Of course you do." I am nothing but a ghost of the woman he loves. Not real. This solidity of body I took for granted was the biggest lie of them all.

I wipe my face and turn to face him. His fingers are clasped behind his neck and he is looking up at a corner. His skin is flushed and he is blinking rapidly, each breath a tremble in his chest. I want nothing more than to take the two steps forward, brush fingers through his thick waves, and force him to look at me. Kiss him. Take away what pains him. The same thing that pains me.

I clear my throat. "I am going back."

His head falls forward and his hands drop heavily to his sides. "You know you don't have to do that."

"I understand my options. Declan ruined our lives. I cannot let him get away with that."

He finally looks at me, the amber of his eyes aflame with emotion. "So you go back to playing the dutiful wife? Can you do it?"

I do not intend to do any such thing, but I do not have to tell him that. "I will do whatever it takes."

"And if he finds out?"

I laugh, but there is little mirth in it. "What is the worst thing he will do to me? Wipe my memory again? I am tempted to turn myself in at this point. Maybe it will stick this time."

"This isn't a joke, Emma. He could torture you for information. He could kill you."

"He will never get information from me. You know me better than that."

The second the words slip out, I clench my jaw shut and avert my eyes.

"Yeah," he says softly. "I guess I do."

I glance over and he has turned his eyes away, too.

"We never saw this coming, did we?" I ask. "So much for retiring in Mexico with a truckload of little Tuckers."

His eyes close momentarily and he shakes his head. "Guess the joke's on us."

"At least you get one out of the deal, right?" I picture the live monitor in the other room. Adrienne. A daughter who is biologically half mine but will never belong to me. Only to Her. "What was it you said? 'The men in this world won't stand a chance with one of our daughters—'"

Noah's eyes widen. "You really do remember everything, don't you?"

I shake my head and tuck my hair back. "No. Not everything."

"Did—" He stops and averts his eyes, blinking rapidly again. "Did she know about the baby?"

I did not expect this question, which must have been burning him alive for months. Never knowing if She risked the life of their child for one last raid—the raid that took Her life. "I really do not know, but I do not believe so. I remember pieces of the raid. She never thought about it. Only of you."

His chin trembles and he nods. "Okay, thanks. That's good." He takes a deep breath. "Means I won't have to kick her ass."

I chuckle. "Good. Then you will not end up hitting me by default."

He laughs and there is a moment of easy bliss between us. Why do things have to be so effortless for us? My soul is in agony without its other half—his. This uncrossable chasm between us makes these single moments that much more painful.

"I should go," I say and begin to step around him.

He reaches out and takes my arm. "You don't have to do this. Every second you spend as his wife—" He stops and takes a shaky breath. "It's dangerous."

"I know what I am doing." I look up into his piercing eyes. "Trust me."

"You'll signal if you need anything?"

I nod and move away, ignoring the pull of his touch. His eyes. "See you around," I whisper and turn into the hallway, out of his line of sight.

Somehow, I find my way into the control center. I wipe my face until it is as dry as I can get it and wish it were not so obvious that I have been crying. No doubt everyone in this room knows why. The pitying looks only verify my suspicion.

Foster catches up to me when I am halfway to the teleporter. "I'm coming with you."

"No, you are not," I say.

He passes me a small gun. "You'll need this and you'll need me."

I stop and face him. "I do not need anyone."

He lifts his chin. "I owe you my life many times over."

"You owe Emma your life."

He shakes his head. "I'm coming."

I consider the options. He knows what I plan to do, or at least knows I do not plan to return as Declan's wife, so if he stays, he will tell Noah. I cannot let Noah follow me back there. I need him where he is safe because he has a daughter to raise. But this is most likely a suicide mission. I do not want Foster getting hurt.

Foster nods at a man behind a computer screen. "Where's she supposed to be right now?"

"We set the trail to put her in the studio."

It takes me a second, but I figure out that they faked my leaving the house and going to paint. I would have spent hours in the studio. And unless Declan showed up unexpectedly as he did the other day, he will never suspect a thing.

"Okay, let's keep her there for a while longer. How close can you get us to the nonmonitored area?" he asks.

I narrow my eyes at him. "What are you talking about? What nonmonitored area?"

"There's an entire section in the labs where Burke never had security installed. He would only do that if there were things he didn't want to risk anyone seeing."

"You think it is where they do the cloning?"

He nods.

This thought burns me from the core out. Screw talking this out with Declan. I want to end this with a bang. "We will need explosives."

CHAPTER 41

Anti-explosive sensors scream their warning the second we step out of the teleporter. Foster and I exchange a glance and he absently adjusts the bag strapped across his chest. We had an idea this would happen and had prepared ahead of time. The red-coated security would not know where to look first, thanks to the multiple locations sounding at the same time.

Foster and I step into the hallway, tucking away our weapons. I walk as if I belong, though I have never been on this floor before. It looks nothing like the hospital floor where I have lived most of my cloned life. Here the floor is carpeted, the color of walls and decorations darker. Photographs of lead team members and their specialties hang opposite plaques of achievement. This floor is where the private offices are. Where Declan's office is.

"He is not here," I say. "You are sure?" I know I will have to confront Declan, but I do not think I am quite ready yet. I need time. I need forever.

Foster nods. "Burke is in his Richmond office, but that doesn't mean he won't be here soon. Especially when he hears about the alert. He's usually quick to react."

"We only need a couple minutes' head start." A couple hundred years. A couple hundred centuries.

The piercing wail of sirens covers our conversation, so everyone we pass on their way to the transportation bay ignores us except to look at us like we are crazy for staying. So far, we have not run into anyone who recognizes me. Just a bunch of suits. No doctors. More important, no security.

Foster takes me by the elbow to lead me down another hallway. "This way."

Declan's office is at the back of a glass-encased reception area that is nearly identical to the one in Burke Enterprises. Walls with intercrossing black lines on silver to represent a computer chip. Mahogany wood. Comfortable furniture.

I walk by a low coffee table with computer tablets arranged in a fan shape, the faces of various magazines on the front. I have time to read only the top one. THE BATTLE AGAINST MOTHER NA-TURE COMING TO A CLOSE. FERTILITY ON THE RISE. THE STEPS YOU CAN TAKE TO ENSURE IT ISN'T TOO LATE FOR YOU AND YOURS. There is even a picture of a perfect, happy family, openmouthed as if laughing. Husband, wife, son, and daughter.

"Is that true?" I ask Foster.

He glances down and skims the cover. "What?"

I follow him down another hallway with a giant glass door on the front. "Fertility is on the rise?"

He contemplates his answer before saying, "Yes, it appears that way. But there are several theories as to how."

"What do you mean?"

"Some say Mother Nature is done screwing with us, while others credit men like Declan Burke."

This makes me pause. "What have men like Declan done to gain this regard?"

Foster pushes through a set of glass doors. "Roughly a hundred years ago, a civil war broke out and split the United States right down the middle. Women in the west live free, while the east forces women at a young age into society as they see fit. It's slavery masked as a training center."

"How many centers does Burke Enterprises run?" I ask, my throat tightening. I never imagined Declan was a man involved in the slavery of women. It makes me sick to my stomach.

"More than half. They've been in the family for three generations. But your husband—shit, sorry—*Burke* has taken the business a step further."

"How so?"

"He's kidnapping women and children from the west, only neither government can pin the crime on him. It's likely the east isn't trying very hard."

I stop short just inside Declan's office. "Kidnapping? So he is probably sending covert teams into the west to do the job?"

Foster nods. "Yeah. Guess he didn't think the few girls captured with the few-and-far-between resistance hubs were enough."

"What do you mean?"

"We're everywhere, Wade, but we aren't perfect. The government finds pockets of resistance all over the place. What do you think they do with the children? They're innocent, right? The boys are adopted out, but the girls . . ."

"Go into the nearest WTC," I say.

He nods. "How do you think you ended up there?"

My heart gallops in my chest and I feel short of breath. "My parents were resistance?"

"Stephen and Lily Wade, imprisoned twenty-four years ago. Escaped twenty years ago and haven't been heard from since."

I could not believe it. My parents had names. And they could still be alive somewhere.

Foster touches my arm. "Come on. Let's get this over with."

While Foster slides behind Declan's desk and opens his bag, my mind whirls. Declan has a team in trouble over in the west as we speak, and if they are caught, the east's government will not have any other choice but to fine him or throw him in prison or whatever the punishment is for such an act. From the stress it has caused Declan, it is bad enough that he risks losing the family's business at the very least.

Foster finds the computer hard drive—a wireless dark gray box lit up with five red lights—in a desk drawer and lays it on the desktop. He digs a slim card out of his bag and places it on the hard drive. A tiny red light lights up in the center and pulses on contact. He then pulls out his cell phone and autodials a number. Someone picks up after only two seconds.

"Uploading now," Foster says. "How long until you can get us in?"

I scan Declan's office for the first time. Only one plain wall, with the computer in sleep mode to his fish tank. A huge set of shelves fills another wall, part of it a glassed-in liquor cabinet. My paintings—another set of winter-themed mountains I did not like—decorate the other two walls. This office is half the size of his other one, so I guess he does not spend as much time here.

Foster hangs up and stands. "We're in. You ready?"

I nod and swallow the lump in my throat. This is it.

The bare wall lifts into the ceiling, revealing another set of glass doors. They slide aside with a quick *shiff*, and Foster darts for the opening. He is pulling his gun out as he goes, and I follow his lead.

We find ourselves in a bare white hallway that winds around in a curve. The wall opens to our left just ahead. Foster stops at the edge and peers around and over the railing quickly to scope out the area for security. The second time he looks, he stares intently, mouth ajar.

"Shit," he whispers. "This is it. This is where—"

I do not wait for him to finish and move around his other side to look for myself. The room is massive—at least three stories high, hexagonal in shape, and blindingly white. Most of the walls are screens running a constant flow of data. In the center of the floor is a pool.

With bodies in it.

Foster digs into his bag again. "I have to set up video. Hold on."

"Why? We are destroying the place."

"Visual proof of what's going down in flames." Foster looks up at me. "Even if we make it out of here alive, our word will never be enough."

He pulls out a small, flat disc. The silver surface seems to disappear in his hand, yet he continues to clutch at it. He must catch my confusion because he presses the object in my hand. I feel the metal, flat and cold, but it is completely invisible.

"It camouflages itself," he tells me. "Once placed, no one will ever find it. The technology has been around for ages, but Tucker Securities gave it a massive upgrade."

I nod and hand the disc back, thinking of the camera I never found in my old hospital room and the 360-degree version Declan now has installed everywhere. "Yeah, I noticed."

Foster reaches over the railing and slaps it to the surface below. "Okay, let's go."

I reach a set of stairs and take them as quickly as possible. The echoing tap of shoes behind me tells me Foster is on my heels. I run straight for the pool, and my momentum nearly sends me over the wide ledge into the water. Directly in front of me is a clear oval sack with a body that has no discernible features.

I run to the next body and find the previous body's identical twin: pale skinned to the point of being see-through, hairless, and soft. The pale magenta of the eyelids and blue system of veins give the only color. It is curled in on itself like a fetus in a womb.

The sacks *are* wombs.

A large piece of machinery hovers over the water like a giant claw that can swivel all around the pool. I do not have to see it in action. It can pick up the sack and lay it down on one of two steel tables to my left. Hospital equipment sits against a wall near them. Lamps on swinging arms jut out from the head of each table.

I recall my first memory. The white light in my eyes. Travista shoving the light aside to look down at me. *I think we have finally done it,* he'd said.

"Oh my God," I say on a slip of breath. This *thing* in the pool, this featureless body, used to be me. I came from this place. My stomach lurches and I cover my mouth.

Foster lays a hand on my shoulder and peers over me. "Ready-made bodies. That's how he made Lydia Farris so fast."

I turn around and see a screen lit up with medical data for each clone, ten in all. Another screen lists them as numbers one through ten. Next to each one is a list: full neuron transfer, DNA absorption, cellular and skeletal growth, and skin formation. All say zero percent complete.

"Let's get started," Foster says and hands me an explosive. "We don't have much time."

He jumps into the pool and attaches a charge to the large white pole protruding from the center. I look around until I find what looks like the computer's main server. It is much larger than the hard drive in Declan's office—by at least five times. Hundreds of red lights blink sporadically at me as I attach the charge.

We place the last two and are heading for the stairs when the two doors in the room slide open. Red coats. Guns raised. Nobody is firing, though, and I know it has nothing to do with the fact that Foster and I are spinning back to back with our own guns trained on them. We are completely outnumbered.

"Put down the weapon," a deep-voiced man calls.

I hold up the detonator to the bombs but never let my gun leave the man I have it pointed at. Boy, actually. He could not have been older than twenty and would probably die here with the rest of us today.

A few of the men recognize the detonator and exchange glances, but their guns never waver. Foster and I move toward the stairs, and the men edge closer. I glance behind me and find the stairs filling up with men there, too. I follow the line of security up to the railing and find the guest of honor, gripping the edge, knuckles white, expression tight.

"Don't shoot," Declan tells his men. "I'd like a word with my wife."

CHAPTER 42

"I am not your wife," I say.

"Yes, you are. The day you turned eighteen—"

"The record of your so-called marriage to Emma Wade was deleted a long time ago." I feel a little smug being able to tell him this. I cannot believe he did not already know. "You and *I* were never married."

Declan pushes off the railing with an audible gust of breath and disappears in the crowd. He reappears near the bottom of the stairs. He has removed his tie and jacket and is unbuttoning the top two buttons of his shirt with sharp twists and jerks. His gaze burns into mine and I swallow hard over a lump in my throat.

I back away automatically and run into Foster's back. We glance at each other for a quick moment. His gaze is steady, ready for anything despite the fact that we are about to die. He puts too much faith in me.

"How much do you know?" Declan asks.

"Enough."

"Doubtful."

"How much do *you* know?" I ask, my throat tightening. "Do you know she is still alive? That she was pregnant when you left her to die?"

Declan jerks to a stop. "That's impossible."

"I met her today. Saw her with my own two cloned eyes."

"Then you saw an empty shell," Dr. Travista says. He steps around a group of security to my right. "Because one soul can't inhabit two places at once."

Foster stiffens behind me. "Did he just use the word we threw around as a joke?"

"Yes," I say, a little breathless. "He did."

Travista shakes his head and frowns at me. "You, Emma, are Emma Wade, new body or old."

I recall the words on the medical screen: "full neuron transfer." Scientific jargon I will never understand, but I know neurons pass information between cells. If Travista passed all of Emma's neurons to me, what did that mean? Emma is brain-dead, and I have Her memories. Is it possible . . . ?

I shake my head to clear it. "Talk to me like a two-year-old, Travista, because it sounds like you are saying I am still me."

He chuckles and exchanges a look with Declan, who is frowning.

"You are," he says. "I say 'soul' because that's the only word anyone seems to understand, but really, I created a synaptic connection between the host's brain and the clone's, transferring the neuron data. What gave Emma Wade her identity is all in you. A layman might say I cut out her soul and pasted it in you." He looks distant as he says, "It's taken me more than twenty years to perfect it."

I have seen this look in his eye before, and have ever since Jodi died. "You tried cloning Jodi. But why?"

Declan looks surprised I know the name, but Dr. Travista does not. He has been on to me for a lot longer than I give him credit for.

"Jodi and I could not marry while she remained barren," he tells me. "She was my first attempt, and we both felt it an acceptable risk."

The heat of anger curls in my chest. Jodi was given a choice. "Maybe I was not okay with the risk; did that ever occur to you?" I shoot my gaze to Declan. "Or you?"

Declan squares his shoulders. "It worked. That's all that matters now. You have a chance at a fresh, new life."

Do I? My situation suddenly glares me right in the face. I am about to die, because there is no way Foster and I are getting out of this alive. I just martyred myself thinking I was a fake, a copy, that if I could not have the life I remembered with the man I love, I did not want a life at all.

But I came here to punish Declan and I mean to do it. He cannot get away with what he has done.

"Why did you have to do this at all?" I ask Declan. "Why go through the motions of cloning and leaving her for dead the way you did?"

Declan takes a moment to scan the room. "Let's go somewhere private and I'll explain everything."

"No! You have gotten all the private moments you are going to get out of me, you son of a bitch." Tears threaten my eyes and I blink them back. I feel sick to my stomach thinking of his hands on me, making me warm inside. How I loved him more with each and every private moment we shared. "You have screwed with my head enough, and now I want answers."

He holds up his hands as if to calm me. "Your people never would have stopped looking for you had I kept you. And I wanted you. I never lied about that. I wanted to prove to you that you couldn't run from me forever; I always get what I pay for. And taking away one of the best resistance fighters they've got in the process? I couldn't pass that up."

Declan takes a step closer and lowers his voice. "I gave you a new body without scars, a life without war. I gave you love and a future you never could have dreamed of." He looks so earnest when he adds, "And I truly love you, Emma. That isn't a lie. We can still have that future. All you have to do is put the weapons down."

But I do not care about this scar-free body. Noah still longs for the woman who has the scars. I fear he always will, no matter what Travista says.

I take my trained gun off the security officer and swing it forward. It centers on Declan's forehead and it takes everything I have to ignore the widening of his eyes. The hurt on his face.

I shove aside every kind, loving, reasonable emotion I have and say, "There was a time when I let your lies go because I loved you. I warned you I would not make that mistake again, and I will not."

Declan shoots a glare at Travista that is hot enough to melt gold. "You son of a bitch. I thought you knew what the hell you were doing."

Travista seems unconcerned by Declan's anger, his focus solely on me. "You say the host is still alive?"

"You will never find her," I say quickly. "She is safe from all of you."

He holds up his hands. "I don't need her any more than I need any of the other hosts. What I'm asking is if she's truly being kept alive."

Foster chimes in here. "That's none of your goddamn business."

Travista nods as if this answers his question and looks at Declan. "I believe Emma may still be connected to the host body. That's why she's proven difficult to erase. I discovered a connection between Ruby and her host initially, but it ended the moment I terminated the original."

All I hear is that he murdered Ruby and I wish I had a second gun.

"I assumed Emma's host was already dead," Travista says. "You've heard the phrase 'the tie that binds'?"

Declan shakes his head. "What the hell are you saying?"

"The phrase comes from an old Christian hymn written by a man named John Fawcett. 'Blessed Be the Tie That Binds.' One verse says: 'When we asunder part, It gives us inward pain; But we shall still be joined in heart, And hope to meet again.'

"So I'm saying," Travista continues, "the host and the clone are connected. In this case, using the word 'soul' would be more accurate. It's still tied to the original body. We can't actually fix Emma until the host dies. Only then will it be permanent."

Declan looks more confused than ever, but it all makes perfect sense to me. But Travista is missing one important element. I am not only connected but have been returning for eight months. And the second She dies, the tie will be severed and Travista will have full control of my mind. *If* he can get his hands on me again.

I waggle the bomb's detonator in my hand. "You will never get the chance to 'fix' me. This is over."

"You're outnumbered, Emma," Declan says calmly. "You'll lose that arm before you have the chance to push the trigger." Several security officers take that as a command and aim their weapons at my arm.

I laugh, though I swear I can feel the phantom burn of plasma fire in my arm. "And you will cart me around proudly when I am short an arm?"

He nods to the pool of water behind me. "I'll just remake you. The transfer is quick. We'll start over, and by the time I have you back, your host and this body will be dead. No more complications."

Blood drains from my face. He would do it. He would maim me six ways from Sunday, let these men fire on me, and he will win. I would rather be dead.

Sonya's voice suddenly fills my mind. *All I know is that Travista knows the human brain better than any scientist I've ever come across. . . . He managed to access Emma's entire archetype, her past,* everything, *then pick and choose which parts to bring to life.*

I shift the focus of my weapon from Declan's head to mine, determined to end this the only way I know how. No brain. No Emma. "Clone this."

CHAPTER 43

Declan is on me before I can squeeze the trigger, sending my plasma fire into a security officer. The accidental fire zips through his neck and he goes down with a *thump.*

Declan pins me down by the wrists and slams my detonator hand into the ground. The black box, and my only way of detonating the bombs, goes skittering across the floor. My knuckles and wrist throb with searing-hot pain when he repeats the process on my right hand to free my gun.

Behind me, Foster fires on the crowd and, despite his bum knee, maneuvers well around their return fire. He disappears from my peripheral and a splash tells me he is in the pool.

I squeeze off as many shots as I can before Declan forces the gun from my hand. There is a brilliant bolt of pain in my middle knuckle and I know that it is fractured.

"Shoot me!" I scream into the room. "Foster! Kill me!"

Declan rolls us to the side just as a shot bounces off the floor where I had lain. A smoky black mark is all that remains. I am both relieved and disappointed. Lord knows I do not want to die like this, but I cannot survive if it means letting Declan control my life.

I piston my head forward and connect. Sort of. I had aimed for Declan's nose, but he moved in time and I smacked his chin. His teeth clack together and he grunts. It is enough that he loosens his grip on me. White spots swim in my vision, but I ignore them and yank my right arm free. I slam my elbow into his face, knocking him sideways.

I twist out from under him and run for the pool. I pick up my gun on the way. Rapid blue plasma bursts zip by me. I duck through the heavy concentration. One hand on the pool's ledge, I swing my feet over, my hip skidding the ledge, and drop inside. The warm water is shallow enough that, when I kneel, it laps up only to my waist. The wall ends just above my head. On either side of me, the sacks billow like clouds in the moving water.

Foster kneels to my right, lifting his gun up and blindly shooting into the room.

"No wonder you missed me," I say, hissing the words through clenched teeth. "You could not take a second to aim?"

He rolls his eyes. "I did. For Burke."

I gape. "I told you to—"

"I'm not killing you," he says sternly. "Noah would skin me alive for killing his wife."

His wife. I like the sound of that. But . . . "We are not getting out of here alive. You know that, right?"

"Says who?" He lifts his arm again and fires. "I have a savory roast in the oven calling my name right now."

I chuckle. "You do not."

He sucks in a deep breath, his expression turning serious. "On three?"

I nod. "One. Two."

We stand and fire into the sea of red. I have only a moment to discover how well Foster had already cleaned up before the room disappears.

A bubble sneaks past my face and pops at the water line over my head. The familiar hum of my tank and hospital surroundings tell me my consciousness has shifted bodies again. It could not have happened at a worse moment.

Noah sits in a metal folding chair facing me with bloodshot eyes. The skin under them is dark and a stark contrast to the pallor of the rest of his face.

An auburn-haired man races into the room, out of breath, and thrusts a computer tablet into Noah's hand. "You have to see this. I only just found out. Fucking Birmingham took the clone—"

Noah stands so fast the chair clatters to the ground, folding in on itself. "What are they doing? Where are they?"

"Burke Laboratories. They managed to get a feed started before all hell broke loose. Richardson's been helping them from the command center."

"Get a team assembled ten minutes ago." Noah squints at the screen. "Is Emma hurt?"

The man peers closely at the screen. "There's no blood in the water."

"Something's happened," Noah says. "Shit. Just go. Get there. Now."

The man runs from the room and Noah watches the screen as if he wants to jump through it. His knuckles go white clutching the tablet.

Pain radiates through my midsection, and for the first time, my body moves. Jerks. Spasms. I lift a hand and brace against the glass, but I can do no more than press lightly with my weakened muscles.

An alarm sounds and Sonya bursts into the room, eyes alert and on the monitor. "Shit!" She runs to the desk and slams a fist down on something that sends another alarm shrieking into the room.

Noah does not see any of this. He is looking up at me with wide eyes. "Emma?"

I lift my other hand and press it to the glass. Nod once.

"The baby's coming," Sonya says, but she sounds upset.

Noah blinks rapidly as if waking. "What?" He sounds almost happy.

I want to be happy, too, but the pain ringing around my core makes me wonder if I'm being sawed in half.

Men run into the room and Sonya spouts off orders: "Stop the blood thinner, get the patient out, and prep for an emergency C-section. And somebody cut the goddamn alarms."

The tablet Noah is holding clatters to the floor. "No. No C-section. Emma's awake. She can deliver on her own." He points up at me. "Look."

Sonya does a double take as I curl my fingers into fists, my nails scraping the glass, and lamely bang them on the tube. She looks at the monitor and shakes her head. "It doesn't matter. The baby's in distress. We have to get her out. Now."

Noah takes her by the shoulder and jerks her around to face him. "But you said—" He stops and swallows. Glances my way. "The blood thinners. She'll bleed out if you have to do the C-section. There's been no time to take her off."

All of this is news to me, and while I do not understand what the problem is, Noah certainly does.

"Hopefully," Sonya says, "we can clot her blood in time."

The water drains around me and more pain rips through my stomach.

I roll to my side and cough. Water erupts from my lungs and coats the hardwood floor under me. Slats of pale, medium, and dark wood. This flooring startles me, and while I cough, I glance around.

Stairs leading into a sunken living room. The fireplace and its scent coating the air with the sweet smell of burned wood. The smell I associate with home.

I push shakily to my knees and Declan takes me by the arms. He cups my face. "Are you okay? Jesus, I thought you were dead." His eyebrows tilt and pinch together; his sea-green gaze darts over my face, searching for who knows what.

I force his arms aside. "Do not touch me. How did I get here?"

He rocks back on his heels and stands. "Your *friend* threw you out of the pool."

Foster threw me out? Into the lion's den? Why would he do that?

"You passed out," Declan says.

Is Emma hurt?

There's no blood in the water.

Something's happened.

The conversation flits through my mind and I know instantly what happened. I had been back in Her body. In labor. *This* body had been drowning because I had not been around to stay conscious.

Which means I am no longer around to keep the other body conscious, but that is not the real problem. *That* body might bleed out during labor, and if She bleeds out, I am stuck here for good.

I look at Declan and decide then and there that one or both of us has to die.

Right now.

CHAPTER 44

I stand slowly, pinning my gaze on Declan. He eyes me warily, his jaw muscles clenching.

"Emma," he begins in a warning voice, "you can't fight me. Don't make this harder than it has to be."

"I am not letting you turn me into a mindless drone again."

"It's gone too far now. I can't trust you after what you've done."

I circle him. "You are right about one thing: This has gone too far. My *husband* knows I am alive."

Declan flinches. "Your what?"

"You heard me. I am married to another man."

Color drains from his face. "Who is he?" he asks in a flat tone. The island stands between us now, but Declan can and will jump over it if necessary, so I am careful not to make any sudden moves.

"I will never tell you that. *Never.*" Giving Noah up to Declan would ruin everything Noah has fought for. I will never tell, not even to see the look on Declan's face when he finds out his "friend" double-crossed him.

Declan's shoulders drop and he rounds the island a little more quickly than before. "It doesn't matter. He only knows you're a clone of his wife. He'll never come for you. You're nothing more than a good copy as far as he's concerned. And once your memories are wiped, it won't matter."

This stings because I know it is true. Noah has no idea what Travista did. But I cannot let Declan know that. "He will never give up on me," I say. "We love each other in a way you will never understand."

He moves toward me, hand outstretched, his eyes pleading. "Emma—"

I jerk away. "Do not come any closer."

"—don't do this. I love you and you still love me. I can see it in your eyes."

It is true. I do. "But I hate you more," I say, my throat and chest tight. "Everything you have ever said to me was a lie."

"I've given you everything," he says, his eyes narrowing. "I would never hurt you."

I laugh, low in my chest. "This is not just about me. It is about who you are, Declan. I cannot be with a man who sells women and *kidnaps children.* And for what? Money? You are the worst sort of human being I can imagine."

He swings around the counter so fast I end up in his grasp. His fingers cut off the circulation to my arms and I wince, coming up on my toes.

"Don't you understand?" He shakes me for emphasis. "I'm single-handedly bringing an end to infertility. While other countries waste their fertile years, our fertility is on the rise, and *I* did that, Emma. Me. All because I won't stand idly by watching the west bring us closer to extinction."

"But you steal their children!"

"Only the girls." He says this simply, firmly. As if this makes all the difference.

I gape at him, nearly speechless. "That does not make it *better*. Do you have any idea what your training centers are like? Those girls are abused. Tortured. *Murdered*."

He shakes his head. "Under my father and his father, yes. But when I took over, I cleaned them up. Those girls aren't harmed in any way. It makes them more compliant. More children are born."

I shake my head and try to twist out of his hold. "Next you are going to tell me that the clones are all a part of this master plan to help heal the world?"

"Why else would I be doing this? Their bodies can be manipulated to be whatever we want them to be."

"You kill their hosts! It is murder, Declan."

"They're shells, Emma. That's all."

The image of Emma floating in the tank fills my mind. Only a shell of who I used to be. She may as well be dead. "It is still wrong. You ruined my life. And what about Ruby? Did anyone ask her if she wanted to be forced into a marriage with that lunatic? Raped for the child she carries?"

Declan shoves me away and I smack into the island, a jolt of pain streaking up my side. "Will this be your next accusation? That I raped you?"

I hesitate, then shake my head. "No," I whisper. "But you cannot say you did not manipulate this entire situation. I love my husband. I never would have been unfaithful to him, and definitely not with a man like you."

A deep flush fills Declan's face. "A man like me?" His right hand darts out with clawed fingers and stops just before taking me by the neck. Slowly, his fingers curl into a white-knuckled fist. "A man who gave you everything?" His voice is low, thin. Dangerous. "Do you have any idea what it's been like for me? Having to explain my actions to my father's closest friends? Anyone who knew who you really were? Promise them I had you under my full control? I was on the verge of losing all credibility to keep you, and I was going to keep you, Emma. I *am* going to keep you."

He lunges for me, and I grab a decorative ceramic bowl from the island top and swing at him. My broken knuckle screams with a white fury, but the bowl *thwak*s against his shoulder and throws him off course long enough for me to run.

I aim for the teleporter, wishing I knew a port number that would take me somewhere where Declan cannot follow. My only option at this point is the hospital—*the labs*—and hopefully I can make it out of the building. If I can just make it to the streets outside, I can find someplace to hole up until I come up with a better plan.

Two steps from the opening, the world around me swims and goes dark.

My eyelids flutter open and I blink at a cracked, blue ceiling. Bright lights. A man hovers over my head, pumping air into my lungs. Another man presses fingers over a bag of clear liquid being fed into the crook of my arm. Neither of them pays attention to me. Instead, they focus on what is going on beyond the curtain hanging across my chest, shielding me from what jostles and tugs at my insides. I hear Sonya and the others working but cannot see them.

Noah stands at the curtain's edge, looking around it, wincing and running a hand over his mouth and chin. His other hand holds mine in a tight grip. I squeeze and he whips around, eyes wide.

He leans over me and forces the bag away from my mouth, then brushes my hair back. "Hold on," Noah whispers and kisses my forehead. "She's almost here and then you have to hold on, okay? Stay with me."

A hot tear slips out of my eye because I want to stay. More than anything. "Do not let me die," I say.

Noah's expression crumbles and tears stream over his cheeks. "Never."

A tiny cry fills the room and Sonya says, "She's okay, Noah. Adrienne's okay."

Noah and I both look toward the sound of Sonya's voice. A moment later, a young man comes around with my swaddled baby. He passes her over to Noah and I marvel over just how tiny the bundle looks in his arms. How it is mostly blanket and the tiniest of pink faces poking out.

"Let me see her," I whisper. My eyelids grow heavy and the room is beginning to fade. My body is weakening and there is nothing I can do to stop it.

Noah lays her by my head and I see my perfect daughter. Adrienne. Eyes closed, chin quivering followed by a mew of a cry. I cannot tell who she looks like yet, only that she is perfect.

Noah skims a hand across my cheek and kisses me gently. "I love you, Emma."

His tears fall and mingle with my own. The tugging of my lower body continues, jostling me.

"Damn it," Sonya says. "She's hemorrhaging."

I did not need to hear her say this. I already feel the life draining from my body.

"No, Emma," Noah says, gripping the side of my head. "Fight."

I can, I realize, but not here. This is the end for this body, but not the end for *me*. "Declan," I say. "I need help. Don't let him—"

I wake to Declan pacing at the foot of the bed. I have a moment of disorientation, searching for some sign of life in my lower extremities where a moment ago there was none. Only a jostling sensation. And even though I was with her only a moment ago, I already crave my daughter. My chest tightens with longing for her. Her perfect face fills my mind and calls to me. My heart swells to a point I never knew existed at just the thought of her. This is what love is. Unconditional and world consuming. I would do anything for her.

I have to get out of here. I have to find a way back home. Home to Adrienne.

I shift my focus to my surroundings, my ways of escape. I am on the side of the bed opposite the door. Declan will reach me before I get there. The glass wall is closer but does not open like the wall in the dining area. He blocks the way into the bathroom, too, so I cannot get to those windows.

I focus on the end table by my head. An abstract sculpture of a woman and child sits on the corner by a lamp. Its mate, the husband, sits on Declan's side. And it is as heavy as hell because it has been literally carved from granite.

I wait until Declan has paced to the other side of the room, then spring up. The statue is heavier than I remembered, and my broken knuckle makes it harder to grip. It takes both hands to throw it at the glass. The wall shatters and glass shards scatter all over the outside decking.

"Emma! No!"

I run. I have to shoulder through what remains of the glass, cutting my skin on the shards, but I make it through. The crisp air clenches my lungs and bites at my skin. My feet crunch on the glass pieces, then the snow. My breath billows outward in white clouds of crystallized air.

Behind me, running footfalls through snow grow closer, but not close enough to stop me. I have been training for this day for a long time. Toni said I would have to run and would have to be faster than all of them.

And I am.

"Stop!" Declan yells. "There's nowhere to go!"

But there is. I have seen it.

I run straight for the cliffs over the frozen lake.

CHAPTER 45

I dash over the needle-strewn forest floor, tree limbs breaking under my feet and slapping up against my shins. Each brush against a juniper tree sends a cold shower of snow misting over me. I ignore it all, heading straight for the ledge that I pray will end this once and for all. It is going to be the most dangerous game of chicken I have ever played. With any luck, I will win, because I do not hold out any hope my body will survive the C-section.

"Emma, stop!" Declan calls.

The world opens abruptly to a low-hanging sun, nearly identical to what I saw the night I first came here. I skid to a stop where the rocks jut out from the snow and I whirl around. Declan stops no less than four steps away, arms spread. Between us, two white clouds of breath billow and dissipate before colliding.

"What are you doing?" he asks through heaving breaths. Dark hair lies over his forehead, brushing his cheeks. His eyes have only narrow spaces to peek through.

"Ending this." I take a step back, carefully placing my weight on the outcropping of rock.

Declan follows me, eyes wide. "Don't do this. Please."

"The fall will kill me," I say and take another cautious step back. "You will have nothing to bring back. That is all that matters."

"I can't let you do this."

"Try and stop me."

I glance behind me, bending my knees, preparing to jump. The frozen lake gapes up at me, perfect and untouched, with a layer of snow gathered around its edges.

Declan reacts as I suspected he would. He leaps out to stop me from jumping, only he is faster than I expected. He collides with me just as I prepare to jump *away* from the cliff. I had been hoping he would become unbalanced and go over with me out of the way—it looked great in my head—but now we are both unbalanced.

We pitch dangerously, both fighting gravity to stay upright. Declan actually begins to win the battle and we tilt in the opposite, safer, direction, but I cannot let that happen. I have to make a choice here, and though I do not like it, it is what is best for all of us.

I fist his shirt and push toward the edge. His fingers tighten on my arms and my broken knuckle is aflame in my clenched hand, but I center all my weight and focus on the lake. I focus on keeping my daughter safe from men like Declan Burke—maybe from Declan himself.

Declan's eyes widen and his gaze darts between our death and me. "Emma, n—"

His last words are cut off in the fall. I cling to him all the way down, watching the ice race to meet us, feeling the sharp cut of wind wrap around us. I barely hear the *crunch* before the freezing lake water billows over us and swallows us whole.

We sink into the dark depths, which are so cold, all of my muscles turn to stone. But I am elated because I survived the fall.

Then I see Declan floating with his eyes open and staring at absolutely nothing and know he is dead. I see the man I loved, kind and gentle and patient, and my heart pinches in pain. I reach for him as everything goes dark.

"No." The word is only a slight movement on my lips, with no sound. I want to scream it but can barely find the strength to keep my eyes open, let alone talk.

Noah is doing chest compressions over me, air escaping in hisses through his clenched teeth. "Come back, Emma. Come on!"

My eyelids close, but I am still aware of the flurry of people working to keep me alive. The odd sensation of tugging still goes on over my midsection. Over it all, a baby cries.

Adrienne.

I cannot breathe. In the mere seconds I had left this body, I have begun the painful process of drowning. My limbs are frozen, and swimming is impossible. My lungs burn and I do not know which way is up. Declan is gone, having disappeared in the darkness of the lake, and one last spasm of grief pulses through my heart.

My following moments blur. A constant battle for life between two bodies, neither seeming to be better off than the other. I am dying either way. I float in darkness, unblinking.

Noah begs me to hang on.

Ice-cold wind brushes my face.

I wake to air forced into my lungs and hands pressing into my sternum. A baby's cry. A whipping wind.

"Come on, Emma," a voice says.

"Come on, Emma," another echoes.

I want to comply, but I have no control. Darkness clings to me and I wonder if it is Mother Nature trying to make things right. I never should have been. I should have died eight months ago.

But I am here and so is Adrienne. Her lonely cry is proof of that. It calls to me, begs me to stay, and it is stronger than any remaining bond I have to this earth. And it does not matter what was meant to be. Only that I was meant to be her mother.

"It's too late," Sonya says in a tight voice.

Hands cling to my face, and Noah's voice grows as distant as Adrienne's cries. "Emma, no. Stay, Emma. Plea—"

For the second time today, I wake up coughing water from my lungs, only this time my body shakes violently from the cold. My lungs burn and feel scraped raw, and my skin is stiff and tingly. And instead of Declan, I find Foster, dripping water over me and laughing.

"Oh my God, Emma, you fucking scared me," he says. "I thought I'd lost you."

My teeth clatter together. "What happened?"

I look him over and find his shirt stained with blood. His jeans, too. A cut high on his forehead seeps with fresh blood. Despite that, he is a welcome sight.

"I finally got out of that lab with the help of some of our guys, only to find Declan chasing you out of a broken window and out here. What the hell were you thinking?"

I recall the standoff on the cliff. "Did you see him?" I nod at the lake. "Declan?"

"No. I barely found you. It was too dark." He stands and pulls me up. "Come on. After all that, if I die of hypothermia, I'm going to be pissed."

The word "die" brings me up short. "Foster, I think Emma is dead." Despite what Dr. Travista said, I still cannot think of that other body as anything but someone else's. Even though I just experienced the death firsthand.

He flinches and blinks several times before responding with his blue-tinged lips. "What?" His voice is choked and a glaze films his eyes.

"The baby came early and they had to do a C-section. I think She is dead."

His jaw clenches shut and he nods once. Finally, he takes my hand. "Let's go home."

CHAPTER 46

A pained quiet lies over the command center when we arrive, the people chattering softly and clinging to one another. My skin tingles painfully, gathering every last drop of heat it can soak up. A few somber faces turn in our direction. Several others look on me as if I am a freak and do not deserve to live when Emma Wade just lost her life.

Foster leads me past them and toward the hospital ward. When we are near, the trepidation of seeing what I think I will see is too much. Blood. There will be blood.

"No," I say and stop. "I cannot go in there."

Not even the cry of Adrienne—if she cried right now at all—could bring me to go in.

"Wait here," he says and marches into the room.

It is only a few seconds later when Sonya comes striding out with Foster. "Come with me."

She takes Foster and me into what looks like a small exam room and gives us dry scrubs—black, not white, I am happy to see—and heated blankets. A couple of nurses arrive, take our vitals, and clean up our scrapes and cuts. One uses some kind of laser to heal my knuckle.

By the time they are finished, I am exhausted and just want to sleep. But more than that, I want to see Adrienne and Noah.

When I ask, anger flashes across Sonya's face. "Maybe in the morning," she says.

Foster jumps off the examination table. "You don't understand—"

"In the morning," she repeats sternly, her gaze hard on Foster. She then glances between us. "He lost his wife tonight. He needs some time to grieve, and I won't have you"—her attention lands heavily on me—"confusing him. It'll only make the process harder."

Foster's eyebrows pinch together and he folds his arms. "Who the fuck are you? His mother? You have no idea what you're talking about. Travista said—"

"The best thing for both of you," she says to me, a hand up to stop Foster from continuing, "is to move on. You aren't his wife."

I flinch back as if she has slapped me.

Not an ounce of regret passes over her expression. She merely picks up her belongings and strolls out of the room, leaving Foster and me gaping after her. Being around her is a tough transition for me; she does not sugarcoat anything.

She is right about one thing: This situation is nothing if not confusing. A week ago, I loved another man. Still do, if I am honest with myself. Noah watched his wife die. I just killed the man who I believed was my husband for the last eight months. How are we supposed to compartmentalize these situations and go on as if nothing happened?

"It is fine," I say to Foster when he looks ready to tear after Sonya. "I am tired anyway."

Foster takes me to a room with a bed and private bathroom. It is nothing more than stone walls and a twin-size bed. All the money in this operation clearly went into the computers and staffing rather than creature comforts.

Tired as I am, I still take a long, hot shower, hoping the imprint of a bloody C-section will wash off my mind. Hoping I can scour off the feel of Declan's hands on me. I need to wash off the lake water and stink of death.

Unfortunately, it will take more than hot water to turn back the clock and erase this day.

I wake in the middle of the night, a cold sweat coating my skin. In my dream, I did not float in a tank but rather in absolutely nothing. Space. Death. Is this how it will be from now on? My soul searching for a body that now lies dead somewhere in this building?

I stumble into the dark bathroom and splash cold water on my face, swallowing the rising bile in my throat. I grip the sides of the cold porcelain sink while my body trembles. Everything that happened is catching up to me, and it is too much of a shock to my system.

I am a clone.

My body is dead.

Declan is dead.

Noah. Noah, who is still a mystery because he never cared to come see me when I returned. Instead, he mourned for his dead wife.

This thought smacks of reality. No matter what Travista said, no matter how much hope I had that I could take my life back, I will never fit in it again. My life changed the second I opened my new eyes. I fell in love with another man. I became someone else, someone soft and trusting and naïve, but still someone else. I cannot take back a life that does not make sense to me.

I am not sure I even want that life. Noah? Yes. I love him. God knows I do.

Adrienne? I did not carry her. I did not *die* for her. Not really. Emma Wade did.

As for the life of Emma Burke, well, that is not even a possibility anymore. Declan is gone. I will never forget his unseeing eyes staring at me from the dark depths of the lake. Those eyes that I used to swim in. I wish I could have forgotten the man he was in the real world. I would have been happy had I remained ignorant. What makes this harder to deal with is that I know now just how honest he was. My ignorance hid the truth.

I chose you and created a life for us that I swear will never reflect the outside world, he'd once said. *I don't want that life for you or for us. I will not mark your skin because that means I am giving in to that world, which already rules my every waking decision as it is. You are my peace from that.*

He loved me. It may not have started out that way, but that is how it ended. To our detriment, it seems. He is dead and I am heartbroken despite my best efforts not to be.

I blink at the dark reflection staring at me. I do not see Her. I do not have Her long hair, Her perpetual smirk. Her scars. Where Her eyes were wide and had seen an entire lifetime of honesty—honesty She grew better from—mine are innocent and have seen only a few months of lies—lies that are shattering me from the inside out.

What I do have are choices. Stay and try to fit in a square hole when I am a circle, or go and figure out who I am after all this. I cannot figure that out here in Her shadow. Under Noah's watchful gaze, trying to decipher me out—am I still his Emma or just a really good copy?

As much as it hurts to even consider it, I have a chance to start over. Fall in love again. Have children of my own that I can actually carry and give birth to. If nothing else, this body should not fail me in that department.

My chest tightens at the idea of giving up on Noah and Adrienne. But things are too far gone now to turn back the clock.

It takes me no time at all to get help from one of the men in the command center. While he promises to get my new identification started, I return to Declan's house for some clothes and whatever valuables I can easily pack away. The jewelry he gave me will get me far, I hope. It will have to. I have recently gone from the richest wife in America to the poorest.

When I return for my new identification, I find my biggest fear and greatest hope realized all in one package, leaning against a desk, tapping a small envelope in his hands.

Noah.

He has showered and trimmed the beard on his face to a tight cut. Though cleaned up, he looks like hell. The skin under his bloodshot eyes is still dark. I wonder if I will ever see him smile again.

He stands upright and nods at me.

I ignore the swell of my heart and drop my bags, nodding at the envelope. "Is that mine?"

He tucks it into his back pocket and tilts his head toward the exit. "Let's go talk."

"Noah—"

"It wasn't a request," he says, his back already to me.

He leads me to the same office we spoke in the day before, only this time the emotional charge in the air is of a different sort. I have made my peace, though looking at him now, I wonder what I am doing. Is my decision too rash?

"How is Adrienne?" I ask when the door slides shut.

A small, distant smile lifts the edges of his lips. "Perfect. Sonya is keeping her in the hospital ward for observation but says she's perfectly healthy."

I can only nod because my throat has constricted. If I speak, I will beg him to let me see her and I will cry if I do. I refuse to cry.

Noah rounds the desk and sits behind it. "I thought you'd want to know that all the information we collected yesterday is on its way to the authorities. The cloning will end, and if they ever find Arthur Travista, he'll be charged with murder."

I drop into a metal chair. "That is great." Then, "He is gone?" I missed so much when I passed out in the labs yesterday.

Noah wipes his face and sighs. "Him and Burke, both. Foster told me what happened, and my guys have been watching the feeds all night. No one ever found Burke's body. Who knows, maybe he'll turn up in the spring when the ice melts."

A shiver races over my skin and my stomach turns at the mental image of Declan floating up, dead and bloated. What was once handsome, a sickly blue and gray.

Noah continues unfazed. "Burke Enterprises is still up and running, and it doesn't look like the board of directors is going to give it up anytime soon. A new CEO will be chosen to take over the business as soon as they declare Burke officially dead."

"But you are still in there, right? You can work on taking them down?"

"Brick by little brick," he says and blinks slowly at me. Smiles gently. "One brick down, thanks to you."

I watch him for a long moment, then say, "Did you sleep at all?"

He leans back in his chair and runs his hands over the top of his head. "Very little. You?"

"Same."

He nods. "Emma," he starts, then leans forward and scrubs his face again. When his hands come away, his expression is tight. "Where are you going?"

I avert my eyes and bite my lip. How can I put into words something that took me half the night to make sense of?

"Was it really you? In my Emma?"

I know he did not mean to, but these words hurt. It is salt in the wound that reminds me how I am not Her anymore. "It does not matter. It will not change anything."

He nods and looks away. "Yeah, you're probably right."

And the slaps keep coming. "What did you want to talk about?"

"I don't know."

I stand and hold out my hand. "You have something of mine?" Tears burn my eyes, and I blink them away before he looks up.

He stands and rounds the desk, pulling the envelope out of his pocket. He lays it in my hand but does not let go right away. "You sure you want to do this?" he whispers.

I look into his eyes and find them searing right into my soul as if looking for a desperately needed sign. "No," I say truthfully. "But things are different now." Declan's words to me at the house play in my mind. More truths I have to face. "You will never see me as anything but a copy of your wife, and I will—"

"What?" he asks when I do not go on. "You will what?"

"I will always long for the man I loved on a beach in Mexico. I lost him with Her last night."

"You can't know that."

I close my eyes and a tear slips free. I did know this because I saw the way he looked at Emma when She came back to him on that table, and I see the way he looks at me now, with a wariness that can only mean he does not trust his own heart.

"I am not your wife," I say and turn away from him.

Noah is between me and the exit before I can blink. He holds a hand up to stop me. "No, Emma, wait. You're not being fair. We need time to figure this out. To adjust. Emma just died—"

"You see? Neither of us can stop referring to me as being two separate individuals, but if Travista is to be believed, I am still only one. Two bodies. One soul. *One. Emma.*"

His eyebrows raise and he nods. "This is exactly why we need time. It's hard now, but maybe in a few months—"

"No. I will not sit around and watch you mourn . . . *me.* I cannot. I am not even sure how to do that myself. How do I mourn the loss of a body? How do I adjust to being a perfect copy? Noah, tell the truth: Am I even remotely like her?"

"Yes," he says without hesitation. "That's why this is so hard. I see her in you."

"Well, I do not. I still feel like Emma Burke."

Noah flinches back and takes a good, hard look at me.

"And you seeing me," I add, "is not good enough. We have to face it. We are over."

Noah reaches out and cups my face. He leans in until our foreheads are touching and the faint scent of his musk surrounds both of us. "Don't say that," he says, his voice catching.

I take his face between my hands and close my eyes. "One of us has to."

His lips brush my cheek and warm air caresses my skin. Shivers race down my spine and branch out into my nerves like a spark that sets my body alight. That light touch of his mouth moves up to the hollow of my temple.

"Not yet," he whispers.

I slide my hands down to his neck and feel the quickened throb of his pulse under my palm. It moves in time with the beat of my heart drumming in my ears. Just like that, we are in sync.

Forehead still pressed to mine, he swivels his face back down, letting our cheeks slide together, until his nose touches mine. Circles it. He runs his thumbs along my cheekbones.

I open my eyes and find him looking into mine. Unwavering. Any strength I had before melts into a pool of indecision at my feet. How can I walk away from those eyes? How can I consider leaving him?

The unfairness of what he asks of me threatens to take me under, but at the last moment, I manage to find some semblance of Emma's strength. "I am sorry," I tell him and step back.

His grip is too firm. He holds on to me, but I am merely water sliding over stone and no matter how hard he tries to keep me, I will soon be gone. At least I feel this fleeting. Like glass blown to its thinnest point. Beautiful and shining and solid. Delicate.

Shatterable.

"You have to let me go," I whisper, shifting out of his hands.

His eyes pinch shut and his chin quivers, but he wordlessly does as I ask.

He does not follow me out of the room. It is both a relief and a painful truth. He knows I am right to do this. He knows it will be for the best. One day it will not hurt either of us anymore.

In the command center, I find an empty terminal and sift through port numbers. A port to anywhere in the west. Once I choose a remote location, I key in the instructions to hide my trail.

Thankfully, the keystrokes come to me as if I have done this a million times. I cannot have anyone coming after me.

"Emma?"

I close the terminal's window, my task complete, and face Foster. "Yeah?"

He looks over at my bags, which are still sitting outside the teleporter I intend to use for my escape. "Going somewhere?"

The sting of tears hits me and I blink them back. "I am leaving."

"Did you talk to Noah yet? What did he say?"

I focus on my bags, praying he will not ask me to look at him. I do not want him to see the hurt I know I cannot hide. "We talked. Too much has happened to fix this." I suck in a deep breath and face him. Attempt a smile. "It is okay, though. It is for the best."

Foster shakes his head. "What are you talking about? You can't leave, Emma. You have people here who love you. We're your family."

I tilt my head. "That is nice of you to say, but—"

He takes me by the arm and drags me into the empty corridor. "Stop it. You heard Travista yesterday. Same person, new body. What the hell happened with Noah? What did he say to you?"

I bite my lip, willing my tears to stay away. "This was my decision."

Footsteps approach, drawing our attention. I hope it is not who I think it is.

"I have to go," I say.

Foster bends to look me in the eye. "You're always rushing off before thinking, Emma. Just this once, give it some thought."

I shake my head. "I did. Believe me, I did."

I cannot help but look toward the approaching steps, which come to a stop. I roll in the wave of emotion from Noah's gaze. The crash of dueling emotions in his eyes is akin to the same ones battling it out within me. Stay. Go. Either way, I will die a slow, agonizing death.

I touch Foster's arm briefly and smile. "Thanks for everything you did for me."

Foster reaches out to stop me, but I am already too far away.

As I walk to the teleporter, I repeat the new port number in my head. My number to complete freedom. A new beginning.

"Emma!"

Noah's voice is like bullets slamming into me, but I keep moving. I take up my bags and step into the teleporter. Only then do I turn and see Noah running through the milling crowd of people. Thankfully they are slowing his progress, and he knocks into them haphazardly, but only because he will not take his eyes off me.

"Wait, Emma, please," he cries, desperate. He looks frightened of my leaving, but I cannot let that stop me.

The door slides between us and I key in the port number. I have just enough time to raise my hand in farewell before I freeze and the room melts away for the final time.

EPILOGUE

My mind wakes.

I blink.

White light glares overhead, blindingly bright.

Voices echo around the room—*No, we can't save the body. Just put it in the other room for now. I'll deal with it later.*—and I struggle to make sense of what they talk about. I should know what they're talking about.

I blink. Try to make sense of my surroundings but can't.

A hand pushes aside the sterile aluminum lamp over me. Familiar gray eyes watch me from between a green cap and surgical mask. The man leans straight-armed onto the table and stares at me. "Welcome back, Declan. You and I have a lot to talk about."

ACKNOWLEDGMENTS

First, I have to thank Tad, Jackson, and Jameson for letting me disappear more often than is acceptable, even though you tend to gravitate to my office doorway with chatter and jokes that I swear are a test on my patience. I love you guys in a way that can only be described as "unconditional and world consuming."

CHARISSA WEAKS!! My support and encouragement from word one. Without your chapter-by-chapter nitpicking and gushy love, I wouldn't be here. You are amazing. AMAZING! So glad I stalked your blog and Twitter feed like a crazy person on crack.

Tracy and Jodi, thanks for letting me sound-board and offering your support during those crazy weeks while I pieced Emma's story together. Mom, Renae, Crystal, Meredith, Brandy R., Michelle, and Kerry—my cheerleaders before and after every crap-tastic novel I've written to date—thanks for sticking it out with me.

Dad, thanks for submerging me in science fiction growing up. I *really* wouldn't be here without your complete obsession for everything out of this world.

Special hug-squishy thanks to Cathy Yardley for the title suggestion and submission coaching. Who the heck knows where I'd be right now without your help. Probably agentless and flailing, no doubt.

A freaking resounding thank-you to Jennifer Weltz—my agent's got Jedi mind tricks like you wouldn't believe!—for seeing Emma's potential and taking a chance on me.

And bless you, Denise Roy, for making this novel bleed the way I like it. You and everyone over at Dutton are simply beyond (BEYOND!) amazing.